* * * * * * *

"Please, come in and sit down."

I watched her as she walked across the room and sort of sidestepped around to the front of a chair that patiently waited for her to sit down on it. She moved with grace and smoothness that showed she knew how to get a man's attention, and keep it.

As she sat down, I stepped around in front of my desk and sat down on the corner. I found it very difficult not to watch her long legs and trim ankles as she crossed them.

She was wearing a perfume I found to be subtle and, I might add, quite pleasant. It was one of those very expensive brands of perfume found only in the very best stores. Everything about her suggested she was a woman of wealth and class.

"Now, what is it I can do for you?"

"It's my husband," she said as she looked up at me with those big blue eyes.

"What about your husband?" I asked.

"It seems he has lost interest in me."

"I find that hard to believe."

I couldn't see how any man in his right mind could lose interest in a woman who was obviously as beautiful and sexy as she was. She looked as if she had everything any healthy American male could want in a woman.

* * * * * * *

Other titles by J.E. Terrall 1

Western Short Stories
The Old West
The Frontier
Untamed Land

Western Novels
Conflict in Elkhorn Valley
Lazy A Ranch
(a modern western)

Romance Novels
Balboa Rendezvous
Sing for Me
Return to Me
Forever Yours

Mystery/Suspense/Thriller
I Can See Clearly
The Return Home
The Inheritance

Nick McCord Mysteries
Vol – 1 Murder at Gill's Point
Vol – 2 Death of a Flower
Vol – 3 A Dead Man's Treasure
Vol – 4 Blackjack, A Game to Die For
Vol – 5 Death on the Lakes

Peter Blackstone Mysteries
Murder on the Crystal Blue
Murder of My Love

Frank Tidsdale Mysteries
Death by Design

MURDER IN THE FOOTHILLS

A Peter Blackstone Mystery

by
J.E. Terrall

ISBN: 978-0-9844591-4-8

Printed in the United States of America
First Printing / 2009   www.lulu.com
Second Printing / 2013 www.creatspace.com

Cover: Covers photos taken by J.E. Terrall

Book Layout/
Formatting: J.E. Terrall
                    Custer, South Dakota

MURDER IN THE FOOTHILLS

A Peter Blackstone Mystery

To Terry and Colleen Ramsdell

CHAPTER ONE

IT HAD BEEN PRETTY QUIET the past few weeks and things were a little slow. I had finished making out the final bill for one of my clients and had turned my attention to the morning newspaper. I was finding nothing of interest when my thoughts were disturbed by the sound of a light knock on the door to my office. I looked up to find a stunning young woman standing in the doorway. She was smiling at me.

"Can I help you?" I asked, hoping there was at least something I could do for her. After all, she had already made my day by just standing in the doorway.

The woman was tall and slim with long blond hair that fell loosely over her smooth bare shoulders. The dress she was wearing was a colorful summer dress with thin string-type shoulder straps and a low cut neckline that showed a good deal of cleavage. The dress tapered down to her narrow waist and flared out slightly at the hips, which gave her figure the most desirable shape. The skirt of her dress was short, well above the knees, and showed off her long tanned, shapely legs. She had the toned body of a woman who worked hard at keeping herself in shape.

"I'm looking for Mr. Peter Blackstone," she said, her voice was pleasant to the ears.

"I'm Peter Blackstone. How may I help you?" I asked as I stood up.

I didn't miss the fact that she took a moment to look me over. It was as if she were sizing me up for something. I'm not sure what she thought, but I knew I was in pretty good shape. I try to work out a couple of times a week at a local health club, but don't always get there.

"Help is what I need," she said, her big beautiful eyes sparkling as she looked into mine.

"Please, come in and sit down."

I watched her as she walked across the room and sort of sidestepped around to the front of a chair that patiently waited for her to sit down on it. She moved with grace and smoothness that showed she knew how to get a man's attention, and keep it.

As she sat down, I stepped around in front of my desk and sat down on the corner. I found it very difficult not to watch her long legs and trim ankles as she crossed them.

She was wearing a perfume I found to be subtle and, I might add, quite pleasant. It was one of those very expensive brands of perfume found only in the very best stores. Everything about her suggested she was a woman of wealth and class.

"Now, what is it I can do for you?"

"It's my husband," she said as she looked up at me with those big blue eyes.

"What about your husband?" I asked.

"It seems he has lost interest in me."

"I find that hard to believe."

I couldn't see how any man in his right mind could lose interest in a woman who was obviously as beautiful and sexy as she was. She looked as if she had everything any healthy American male could want in a woman.

"But he has," she insisted.

"I still don't see how I can be of help."

"I would like you to find out why he has lost interest in me."

"Do you suspect he is seeing another woman?"

I only asked that question because it was the most logical reason for a man to lose interest in a woman as good looking as the woman sitting in front of me. At least, she hadn't given me any reason to lose interest in her, so far.

"I don't think so, but that is what I want you to find out."

"As a private investigator, that is what I do. But before I decide if I will look into this for you, I think it would be a good idea for me to know who you are."

"I guess that would be important to a good business relationship."

"Yes, it does help."

"My name is Samantha Williams," she said with a note of pride in her voice.

I immediately recognized her name. I would think she should be proud, especially if she was the Samantha Williams that I knew to be the wife of Arnold P. Williams, a very prominent and wealthy businessman in the Denver area.

To my knowledge, Arnold P. Williams was involved in almost everything you could imagine in the city of Denver. He was on the board of several well-known companies, as well as on the board of the Performing Arts Council. He was well respected in the community. And as far as I knew, it was old money that made him what he was. It was the kind of money that comes down from one generation to the next with each generation increasing the family assets.

I was also well aware that anyone who knew Mr. Williams thought very highly of him. And if I remembered correctly, he had to be much older than the woman sitting in front of me. He was certainly not the first older man that I knew who had a wife young enough to be his daughter.

"Let me see if I understand you. You want me to follow your husband around and find out what he is doing. Is that correct?"

I couldn't help but notice her smooth legs and slender ankles as she shifted in the chair. She moved as if what I had suggested had made her feel a little uncomfortable. I got the impression that she didn't like the way it sounded when I described what I thought she wanted me to do.

"Well, in a way, I guess," she finally replied after giving it some thought. "I mostly want to know what he does on Wednesday evenings."

"Wednesday evenings?"

I was instantly curious and somewhat confused. I had never been asked to tail someone at a specific time.

"Yes," she said as if it was the most natural thing in the world.

"What is it you think I will find?"

"I'm sorry?" she said as she looked at me as if she didn't understand the question.

"Most people have some idea of what they expect me to find. I want to know what you think your husband is doing on Wednesday evenings."

"Oh. I really don't know what I expect you to find. I simply want to know what he is doing."

"How long have these Wednesday evenings away from home been going on?"

"For the past six, almost seven months. Is that important?" she asked.

"It could be. What is it you want to know?"

"I want to know where he goes, who he is seeing and what he does," she explained as if what she was asking was as normal as ordering a cup of her favorite cappuccino.

"I know this may sound a little peculiar, but why just on Wednesday evenings? Is there something unusual about Wednesdays?"

"Yes, there is. It is the only time he goes out in the evening and does not take me along. He likes to be seen with me."

I didn't have any problem understanding why Mr. Williams would like being seen with her. She was a very attractive woman.

"I see," I said, but I had a feeling I wasn't seeing everything.

I didn't have any problem understanding why she might think Mr. Williams was doing something strange by not spending every single night with her. However, I had a problem as to why she had to know where he was all the time. One night out of the week without her didn't seem like too much to me. Even men with the best wives have to have some time away from them.

"Maybe he wants a night out with the boys. You know, a little poker or something. I see no harm in that."

"Oh, I don't, either. But I don't think it's a night out with the boys. If it was, I'm sure he would have told me."

"Then what do you think it is?"

"That's what I want you to find out."

The expression on her face indicated I should have known the answer to my own question.

"How is he the rest of the week?"

"Arnold is very attentive, very giving and very loving. We enjoy our time together, especially while we are in bed."

I didn't need to be hit on the head with a hammer in order to figure out what she was getting at. From the look on her face, she was telling me the truth. Either that, or she was one very good actress.

I still couldn't get it out of my head that there had to be a good reason for her to want to know what was going on with her husband on just one evening a week. Maybe he needed a night without her. After all, she was much younger than him.

She had me wondering what this was really about. It appeared the only way I was going to find out would be to take her on as a client. I had little else to do at the moment, plus I could use the money. I decided I would accept her as a client. Since it was going to be just one day a week, I could see no reason not to take a shot at it. It would give me time to take on other clients, should one come along.

"I have to tell you, I don't do this type of work for nothing. I'm rather expensive," I said as I looked into those baby blue eyes.

"I'm sure you are. But then they say, 'you get what you pay for'. Don't they?"

"Yes. Yes they do."

"How much do you charge, Mr. Blackstone?"

I took a few minutes to explain my fee. I also told her that I expected to have a sizable retainer before I would even start. She didn't seem to have a problem with the fee or the retainer. She reached into her purse and pulled out a plain white envelope that was almost as large as her purse and handed it to me. I opened it and looked inside. There was fifteen hundred dollars in nice new crisp one hundred dollar bills in the envelope. I looked up at her, a little surprised she had that kind of cash on her.

"I assume you prefer cash?"

"Yes. Cash works for me."

"I would think that should be enough for you to get started," she said with a smile.

"It will do nicely," I replied.

"By the way, I would like our meeting to be strictly between the two of us. You understand. It would be difficult to explain to my husband why I visited a private investigator, if he should find out."

"Certainly. All my clients are confidential," I said in an effort to reassure her that I would say nothing to anyone.

"Good," she said as she uncrossed those sexy legs, stood up and turned to leave.

"There is just one other little matter we need to discuss," I said as I straightened up and she stepped around the chair.

She stopped, turned and looked at me.

"And what might that be, Mr. Blackstone?"

"How should I get in touch with you? I'm sure you would prefer I not call you at your home."

"Oh. No. Calling me at home would not be a good idea. It would be best if I call you. When do you think you might have something to report?"

"Why don't you call me Thursday, say Thursday morning? I will have had a chance to follow Arnold for one day," I said as I handed her one of my cards. "I may have something to tell you, but don't really count on too much. It sometimes takes awhile to find out what is really going on."

"You wouldn't withhold information from me. Would you?"

"No. I wouldn't think of it."

"Good. I will call you on Thursday morning," she replied as she stuck out her hand.

I gently shook her small delicate hand and smiled at her. She turned around and walked out of the office. I found it difficult not to watch her short skirt sway from side to side as she walked away. The faint smell of her perfume lingered in the office for several minutes after she had gone.

NOW THAT MRS. WILLIAMS had left my office, I wondered what was really going on in the Williams household. A prominent figure in the Denver community was going out on one night a week and wouldn't tell his wife where or why he was going out. If their life was so great the rest of the week, why was his wife so concerned that she would hire an investigator?

What was it she was not telling me? There had to be a reason, but I had no idea what it was. With so many years in the business, I was used to clients not telling me everything I needed to know. I doubted Mrs. Arnold P. Williams was any different.

I felt a trip to the library was a good idea. I have always been a believer in reviewing newspapers to find out about people, especially prominent people. They were often the subjects of local news, predominantly in the society columns. I could find out a lot about Mr. and Mrs. Williams from past newspapers. The best place to do that without causing suspicion was in the public library.

I needed to find out if there was anything in the past seven or eight months that might give me a clue as to why Mr. Williams had suddenly started going out on Wednesday evenings without his wife. It might give me some idea what I was getting myself into as well.

THE DOWNTOWN PUBLIC LIBRARY was about fifteen minutes from my office. It didn't take long before I was up to my neck in old local newspapers. They covered a period of the past seven to eight months.

Mr. Williams and his wife appeared to be in the society section quite often. In fact, it seemed as if they were always pictured together. They made a very nice looking couple.

I discovered Mr. Williams was involved in several companies in the Denver area, to say nothing of leading a very active social life. His name appeared quite often for giving charitable fund raising dinners, sponsoring fundraisers for the performing arts, and attending those charities and fundraisers sponsored by other influential Denverites or by companies he had an active interest in.

The type of information I was seeking caused me to drift back and forth between the society section and the business section of the newspapers. I jotted down the names of any companies he had any kind of a connection with, no matter how insignificant it seemed. I wanted to cross check them against information I found on the companies to see if any of them might be having financial or legal troubles. If they were having difficulties, I wanted to know what kind of problems the company was having and who was involved. I also wanted to know how deeply involved Mr. Williams might be with the troubled company, if I should find one.

I also jotted down the names of the organizations Mr. Williams had some interest in. I quickly discovered I was likely to find his name connected to any number of organizations in the Denver area. He was either a patron and financial supporter, or a member of the board of directors.

As I waded through the pile of newspapers, I had no idea what I was expecting to find. I simply needed to know as much as possible about Arnold P. Williams. I wanted to know more about Mrs. Williams as well.

One interesting thing I discovered was their life together seemed to be a very public one. There was hardly a newspaper that didn't have something about the two of them in it. They were apparently at every major social event in town. I found it interesting that they were always together. He seemed to be one of those people who survived on publicity. With such a public life, it made the fact that he kept Wednesday evenings so private harder to understand.

After a while, I had been searching through so many papers my brain was beginning to turn to mush. I decided to take a break in an effort to clear the cobwebs. I needed to start putting what I had learned into some sort of order.

I RETURNED TO MY OFFICE. I took a few moments to reply to the messages on my answering machine. I still had a lot to do before I would be ready to follow Mr. Williams, but I wasn't ready to return to the library and bury my head in newspapers again.

I sat down at my desk and looked up the address of Mr. and Mrs. Arnold P Williams. Their home was located in the foothills above Denver. I knew from the address it was a very exclusive area. A trip to the foothills was in order, but not today.

CHAPTER TWO

I HAD PUT OFF RETURNING to the library for as long as I dared because it is the most boring part of an investigator's job. It was also one of the most important parts. I finally returned to the library to continue my search for information.

There were not very many people in the library in late afternoon. I was able to get the help of a young woman who seemed to have nothing better to do. She quickly became a source of information as well as someone to run and get reference material for me.

In my search for information, I discovered Arnold P. Williams had had a brief association with a fairly well known criminal by the name of Frank Waterman. Waterman had been convicted and jailed for extortion and theft of union funds several years ago, but had been released maybe a year ago. The union he had stolen money from was for construction workers. I wondered if he was still involved in the same sort of activities after he got out of jail.

With a little digging I discovered Williams had known Waterman before Waterman's troubles with the law. I noticed Williams had quickly distanced himself from Waterman as soon as the allegations of embezzlement and extortion became public. In one article from an older newspaper, Williams stated he knew nothing of what Waterman had done except for what he had read in the newspapers. He said they only knew each other because "we happen to be members of the same country club". Williams had wasted no time in making it clear he had never had any "business dealings", as the newspaper put it, with Waterman.

It was obvious that Williams had done everything he could to make sure their names were not connected in any way. It had apparently worked, as there was never any mention of Williams in stories about Waterman after that article appeared.

I came across an article about one of the companies where Williams was a member of the board of trustees. It seemed the company was having some legal problems. I gave the article my undivided attention.

The company was Ace Diamond Construction Company. It was a construction company that built mainly large high-rise buildings. The interesting part was there didn't seem to be any outside contractors. That was not a common practice in the Denver area. Ace Diamond handled every phase of construction on its own, from start to finish.

The article indicated a downtown building being built by Ace Diamond Construction Company had inferior materials used in the construction causing the building to be unsafe. The allegations had been made by a foreman of the construction company. The article was quick to note that the foreman was a "former employee". I wondered at what point he had been fired. Was it before or after he reported his findings of inferior materials?

A more recent article indicated the foreman had told the board of trustees about the problem six months ago, but they had done nothing about it. It was only after the board had ignored the foreman that he sent a letter to the newspaper accusing the board of trustees of failing to take him seriously. The article indicated the state building inspectors were investigating the report and questioning the foreman, but gave no indication as to what had been discovered or whether the allegations were true or not.

If the foreman had told the board of trustees about the problem six months ago, that would be about the time Williams started going out every Wednesday evening without Mrs. Williams.

It made sense that the board of trustees would want to meet and discuss how to handle any fallout once the allegation became public. They would want to keep up on any developments along the way so they could plan strategies to counter any negative press or other problems.

An article in the next day's newspaper had a picture of Arnold Williams behind a podium. The article said the state inspectors were looking into it and that he was "confident" the allegation would be proven false. It said the foreman had written the letter after he had been fired from the job for trying to cause trouble for the company over non-union workers.

The more I learned about Williams, the more it became clear he would not like the idea of being connected to a company that did shoddy work, especially if the shoddy work caused the project to be unsafe. It would not be good for his image, or for his position on other boards and in the community. He had a reputation to protect. I wondered just how far he would go to protect it.

I also wondered if the articles I had read had anything to do with his Wednesday evenings away from home. It was possible, but I had my doubts. However, I couldn't ignore the fact that the secret meetings on Wednesday evenings had apparently started about the same time the board was notified of problems. It also appeared to be at about the same time that Mrs. Williams said that he started going out without her.

If the meetings were about the "Unsafe Building", I wondered why just Wednesday evenings. It would make more sense for them to meet anytime something new came up so they could keep ahead of any fallout.

As I closed the book of newspapers, I thought about Mrs. Williams. One other thing came to light while looking into Mr. Williams's activities. It seemed a bit peculiar to me that Mrs. Williams was never mentioned without her husband.

Often times in the upper crust of society, the wives of such prominent men as Williams had charities of their own to work on. They often appeared in the newspapers without their husbands when their charities were mentioned. I had not found Mrs. Williams mentioned even once without it being simply a footnote to something involving her husband. There was no indication she had any interest in any organizations or charity. In all the articles I saw, Mrs. Williams was nothing more than a very nice looking woman who stood at her husband's side to help make him look good. There was no doubt she did that very well.

I could find nothing in all my research that would lead me to believe Williams was anything but what he appeared to be. Yet, I still had a nagging thought there was something going on that needed, no, required me to look into it.

There was something even Mrs. Williams didn't know about her husband. I wanted to know what it was. The fact he was doing something that seemed out of character for him was enough to keep me interested, even if I had no proof.

I sat back in the chair and looked at all the newspapers and magazines surrounding me. There was nothing in any of them I could consider to be proof that Williams was involved in anything illegal, or even a little shady. There didn't seem to be any evidence to back up the foreman's accusations that the building built by Ace Diamond Construction Company was unsafe. There was no evidence that Williams knew about any problems with the building until the foreman reported it to the board. There was nothing to indicate he had anything to do with anything other than to launch an investigation into the allegations, which was certainly the appropriate thing to do.

As far as I was concerned, there had to be some other reason for Williams to be away from home on Wednesday nights. It again crossed my mind he might be playing poker with the boys, or something as simple as that.

I closed my eyes and let out a deep sigh. The day had proven to be very interesting, but nothing more. I was no closer to figuring out what my client really wanted to know. Mrs. Williams had given me nothing to work with, which didn't help matters.

"EXUSE ME."

I opened my eyes and found the young woman who had been helping me standing next to the table looking at me.

"We have to close up," she said almost apologetically.

"Oh. Say, what's your name?"

"Lisa," she replied with a slight grin.

"Well, Lisa, you have been a great deal of help. Have you had dinner?"

"No," she replied shyly.

"Do you get off soon?"

"I'm actually off now."

"I would like to do something for you for all your help. Would you care to join me for dinner? I would certainly understand if you decline, but you deserve it and I hate to eat alone."

"I'd be happy to have dinner with you. And thanks for asking."

"Great," I said as I stood up.

I took her gently by the arm and we started for the front door of the library.

"There's a little restaurant a couple of blocks from here. How would that be?" I asked as I led her down the steps of the library.

"That would be fine," she said with a smile.

I left my car in the library parking lot while we walked down Broadway to a diner I knew was open late.

ONCE INSIDE THE DINER, we found a booth in a corner and sat down. For the first time I really looked at her.

Lisa was a nice looking young woman, probably in her early to mid-twenties. She had mousy brown hair cut in a pageboy. Her eyes were a deep brown and sparkled in the light. Her face was small and rather cute making her look younger than she really was. She had a slim figure, giving her an almost teenager appearance. It crossed my mind I probably had ten to fifteen years on her.

"You're pretty brave to go out with a man you hardly know."

"You seem harmless enough," she said with a smile.

"Ouch. You sure know how to hurt a guy."

"Oh, I'm sorry," she said with an embarrassed sort of giggle. "I didn't mean for it to sound that way."

"It's okay."

"I get a little nervous the first time I go out with someone."

"You don't seem nervous."

"I haven't dated much since I moved to Denver. It's kind of hard to meet men in a library."

"I take it you like a man who isn't afraid of books."

"Yeah, I guess so," she replied with a hint of coyness in her voice.

The waitress stopped by our table and took our order, then we continued our discussion.

"Are you a reporter?" she asked after the waitress left.

"No. What gave you that idea?"

"You were doing a lot of research on one of the more distinguished members of the Denver Community. I thought maybe you were working on some sort of article about him."

"Actually, I'm a private investigator."

"Really," she said with a hint of excitement in her voice.

"Really."

"I thought private investigators existed only in mystery novels and the movies. Well, I mean, I . . ah."

"It's okay. I know what you mean. There are a good number of private investigators around. I can assure you it isn't as exciting a job as most people think. There's a lot of research done in libraries, courthouses, newspaper archives and on computers.

"Why don't you look up everything on the computer?"

"I prefer to read it in the paper. It has more life to it than sitting in front of a computer screen trying to find details and trying to figure out what is the truth."

"It seems interesting."

"It's not as interesting or exciting as the books and movies make it out to be."

"Then why do it?" she asked.

"Being a private investigator gives me a lot of freedom. I can usually work when I want. If something comes up, I don't have to ask for time off. I'm my own boss. I can take a case or refuse it. I have no one looking over my shoulder telling me what to do and when to do it. It's all up to me," I explained.

"It still sounds exciting."

"It can be, but like you saw tonight, it can be pretty boring, too."

When the waitress showed up with our meals, I leaned back and looked at Lisa while the waitress set our dinners on the table. Neither one of us wasted any time digging in. I guess we were both pretty hungry.

After we finished eating, I leaned back and sipped at my iced tea. The young woman sitting across the table seemed nice and unspoiled, even a little naïve.

We talked about her and what had brought her to Denver. I glanced at my watch and realized the time had slipped away rather quickly.

"It's getting late. Maybe I should walk you home," I suggested.

"You don't have to," she said.

"A pretty girl like you shouldn't be walking around this part of town alone. I would be pleased to walk you home."

She smiled and nodded her head slightly. After I paid the cashier for our dinners, we left the diner.

"Okay, you've told me you live near here, but didn't say where. You'll have to point me in the right direction."

Lisa smiled, took my hand and led the way. As we walked along, we shared a little small talk. It was only six blocks to her apartment house.

I walked her up to the security door and waited for her to unlock it. Once the door was open, I stood there and waited for her to go inside. She turned in front of me and looked at me as if she expected me to say something romantic.

"Again, thank you very much for all your help today."

"Ah, would you like to come up, ah, for a little while?" she asked nervously.

The way she said it, and the look on her face, gave me the impression she wanted me to come in with her, but she wasn't completely sure it was a good idea. She seemed to be a lonely girl who wanted company. It would have been easy to take advantage of her, but that's not my style.

"I would love to, but I have a very busy day tomorrow. Would it be okay if I take a rain check?"

She looked into my eyes, presumably to help her decide if I was trying to get away from her, or if I really meant it. A smile slowly came over her face.

"Sure," she said as she squeezed my hand.

I leaned close to her and kissed her lightly on the lips. As I stepped back away from her, I smiled.

"See yah soon," I said softly, then turned around.

As I walked down the steps to the sidewalk, I heard the security door close behind me. I glanced over my shoulder and saw her standing inside the building watching me leave. I gave her a brief wave and turned toward the corner.

The walk back to the library parking lot gave me time to think about Lisa. She was a sweet young woman and nice looking as well. She didn't have a drop-dead sexy figure like someone I knew very well, but she was still very nice looking. A night with her could have proven to be interesting, and neither of us would have had to be alone. But I prefer to know the women I sleep with better than I knew Lisa.

IT DIDN'T TAKE LONG to get back to the library parking lot. By the time I got to my car I was wishing, at least a little, that I had taken Lisa up on her offer. I wasn't looking forward to going home to an empty apartment, but deep down I was feeling pretty good about myself for making the right decision.

As I unlocked the car door, I glanced over the top of it. Off in the distance I could see the tall building that had come under question. I could only see the top four or five floors, but I could see lights on a couple of levels. It caused me to wonder if the report made by the fired foreman was true. If it was, there were some serious problems coming Williams's way, whether he was responsible or not.

I realized I didn't know much about the building. I had no idea if it had been finished, or if it was still under construction. I felt it might be a good idea to find out.

It was not the time to be checking out the building. I was tired and it was getting late. What I needed now was to rest my brain. I could check it out tomorrow.

I GOT IN MY CAR and drove across town to the apartment complex where I lived. I parked my car in the garage and went inside. I hardly had time to drop my keys on the table next to the door when the phone began to ring.

"Hello."

"Did you just get in?"

I had no trouble recognizing the voice. It was soft and sexy, and had a hint of concern in it.

"Hi, Jennifer. Yes, I just got in."

"Where have you been so late?"

"I was at the library doing some research."

"Oh," she said, but there was a tinge of disbelief in that single word.

"I also had dinner after the library closed."

"Oh."

Her last "Oh" didn't have the same ring to it the first one had. She could understand why I was so late getting home.

"Why the late call?"

"I thought you might like to hear my voice."

"I do, but I've never known you to call this late before just to chat."

"Would you prefer I call you tomorrow?"

"No. Of course not. I was concerned there might be something wrong."

"Well, there is, sort of. Jason and I have split up."

"I'm sorry to hear that."

"Don't be. It was for the best. I'm glad I found out how possessive he can be before things got too serious."

"Then I'm glad, too. You're too nice for the likes of him."

"I was thinking, ah, maybe we could get together sometime soon. Maybe have a drink somewhere and talk," she suggested hopefully.

She needed someone to talk to. Since I was her best friend, it was only logical for her to call me.

"Good idea. I'll call you. I'm in the middle of an investigation right now, but maybe we could get together this weekend. Would that be okay?"

"That sounds good. Give me a call."

"I will," I said without setting any definite time.

"Goodnight, Peter."

"Goodnight, Jennifer."

I hung up the receiver and leaned back on the sofa. I closed my eyes and thought about Jennifer. It wasn't hard to conjure up an image of her in my mind.

Jennifer was a very nice looking woman. She was about five foot five inches tall with an hourglass figure. There was nothing out of proportion. She was all woman. There were few women who could claim to have a body as nice as hers. She had all the right curves in all the right places.

Along with her fantastic figure, she had long curly brown hair with reddish highlights. In the bright sunshine, her hair looked more red than brown. She had a cute face with a few tiny freckles on her nose. Her eyes were green like Irish clover and sparkled when she was happy or excited. She had the temper of a redhead and a sense of humor that could keep me smiling as well as keep me on my toes.

Jennifer was the perfect woman for me right now. She didn't ask for any commitments and took me the way I was. There was never any pressure to make our relationship any more than what we could handle at the moment. When either of us needed someone, we were there for each other. Yet, at the same time, we led our own separate lives.

I suddenly yawned again. A quick glance at my watch told me it was really late. I knew I had a lot to do tomorrow and needed to get some rest.

It didn't take long for me to get ready for bed, but I found it difficult to get to sleep. There was too much going on in my head to shut down my brain so easily. It took what seemed like forever before I finally dozed off.

CHAPTER THREE

I WAS WIDE AWAKE as the sun came up over the row of apartment buildings behind the one I live in. It was still early, not yet six-thirty. I was thinking about the building that had come under question as to its safety.

It was strange how a person seems to wake up thinking about the same thing he fell asleep thinking about. I had been thinking about the Ace Diamond Building when I went to sleep, and here I was thinking about it again.

Since I was already awake and doubted I would be able to go back to sleep, I decided it best if I got up. I swung my legs off the side of the bed and headed for the shower. After a warm shower, I got dressed and went to the kitchen.

The first thing I did was fix myself a cup of black coffee in the microwave. While it was "brewing", I fixed a bowl of Cheerios with sliced peaches and milk, and poured myself a glass of orange juice.

It's a habit of mine not to turn on the radio or the television to find out what had been going on in the world and in the city while I was sleeping. I treasured my few minutes of ignorant bliss every morning before I let the problems of the world rush in to invade my tranquility. I don't even read the newspaper during breakfast. Breakfast is the most important meal of the day, so I'm told. I don't want anything messing it up. However, everything changes after breakfast.

It takes about twenty minutes to drive to the office, during which time I do listen to the news. This morning there was nothing very earthshaking to my part in the order of things, not that I really expected there would be.

IT WAS A FEW MINUTES BEFORE eight o'clock when I walked into my office. I sat down, kicked back and reviewed my notes from yesterday. Two things became very clear. One was I needed to find out more about the Ace Diamond Building. The second was I should take a drive out to the Williams house in the foothills.

The building was located not very far from my office. It was a nice morning and a good day for a walk. With that thought in mind, I left my office and began walking the few blocks to where most of the high-rise buildings could be found.

It wasn't long before I was standing in front of the Ace Diamond Building. It looked very much like most of the newer tall buildings in the downtown area. From the outside it appeared to be made almost entirely of glass.

There was a sign on the front of the building publicizing space available for offices. It looked like there was space available on the ground level for some kind of a retail business as well. It was obvious the building was not finished.

From the sign, it appeared the Ace Diamond Construction Company was handling the renting. It was not a very common practice in the Denver area. However, I knew from what I had read about the Ace Diamond Construction Company that they did everything themselves.

Not sure what I might find by going inside, I pulled opened the door. As I stepped into the large and pleasantly appointed lobby, I could see nothing had been spared to make it look expensive. It was an obvious case of wanting to make a good first impression, but that was only the surface. I wondered about what was underneath the fancy exterior.

I checked the Directory next to the elevator. There were about five or six companies listed on the directory, but it was clear there was still room for more.

The directory showed two insurance agencies, an investment agency, and a law office with a long list of attorneys. The only retail type business listed was Baby Gap, a store that sells baby clothes and other baby items. Baby Gap was located on the ground floor, but it was not open, yet.

For a building this large, it didn't strike me as very many tenants. The insurance agencies took part of one floor, as did the investment agency. The law firm took another floor. That didn't seem like a lot for a building with sixteen floors. I wondered if the building had been built on speculation. If it had, it was a risky undertaking at best.

I was curious as to how they got Williams to be a part of it. He didn't seem to be the type to take unnecessary risks with his money. What had driven him to take such a risk, I wondered.

Common sense told me there had to be a good sized company planning to move its offices here. My only question was what company? It didn't seem logical that a man with Williams's background and experience would be involved in such a project without having a strong commitment from a major company for the majority of the space in the building.

I looked around the lobby for the rental office. There was a glass door to the right of the elevators that had "Ace Diamond Rentals" neatly printed in gold on it. I figured it would be a good place to start.

As I stepped into the office, I saw it had the same attention to detail as the lobby. It was well lit and the walls were papered with gold-flocked paper. The carpet was a thick plush deep red with a delicate gold pattern running through it. On the walls were a number of framed prints by some well-known Colorado artists. Most of the paintings were of scenes of the Colorado Rockies.

There were several dark cherry wood chairs with dark brown leather seats and backs. The desk was also of dark cherry wood with a matching chair and a brass desk lamp setting on it. The only thing missing was someone sitting behind the desk. The name on the nameplate indicated it should be Jackie L. Bradley.

Looking around, I found nothing I wouldn't expect to find if Arnold Williams had anything to do with it. I expected nothing less than perfection, but there was someone who didn't think the building was so perfect.

I was about to leave to see if I could find someone who could help me when the door behind the desk opened. A woman in her mid-forties stepped into the outer office. She was wearing a tailored gray suit with a white blouse and dark gray tie. She looked every bit the serious businesswoman. She also looked a little surprised to see me.

"Oh. I'm sorry I kept you waiting. Is there something I can do for you?"

She had a very pleasant voice and an equally pleasant smile. It was easy to see she fit into the office.

"It's all right. I was just admiring the building, Miss?"

"It's Ms. Bradley," she replied with an emphasis on the Ms. and an overly polite smile.

"Of course."

"It is very nice, isn't it?"

"Yes. I was wondering who I need to talk to about renting space in this building?"

"Mr. Hamilton would be the person in charge of rentals, but he isn't in at the moment. Maybe I can help you? Can you tell me how much space you will need?"

"Before we get into that, I would like to know what percentage of this building is currently occupied?"

"Ah, right now we have only about ten percent occupancy, but once the building is finished we should have about eighty-five percent occupancy."

"Oh. I take it you have a large firm moving in?"

"Well, ah, yes. However, the management is keeping it quiet for the time being."

"And why is that?"

"I believe the board of trustees made that decision. I don't really know their reasons."

"It would seem to me that it would be a drawing point for anyone thinking about moving here."

She looked at me as if I had caught her off guard. If the anchor firm had not announced its intentions to move here, they must have some concerns about the allegations that came out in the newspaper. If that wasn't the case, the only other reason for not telling was they didn't have an anchor firm totally committed to the building. That alone could prove to make it difficult to get other businesses interested in moving in.

"Could it be the anchor firm has chosen not to commit to your project with the allegations of the building being unsafe hanging over it?" I asked, and then watched her for a reaction.

This was one woman who should never play poker. From the look on her face, I was sure I hit the nail on the head. It was easy to understand why a company would hesitate to commit to a project that might be closed down or its opening indefinitely delayed.

"I can assure you, sir, the allegations will be proven unfounded. The state building inspectors have not found anything to support the allegations," she said, her voice a little shaky.

"I see. I'll tell you what. I'll give Mr. Hamilton a call later in the week to set up an appointment."

"I can take care of it, if you would like."

"I think I'll call back later. Have a nice day," I said with a smile.

As I turned and left the building, I began to think about Williams. Investing in a project of this size, then have it fall under suspicion of being unsafe would have to worry him. If it turned out the building was unsafe, he stood to lose a lot of money to say nothing of the damage it would do to his reputation. Even if the allegations were proven unfounded, it could still leave a mark on the project it might not be able to overcome for many years.

The next thing I needed to do was to take a drive up into the foothills and get a look at the Williams house. If I was going to follow Williams tonight, I wanted some idea where I might start.

I returned to my office and opened the morning mail. After tossing all the junk mail and setting the rest in a basket to take care of later, I left the office.

I HEADED OUT TO THE INTERSTATE that would take me into the foothills. As I drove along the interstate, I began to wonder what was going on between Mr. and Mrs. Williams. A woman who is happy with her life doesn't go looking for trouble. There had to be more to it than meets the eye. I started up into the foothills above Denver with no idea of how the drive would help me figure out what Mrs. Williams really wanted.

Their home was located on Coyote Drive, a paved road that wound around in the foothills. The drive alone was well worth the time. It was as much a scenic drive as anyone could want.

I found their home and pulled off to the side of the road. It was a large sprawling ranch house with a three car attached garage on one end. The house sat back away from the road giving it a little more privacy than some of the other houses in the area. It was built of a reddish brown brick with dark brown trim around the windows and doors, and a cedar shake roof. There were three rather large chimneys indicating at least three fireplaces.

In the back, there was a privacy fence indicating there was probably a swimming pool in the back yard. There was probably a pool house as well. The front yard had a few trees scattered about giving it an open country atmosphere. The lawn was a rich green and nicely trimmed.

I began to wonder about what I was getting into. The rich often had some very interesting secrets they didn't like everyone to know about. Some of them would do almost anything to keep their secrets from the rest of the world. What nasty little secret was I going to find there.

I wondered if Williams was as good a husband as Mrs. Williams was trying to get me to believe. So far there was nothing to indicate that they were not what they appeared to be, a very happy couple, except for his Wednesday evenings without her.

The vehicle parked in front of the house looked out of place. It was a five or six year old Chevy. It looked more like the kind of car the maid might drive. However, I doubted the maid would be allowed to park in front of the house.

I took my binoculars out of the glove box. If I could get the license plate number of the car, it wouldn't take long to find out who owned it.

Looking through the binoculars, I saw the front door opening. There was a tall, dark-haired man wearing white shoes, white pants and white short-sleeved jacket similar to those worn by orderlies coming out of the house. He appeared to be in his mid-twenties and well built. He had a folding table in one hand. I had the feeling that he was probably Mrs. Williams's personal trainer. I had no doubt she would have one. He could be extremely helpful in keeping her in good shape, and she was in excellent shape.

He had no more than stepped out of the house when he stopped and turned back toward the door. Mrs. Williams stepped around from behind the door into the doorway. She was wearing a white robe that came down to just above her knees. She said something to the young man, then leaned forward and kissed him on the lips. It didn't seem to be a very passionate kiss, but who knows. My first thought was he might be more than her personal trainer.

I'm not a naive person. I've been around the block a time or two. I know there are a lot of women who have lovers and still loved their husbands. Mrs. Williams might be one of them.

It crossed my mind that Williams might not know about Mrs. Williams's personal trainer. Well, he probably knows she has one, but I doubted he knows what kind of a relationship she has with him.

I had to admit that having your lover come to the house as a personal trainer was a good cover for the rest of the neighbors, that is if he was her lover. I really didn't have any hard evidence to support that idea. The fact she kissed him only showed they had grown close.

It would not surprise me to learn that several of the women who lived in the area had personal trainers, and they most likely came to the house. It was important for the women to keep a good figure. The competition among these women could be tough. Their status in their social circle was often based on how much money and prestige their husbands had, and how well they looked with him.

Mrs. Williams quickly stepped back and looked around as if she were afraid someone might have seen her kiss him. After giving him one of her sexy smiles, she stepped back into the house and closed the door.

Even as far away as I was, I couldn't miss the smile on the guy's face as he turned and walked to his car. He had obviously enjoyed the kiss. I wondered what else he had enjoyed while visiting her.

I watched him put the folding table in the trunk, then looked back toward the house. I couldn't help but notice the grin on his face when he walked around to the side of the car and got in. He immediately drove down the long driveway to the road.

Since I didn't wish to be seen, I quickly slipped down in the seat and waited for him to drive by. As soon as I heard him drive past, I sat up and watched him disappear around a curve. I managed to get his license plate number before he was out of sight. I wrote it down and slipped it into my shirt pocket. I would call my friend in Motor Vehicles later to find out who the car was registered to. That bit of information might prove valuable later, although, I didn't know how at the moment.

I turned and looked back at the front of the house. I had a lot of things running through my mind all at once. The kiss the man got at the front door could have been nothing more than a thank you, but a thank you for what? What had he done to earn him that kind of thank you?

I know some people get very close to their personal trainers. Not me, of course. I don't have one. Not that I wouldn't mind having one if she was built like Mrs. Williams.

I knew I wasn't here to investigate Mrs. Williams, but it seemed prudent to find out a little about her. I had no burning desire to get dragged into something that would put me in hot water with the police. With the kind of influence Williams had, it would be in my best interest to keep a low profile. I had to be very careful who I talked to about him, and what questions I asked.

The more I thought about it, the more I thought it wouldn't do any harm to follow Williams for a couple of Wednesdays and find out what I could about him. The one thing I always had on my side was I could drop the case and get out if things got too hot.

AS I WAS ABOUT TO LEAVE, I spotted a large black Lincoln Town Car coming up the road. I watched it as it turned in the driveway to the Williams house. I was able to get a glimpse of the driver. It was Arnold P. Williams.

A quick glance at my watch told me that he had missed Mrs. Williams's personal trainer by less than fifteen minutes. It was eleven-fifteen in the morning. I wondered if that was early for him to be home for lunch, or if it was a normal time for him. From what I knew, I doubted he came home for lunch very often. Everything I had been able to get my hands on so far indicated he worked long hours and would most likely not take the time to drive all the way home for lunch.

He pulled up in front of the house and parked. Since the garages were on the end of the house, it was unlikely he planned to stay home for very long. Parking in front would also indicate he was planning to leave again and probably very soon.

As he got out of the car, he walked rather swiftly as if he were in a hurry. He didn't have a briefcase or anything else. He was the type of man who would have a briefcase almost everywhere he went. It was possible he was stopping off to get something he forgot and left his briefcase either in the car, or at the office.

I sat along side the road for a while longer. There were a lot of things running through my mind, but nothing I could prove. In other words, I had no idea what was going on. I wondered if there was anything going on with Mr. Williams that should concern Mrs. Williams. There might be something happening that should concern Mr. Williams, but he was not the one who had hired me.

I took one last look at the sprawling ranch house before I set my binoculars down and started my car. I checked the road behind me before pulling back onto the blacktop. My car had no more than begun to pick up speed when I noticed a police car coming up behind me.

At first I didn't think much of it. I hadn't broken any laws that I knew about. When the police car got close, the light bar came on with red and blue flashing lights. Out of habit, I glanced down at my speedometer and saw I was still well under the speed limit.

I glanced back again as I took my foot off the gas pedal and slowed down. He slowed down as well. I pulled over to the side of the road, stopped and watched as he pulled in behind me.

While I waited for him to get out of his car, I could see he was talking on his radio. He was running my license plate number to see who owned the car. It wasn't long before the officer got out of his car. With one hand on his gun and the other holding his clipboard, he walked up along side my car.

"Good morning," he said politely.

"Good morning, officer. Is there a problem?"

He was looking across the seat at the binoculars. I'm sure he was wondering what I had been doing.

"I would like to see your proof of insurance, driver's license and registration, please," he said politely, but with a tone typical of a person who says the same thing over and over again, day after day.

I reached over to the glove box and retrieved my proof of insurance and registration. After handing them to him, I gave him my driver's license. I watched him as he looked at them, and then handed them back to me.

"There's no problem, Mr. Blackstone. I would like to know why you were parked along side the road for so long?"

"I was thinking."

"You were thinking?" he asked, his eyes showing that he didn't believe me.

"Yes. I sometimes drive to nice places like this, just to think."

I tried to make it sound as if it was the most logical thing in the world. I wasn't really lying to him. After all, I had been doing a lot of thinking. I didn't believe it was in my best interest to tell him that I had been watching the Williams home while I was thinking. I seriously doubted that would be a good idea.

"I see."

I knew he didn't see. The only thing he saw was a car that looked a little out of place in this neighborhood. My two year old Dodge was not a Lincoln or a Cadillac. He had probably received a call from one of the local residents complaining about a car parked on the side of the road that didn't belong there.

"Have I broken any laws, officer?"

"Well, no."

"Then, what's the problem?"

"None, I guess. We received a call of a car parked on the side of the road. We have to check these things out. You understand."

I understood all right. If I lived in this area, I would want a strange car checked out, too. One never knew when someone was casing a house or planning on doing someone harm.

"May I go?"

"Yes, sir. Have a good day," he said as he stepped back away from my car.

I shifted into drive and pulled away. I looked back in my rearview mirror. The officer was still standing on the side of the road watching me. I'm sure he was thinking about what I had told him, and I don't think he believed me.

CHAPTER FOUR

IT WAS SHORTLY AFTER NOON when I returned to my office. I kicked back, put my hands behind my head, closed my eyes and began to think about where I was going to start following Arnold. I knew if I went back up to the foothills, I might run into the police again. I got away with it once, but a second time could prove to be hard to explain.

There were several ideas that came to mind. The first was to start tailing him from where Coyote Drive intersected with the interstate. I could park off the road just before the interchange where it would be hard for anyone to see my car. The only chances of missing him would be if he passed by before I got there, or he went a different way which was highly unlikely because it would be way out of his way.

The second was to take the chance he would be going to the Ace Diamond Building. I could park in front of the building and watch to see who goes in and out. There shouldn't be too many people in the evening. I could park across the street and photograph all those going in and out after hours. Afterwards, I could figure out who they were, if I didn't already know.

The last idea seemed like a good one. I wasn't sure if it was because it was the best, or if it was easiest for me. I wouldn't have to sit in my car as long, and there was little to no risk of being spotted tailing him. The only problem I could see with my plan was I had no idea if his meeting was at the Ace Diamond Building. The one thing I knew was I had time to decide.

Just as I was getting comfortable with my idea of going to the Ace Diamond Building, the phone began to ring. With a sigh of disgust at being disturbed, I sat up and reached for the phone.

"Hello?"

"Hi. Is this Mr. Blackstone?"

"Yes. How can I help you?"

"Have you heard the news?"

"Who is this?"

"It's me, Lisa, Lisa Tittle. You know, Lisa from the library," the tone of her voice indicating she was disappointed I didn't recognize her voice.

"Oh, hi, Lisa.

"Have you heard the news?"

"What news is that?"

"A policeman friend of mine stopped in and told me that Arnold P. Williams had just been killed at his house. Someone shot him," she said, her voice showing her excitement.

I sat right straight up. I couldn't believe what I was hearing. After all, I had seen him go into his house not much more than an hour ago.

"I don't believe you."

"It's true."

"When did you hear about it?"

"Just a couple of minutes ago."

"Do you know when it happened?"

"I'm not sure, but I think it was about an hour ago. According to my friend, someone broke into Mr. Williams's den from the backyard and shot him."

"This friend of yours, you say he's a police officer?"

"Yeah, he works here in Denver. He stopped in on his coffee break to see if I wanted to go out tonight. That's when he told me."

I quickly realized I could have a problem, a serious problem.

"Lisa, did you happen to tell him about the research I was doing yesterday?"

I asked hoping she hadn't told him, but my luck didn't usually run that good, and I had no reason to believe it would be any better today. I held my breath while I waited for her answer.

"Sure."

The tone in her voice showed she was excited. I got the feeling that having helped me with my research gave her some small part in a real live investigation. But telling her friend didn't do me any good. If this police officer friend of hers was any kind of a cop at all, he would let the officers involved in the investigation know about me and what I had been doing in the library. Between him and the officer that stopped me near the Williams's house this morning, there was little doubt I would be getting a visit from the police very soon. I would most likely be one of their suspects. I needed to know how deep I was in.

"What did you tell your friend?"

"Not much, really. I just told him that you had been doing some research at the library into Mr. Williams as part of an investigation you were working on. That's all."

That's all, I thought. Hell, no matter what I did or said now, I was involved up to my neck. I knew a few people on the police force. It suddenly seemed prudent to call one of them and fill him in on my involvement right up front.

"Thanks for the heads up. I'll talk to you later. I have to go."

"Okay, but I think it's kind of funny that the guy you were investigating was killed?"

"I'm sure you do. I have to go," I said, then hung up the phone before she could say anything more.

I'm afraid I couldn't see the humor in it. It wouldn't take the police long before they would be knocking on my door. I wasn't ready to deal with them right now. I still had a couple of loose ends to figure out before I talked to the police.

I immediately left my office and drove toward the interstate. I needed time to think. It seemed like a good idea to do my thinking some place other than at my office. Driving around in my car seemed like a safer place to be at the moment.

As I ran what little I knew about the Williamses through my mind, I remembered the man that had been at their house this morning. It occurred to me it might be a good idea to find out as much as I could about the man in white. It might come in handy when the police start questioning me.

I WAS LOOKING FOR A PLACE to pull off the road and make a call, when I saw a Denny's Restaurant. I hadn't eaten since breakfast and it was almost two in the afternoon. I pulled off the interstate and into the Denny's parking lot. After finding a parking space away from the street, I made a call to the Department of Motor Vehicles on my cell phone. I had a friend there who might be able to tell me whose car had been parked in front of the Williams house. The phone rang several times before it was answered.

"Department of Motor Vehicles, how may I direct your call?" the voice of a woman asked.

"Jennifer Taylor in licensing, please."

"One moment."

Now I know "one moment" in any government agency can be from now to thirty minutes or more. What I needed to know was important enough to wait for as long it took. Besides, Jennifer and I were more than simply friends. On occasion, we had been lovers.

"Licensing, Jennifer speaking."

"Hi, Jennifer."

"Hi, Peter. What's up? You don't usually call me here. Is there something you need?"

It was clear she knew me better than most people. In fact, sometimes I thought she knew me better than I knew myself.

"As a matter of fact, yes. I need you to run a license plate number for me. I need to know who it belongs to."

"Is it important?"

"It could be."

"I shouldn't be doing this, you know, but give me the number."

I gave her the Colorado license number, then thanked her.

"Give me a minute."

I could hear the clicking of a computer keyboard as she typed in the information.

"You owe me for this, you know," she said casually.

"Okay. How much is it going to cost me?"

"I think a nice dinner somewhere classy. Followed by a little wine and a little of your time to keep me company."

"How much time are we talking about?"

"Say, all night," she said, only this time in her sexist voice.

"That sounds fair. Do you have a time in mind or should I suggest one?"

"If I wait for you to suggest it, it could take awhile for me to collect. I was thinking along the lines of tonight?"

"I can't make it tonight, but how about tomorrow night?"

"That'll do," she replied with a slight giggle in her voice.

It was not hard for me to remember the last time we had been together all night. I don't think either one of us got very much sleep. She was one sexy looking woman, and I have had the pleasure of her company on a number of occasions before her last boyfriend. Thinking about our last rendezvous together made me glad she had split up with him.

"Oh, here we go. That license plate belongs to Randolph G. Pressman. P-r-e-s-s-m-a-n," she said spelling it out.

"Can you tell me where he lives?"

Jennifer read me the address. It was out on East Colfax Avenue. If my memory served me right, the address was a run-down motel. It was a place frequented by the police because of drug dealers and prostitutes. It was not one of the nicest neighborhoods in the Denver area.

"Are you sure of the address?" I asked, a little surprised at where he lived.

"Yes. I'm sure. Were you expecting him to live in a higher class neighborhood?"

"I guess I was. At least a little higher class."

"Sorry, but that's all I have."

"It might explain the car he drives."

"It's a pretty old Ford," she said casually.

"A Ford?"

"Yeah. It says here the plates belong on a nineteen ninety one Ford Escort two door, blue in color."

"Those plates were on a ninety six or ninety seven green Chevy."

"You're kidding?"

"No. I'm not."

"Sounds like the plates might have been stolen, or he took them off one car and put them on a newer car without registering it," she suggested.

"And what would be the chances he simply put them on a newer car and didn't register it?"

"Rather slim, I would think. But it's not unheard of."

"I'm sure its not. I guess I'll have to check it out."

"Anything else I can do for you?" she asked a little less business like.

"Not now, but I'm sure there will be something you can do for me tomorrow night," I said to assure her I would be there.

"Sounds interesting. What time tomorrow?"

"About seven?"

"Okay. See you at seven," she said with a smile in her voice.

I hung up the phone and sat there for a few minutes. By all rights I should have been thinking about Jennifer, but my mind quickly returned to the case. I needed to find out if this Randolph G. Pressman was the man I had seen at the Williams house, but that would have to wait until I got myself something to eat.

I WENT INTO DENNY'S and ordered a meal. There was a lot for me to think about before I had a talk with the police. I figured I might have a few hours at best before they got serious about finding me. The last thing I wanted was for the police to keep me from being parked in front of the Ace Diamond Building. I needed to know who went in and out after hours. I had no idea what it would prove, or what to expect. As far as I was concerned it was still worth a try. Besides, I had no other ideas at the moment.

After I finished my meal, I left Denny's and started toward East Colfax.

EAST COLFAX WAS ON the other side of town. By the time I found the address Jennifer had given me, it was going on four o'clock and rush hour had already started. The place was a run-down old motel with graffiti all over it and a chain link fence around the parking lot. Most of the windows on the second floor were boarded up. There was a gate across the stairs to the second level to keep anyone from going up there. It obviously didn't work very well from all the graffiti on the boards over the windows on the second floor.

As I turned into the parking lot, I saw four men wearing ragged T-shirts and filthy jeans. They looked at me with suspicion, probably wondering if I was the police. They quickly disappeared into rooms.

By the time I came to a stop, there was only one person outside the rooms. It was an old bag lady. She stood in front of her grocery cart as if it would keep me from seeing what she had in it. It was her way of protecting all her worldly goods.

The idea of leaving my car unprotected for even a few minutes gave me cause to question the wisdom of being there. I was sure that if I didn't keep an eye on it, it would be stripped right where it was parked.

After locking the car doors, I walked up to the office. There was a sign on the door that said to knock, so I did. It took a few minutes before anyone came to the door. While I waited, I looked around for the car I had seen at the Williams house. The only car in the parking lot was mine.

I turned around at the sound of the door being unlocked and found an elderly black man looking at me. He gave me a quick going over before he spoke.

"What you want? You a cop?"

"No, I'm not a cop. I'm looking for a man who shows your motel as his address."

"A white man?"

"Yes, as a matter of fact," I replied.

"Ain't got no whiteys livin' here."

"How about a Randolph G. Pressman, does he live here?"

"He did, but he don't live here no more."

"Can you tell me where I could find Mr. Pressman?"

"Yeah. He's dead. You'll find him in the cemetery."

I looked at the man and wondered if he was telling me the truth. If Pressman was already in the cemetery, I doubted that I was looking for him. I could see no use in hanging around.

"Thank you for your time."

The old black man didn't say anything more. He simply watched me as he slowly shut the door. As soon as the door was closed, I could hear the unmistakable sound of the door being securely locked from the inside.

As I turned toward my car, I saw that the bag lady was still standing next to her cart. She seemed to be interested in me, for what reason I had no idea. My first guess was she was looking to hit me up for a few bucks for some cheap wine.

There was no one else around, so I decided to talk with her. There was no telling what she might know. I knew that the street people often knew more about what was going on in the neighborhood than the local police. Besides, I wasn't getting anywhere so far, and a cop was the last person I wanted to see right now. She had probably heard most of my conversation with the motel manager so I walked over to her.

The bag lady looked like she might be in her late fifties or early sixties. The clothes she was wearing were old and worn pretty thin in some places. Several buttons were missing and there were holes in the sleeves of her dingy sweater. She was also filthy and half her front teeth were missing.

"Do you see very many white men around this motel?" I asked.

"Naw. Hardly ever."

"Have you seen one lately?"

"Maybe."

"I'm looking for a white man in his mid-twenties. He's about as tall as I am and he's well built. Have you seen anyone like that around here lately?"

"Maybe."

"When did you see him?"

"A couple of weeks ago."

"What was he doing here?"

"Why you want ta know? You goin' to arrest him for stealin' the plates off Randy's car?"

Now there was a surprise. I hadn't said a word about license plates, or the stealing of anything. Yet, she knew about it.

"How do you know about that?"

"I saw him take 'um."

"Did you happen to see where he went?"

"Yeah."

"Where did he go?"

"He went around on that street over there to a house," she said as she pointed toward the corner of the block.

"Do you know which house he went to?"

"Sure do."

"Which one?"

"The third one on the left. It's an apartment house."

"You didn't happen to notice which apartment?"

I knew I was pressing my luck, but I had to ask, anyway.

"Yeah, the one on the top floor in front."

This was getting too good to be true. My first thought was she was trying to tell me what she thought I wanted to know in order to get some money out of me. But there was the possibility, no matter how slim it might be, that she knew what she was talking about.

"How do you know that was the apartment he went in?"

"He took the plates off Randy's car at night. I followed him to the apartment. All the lights was off, 'cept the one on the front porch. Shortly after he went in, the lights on the third floor in front come on. I saw him in the window when he closed the blinds."

"Do you know you would make a very good detective," I said as I reached into my pocket.

The old lady grinned from ear to ear. The gaps in her teeth did nothing to detract from the sparkle in her eyes. That simple comment had made her day.

"You have earned this," I said as I held out a twenty dollar bill.

As she looked at the money, the smile disappeared from her face. She then looked back at me with a surprised expression on her face. I doubted she had seen a twenty dollar bill in a very long time.

"Take the money, you've earned it."

She looked back at the money again. She reached out and snatched it away from me. She took a quick look around before stuffing the bill down the front of her dirty blouse.

"Thanks, mister," she said with a smile.

"You're welcome."

I walked back to my car and left the motel parking lot.

I DROVE OUT ONTO EAST COLFAX and turned at the next corner. As I passed the alley that ran behind the motel, I could see an old blue Ford Escort with the wheels missing. It was a two door and the rear plate was missing. I couldn't see the front of the car, but I assumed the front plate was missing, too. My guess was the car had belonged to Mr. Pressman.

As I continued on down the block, I saw a green Chevy parked on the other side of the street in front of an old apartment house. The license plate on the front of the car was the one I saw at the Williams house. Bingo. I had found where he lived, thanks to the help of an old bag lady.

I pulled into a parking place across the street and sat in my car as I looked up at the third floor windows. I had found where Mrs. Williams's personal trainer lived. The only other question I had was what difference did it make? There didn't seem to be any connection between him and Mr. Williams. I knew he had been at the Williams house, but I had seen him leave before Williams arrived. I had no reason to believe he had anything to do with Williams's murder.

His only crime that I knew of was that he had stolen a set of license plates off a dead man's car. Right now, knowing where he lived would have to do. What I really wanted to know was his name. I had no idea if it would be important, but it was one more piece of information that might come in handy.

It was a long shot, but maybe he had his name listed on the mailbox inside the apartment building. The U.S. Postal Service insisted on it, but didn't always enforce it.

I went across the street to the apartment house. The building had a security door, but it had not shut completely. I pulled open the door and stepped into the lobby where the mailboxes were located.

The entrance way was dark and dingy. From the looks of it, it had been a long time since the walls had been painted or washed. A quick check of the closest apartment door gave me the method of numbering the apartments. If they had carried it out throughout the entire building, the guy I had been looking for lived in apartment C-1 or C-2, C being the third floor.

I checked the names on the mailboxes for C-1 and C-2. The name on C-1 was Sue Perry. The name on C-2 was J. Jackson. Since there were only two apartments on level C, I assumed it must be J. Jackson. I would file that information away in the back of my mind for now. It might prove useful later, but it was not important to me now.

I returned to my car. I sat looking up at the third floor windows as I thought about what I knew. The one thing I knew for sure was that I knew nothing. The best place for me to be was in front of the Ace Diamond Building to see who might be having an after hours meeting there. I started my car and headed for the downtown area.

CHAPTER FIVE

IT WAS SHORTLY BEFORE SIX when I arrived at the Ace Diamond Building. I found a parking space across the street where I could see down the alley that ran along the side of the building. I climbed into the back seat and settled in for a long evening of waiting and watching. I wasn't sure if anything was going to happen, but I couldn't think of a better place to be to find out. I was soon wishing I had stopped and picked up some coffee.

For the first twenty minutes, all I saw were people leaving the building. They seemed to be in a hurry. I guess they were in a hurry to get home. It reminded me of watching a bunch of rats leaving a sinking ship. The rush of people leaving the building gradually slowed to just one or two every now and again.

It wasn't until I saw Ms Bradley that I recognized anyone. Unlike the others, she didn't seem to be in a hurry. I wondered if there would be someone waiting for her at home.

As she started to turn to go down the street, I saw a man in a gray business suit call to her. He was walking pretty fast and waving in an effort to get her attention. Whatever he wanted, it appeared to be urgent.

When Ms Bradley saw him, she smiled and started walking back toward him. She seemed glad to see him. Maybe he was her boyfriend, or possibly her lover. Maybe he was her husband, although I had not seen a ring on her finger when I talked with her in the office.

Once she was standing in front of the man, I realized he was not her boyfriend or lover. They stood fairly close to each other, but did not touch. She looked at him while he talked to her. She looked at his face as she listened to his every word.

I couldn't hear what they were talking about, but it looked as if he was doing most of the talking. I could only see the back of the man, but I could see Ms Bradley's face. The expression on her face went from that of someone listening intently to a look of shock in short order. She put her hand over her mouth and looked as if she was going to cry. Whatever he had said to her, it was obviously not good news. If I had to guess, I would say she had just found out that Arnold Williams had been murdered.

Ms Bradley said something to the man and then turned and started off in the direction she had been heading. The man stood there watching her as she slowly walked away.

As soon as she disappeared around the corner, he looked down at the sidewalk in front of him. He was apparently thinking about something. He looked up for a moment or two as if he wasn't sure what to do next. After taking a deep breath, he looked first one way then the other as if he wasn't sure which way to go. When he turned and looked back down the street, I could see his face clearly. I took a picture of him using my camera with its telephoto lens, and then watched him as he headed back the way he had come.

I sat in the back seat of my car for the next hour and a half without seeing anything of interest. I was beginning to think I had made a mistake. With Williams's death, there might not be a meeting tonight. But then I wasn't even sure Williams had been attending meetings on Wednesday evening. If he had been attending meetings, I wasn't sure that they were in the Ace Diamond Building.

It became apparent if anything serious was going to happen, it wouldn't be until after dark, especially if it was to be a secret meeting. It could turn into a long night.

It wasn't until the same man who had talked to Ms. Bradley returned to the building that there was anything going on. I watched him as he came around the corner and entered the Ace Diamond Building.

There was a lot of glare on the glass windows, which made it difficult to see him after he went inside. However, I was able to see enough to know he went into the rental office. I began to think that he might be Mr. Hamilton, the rental agent. It seemed to make sense when I thought about it. Ms Bradley had listened to him as if he was someone of authority. Mr. Hamilton had been gone when I was there earlier; so I didn't get a chance to meet him. It all seemed to add up, especially since he came back and went into the rental office.

THE NEXT HOUR or so went by very slowly. Traffic slowed to very few cars as it grew late. The sun was setting and a quick glance at my watch told me it was getting on toward eight o'clock. The canyons of the city were beginning to darken.

I was starting to think that my being there might not have been a good idea when I saw a dark colored Lincoln Town Car pull up in front of the Ace Diamond Building. From the back seat of my car I would be able to see anyone who got out of the car, but they would not be able to see me behind the dark tinted windows of my car.

The Lincoln just sat in front of the building with nothing happening. At first I thought they might be waiting for the man I had seen go into the rental office. Suddenly, the door of the Lincoln opened and a man stepped out. He looked up and down the street, but it wasn't until he looked toward my car that I recognized him. It was Frank Waterman. I took a couple of pictures of him in case I needed to verify that he was there.

Before I had a chance to think about it, another car pulled up in front of the building. It parked behind Waterman's car. The car was a shiny black BMW Sports Sedan. I can never remember the numbers they give those cars, but it looked like it was one of the more expensive models. I took a photo of the car and license plate so I could find out who owned it.

The door swung open and a young man got out. I had no idea who he was, or what business he had there. He smiled, walked up to Waterman and they shook hands. Obviously they knew each other.

The young man was tall with a good build. He had dark hair and was very neatly dressed. He could easily pass for a banker, investment broker or a lawyer. From the looks of him, he had money and didn't mind flaunting it.

Now that it was dark outside, I had no trouble seeing inside the building. The lobby was well lighted. As I watched the front of the building, I saw the man who I believed to be Hamilton come out of the rental office to the front door of the building. I watched him through my camera. The look on his face made me think he was worried about something, but I had no idea what.

He opened the door and motioned for Waterman and the yuppie to enter. There was no formal greeting between Hamilton and the other two. Whatever was about to take place, Hamilton apparently considered it to be serious. I watched as they all went to one of the elevators and got in. From my location I could not see the floor indicator light. The only thing I understood was they were having a meeting and it was not going to be held in the rental office. I could only guess what the meeting was about. I thought that it might have something to do with Williams's death since he was the principal investor in the building. That seemed to make sense.

Just then I noticed some movement out of the corner of my eye. I couldn't see what it was, but there was definitely something moving in the alley. A light coming from a window in the alley lit it up enough for me to see it was a dark colored car with the headlights off. It was moving slowly up the alley toward the street.

It stopped, staying well back in the dark shadows of the buildings. I trained my camera on it in the hope of seeing who it might be. About the only thing I was able to make out was that it was a limo, a Lincoln or possibly a Cadillac. There were no lights on the inside or outside of the car. I hoped to get a picture of the license number, but it was too dark.

When the backdoor of the car opened, I saw the dome light come on. All I could see was the dark image of the driver because the dome light was behind him. There was not enough light for me to be able to identify him, or to see who was in the back of the car. I continued to watch in the hope I might catch a glimpse of someone or something that would help identify who it might be.

Whoever had gotten out of the car had gone around behind the car and disappeared. They had used a door off the alley to enter the building. I swung my camera back to the front lobby in the hope of catching a shot of who came in.

Three people entered the lobby from the side. They were all wearing the same style and color coats and hats. The collars of their coats were turned up and their hats pulled down making it impossible to tell who they were, or to get a picture of their faces. They made an obvious effort to never look toward the front of the building.

I took several photos of them before they entered the elevator, but doubted I would get anything useful. From the back they all looked the same, which I'm sure was their intention. If my deduction was correct, only one of them was important. The other two were most likely bodyguards. If that was the case, it meant there were only four people who were of interest at the meeting, the others were bodyguards. The real question was what was the meeting about? Why all the secrecy?

I looked back into the dark alley. The limousine was still there. It was obviously waiting for the three men to return.

Shortly after the elevator doors closed, I observed two men dressed in work clothes come around the corner. I watched them through my camera lens. At first I didn't think anything about it. They were just a couple of working stiffs on their way to work. It wasn't until a light from inside the building reflected off the shoes of one of them that I became interested.

I thought there might be something wrong with what I was seeing and I took a double take. My suspicions were quickly confirmed. One of the men was wearing dress shoes. I began to think there was a good possibility the man had on some much nicer clothes under the coveralls.

One man had a gray sack that looked like a laundry bag. If it hadn't been for the shoes, I might have thought he had rags for cleaning in the bag. Now I wondered what was in the bag.

The other man was dressed in coveralls, too, only he was carrying what looked like a heavy canvas bag. There were a couple of short handles sticking out of the bag. Under normal circumstances, I might have thought they were brush handles of some kind. Taking a closer look, I could see he had one hand inside the bag. He was probably a bodyguard and had his hand on a gun inside the bag. I took a couple of pictures of them. I felt the pictures might prove to be important, but at the moment didn't know how.

The two men turned and entered the Ace Diamond Building. Once they were inside, I tried to concentrate on the man with the shiny dress shoes. There was something about him that seemed familiar, but his baseball cap kept his face in the shadows.

The two "janitors" got into the elevator. I watched them as the doors closed. I was hoping I would get a better look at them, but no such luck. Neither of them turned and looked my way.

I SPENT THE NEXT COUPLE OF HOURS sitting in the back seat of my car watching the building. No one else went in or out of the building. The limo stayed back in the shadows of the alley without moving.

I thought about getting out of my car in the hope of getting a better look at the limo, but decided against it. My car had been seen by at least two of the men who went into the building. There was also the fact the limo driver would probably see me get out and report it to his boss. That could prove to be very dangerous for me. The last thing I wanted to do was to draw any attention to myself.

I remained in the back seat of my car with my camera in hand. Time went by very slowly. It didn't take long before boredom set in. I couldn't help but smile at the thought of Lisa and how she thought being a private investigator was so exciting. At times it could be, but this sure wasn't one of them.

A police car went by the front of the building. It didn't seem to be anything other than a routine patrol. I know the police cruise the downtown area all night. Just to be on the safe side, I took a picture of the police car and noted the time it passed in front of the Ace Diamond Building. It might help verify my whereabouts should I need it.

IT WAS CLOSE TO midnight when I saw the elevator doors open. The three dressed in the same style coats and hats came out first. They kept their heads tipped down so the brims of their hats covered their faces. They quickly disappeared around the corner and left the building by the same entrance they had used when they arrived.

Waterman and the young yuppie came out of the elevator next. The elevator doors closed behind them. They went right out the front door and directly to their cars without any comment to each other.

As they were getting in their cars, I quickly turned my attention to the limo in the alley. The inside lights came on. I still could not see anything inside that would help me identify who it might be.

I was hoping the limo would come straight out of the alley. If it did, I could get a license plate number, but I was hoping for too much. The inside light went out and the limo backed down the alley and disappeared completely into the darkness.

I turned my attention back to the Ace Diamond Building. As Waterman and the yuppie were pulling away, I saw the elevator doors opening again. The two men I had seen in janitor clothes stepped out into the lobby. They were still wearing coveralls and baseball caps. They both had their caps pulled down which made it impossible to get a good look at their faces.

They walked out of the building and stopped on the sidewalk. The one with the canvas bag looked up and down the street. The one with the shiny shoes stood next to him and looked directly at my car, but I still could not see his face with the lights of the building behind him, and the street light off to his side and slightly behind him.

From the way he was looking at my car, I got the feeling he could see me. It made me feel like I was standing naked out in broad daylight. I knew that was not the case, but it still made me feel very uncomfortable.

I really got uncomfortable when the man in the dress shoes reached over and touched the other man's arm, then pointed at my car. I was afraid I had been discovered. It was only when the one with the canvas bag, looked both ways along the street before stepping off the curb that I really got nervous.

I took one quick shot of the man as he walked toward my car before I stuffed my camera under the seat and quickly covered myself with a dark blanket. I laid down on the floor and made myself as small as possible. The fact my car was parked in a place where it was dark, and the side and back windows were tinted pretty dark, made me hopeful he wouldn't be able to see me.

I laid as still as I could. I could hear him try the doors to see if the car was unlocked. Fortunately, I had locked the doors. I couldn't see him from under the blanket. He probably had his face up against the windows in an effort to see inside. By lying down behind the front seats, I hoped he couldn't see me. I had no idea what would happen if he did, but I knew it wouldn't be pleasant.

I waited for what seemed like forever before I slowly raised myself up and pushed myself back up in the rear seat. I peeked out the window and saw the man stepping back up on the curb across the street.

The two men talked for a moment or so, then turned and started back down the street. I let out a sigh of relief when I saw them go around the corner. I sat up and leaned back in the seat.

THE BACK SEAT OF MY CAR was fairly comfortable to sit in, but not when I'm stuffed down between the seats on the floor. I thought about getting out of the car and stretching. I was ready to reach for the door handle when I saw a car come around the corner. It came from around the same corner the two "janitors" had gone around only moments ago. I quickly ducked down in the back seat so the car's lights would not shine on me. It passed by me very slowly.

I got to thinking. If they had come around the corner to see if my car was still there, they might go around the block for another look. I had a lot on my mind at the moment and needed some time to think. I decided to stay there for a little while longer.

I sat in the back seat thinking about what I had seen. It wasn't until I began thinking about who had come out of the building that I became concerned. I realized Hamilton, or whoever he was, had not come out of the building. He had not even come back to the lobby on the elevator. The question that filled my mind was what happened to Mr. Hamilton, or the man I believed to be Mr. Hamilton. Everyone else had come out of the building. A quick look at my watch told me it was well after midnight.

I turned my attention back to the building. The lights in the rental office were out. I remembered Hamilton had turned them off when he came out in the lobby and opened the door for Waterman and the yuppie. That was an indication he didn't intend to return to the office. He had gone somewhere in the elevator with Waterman and the yuppie. He had not waited for the "janitors", or the three men in matching coats and hats.

I remembered the look on his face before he went into the elevator. He looked serious, almost as if he was worried about something. Maybe he had something to be worried about. The only question was what?

It should be safe to go now. I had waited long enough and was about to get out of the back seat when that same large car came around the corner again. I quickly ducked down and waited for it to go by. I was suddenly very glad I had stayed where I was.

It was my guess they would not take another pass. By now they should be sold on the fact that the car was parked for the night. With everyone gone for over twenty minutes, it seemed there shouldn't be any reason for them to believe my car should concern them. I watched them travel down the street until they were out of sight.

I GOT OUT OF THE BACK and into the front seat. As I started my car, I looked over toward the front of the building one more time. I couldn't help but think that there was a good chance Hamilton would be discovered in the morning, dead.

As I pulled away from the curb and started back toward my apartment, I thought about calling the police, but what would I tell them? I didn't know if Hamilton was dead or not. All I knew was he didn't come out of the building with the others and he hadn't returned to the rental office. I had no evidence to justify a search of the building to look for him. In fact, I had no evidence of anything that could even remotely be considered illegal.

I drove back to my apartment and parked my car in the garage. I had a dark room in the spare bathroom. I developed the film I used at the Ace Diamond Building. As soon as I was finished, I hung the photos up to dry.

It was getting pretty late and I had done all I could for tonight. I had seen nothing in the photos I had not expected to see. It was time to get some sleep.

I climbed into bed and laid there looking up at the ceiling. I began to think about Williams. My first thoughts were that Williams's death was the result of catching a burglar in the process of stealing something. But who would steal anything in broad daylight when his wife was at home? My only answer was it had to be something very important to take such a risk.

What could Williams have at home that would be so important it was necessary to break into his den during the day? It didn't seem to make sense. It was more likely someone had followed him home with the intent of killing him, but I had not seen anyone following him. That brought up the question of what did he know, or what did he have that would be dangerous to someone else?

I had been able to put together some connection between Williams and Waterman, a known criminal. But I didn't see how that connection was serious enough to cause someone to want Williams dead. There had to be more to it, but I just couldn't see it. Maybe the photos I took would reveal something once they were dry and I could examine them more closely.

I decided the best thing to do right now was to close my eyes and clear my mind enough to get some sleep. It turned out not to be that easy, but I eventually did get to sleep.

CHAPTER SIX

I WAS UP AS THE SUNLIGHT was just starting to come in through my bedroom window. It looked like it was going to be a great morning to be alive. That thought caused me to wonder if Hamilton was alive to see it.

I swung my legs over the side of the bed, took a deep breath and then stumbled into the bathroom. After a quick shower, I went to the kitchen to prepare my breakfast. My thoughts turned to the photos I had taken last evening. I hadn't taken the time to study them closely last night because they had not dried before I went to bed.

As I drank my coffee and juice and ate my cereal, I thought about all the people I had seen go in and out of the Ace Diamond Building. There were only two I knew, or I thought I knew, Hamilton and Frank Waterman.

As I thought about Hamilton, I realized I didn't know much about him. I had no idea what his background was or what his real job might be. In fact, I knew nothing about him including his personal life. I figured it might be in my best interest to find out as much as I could about him. The best place to start would be at the rental office where I could have a little chit-chat with Ms Bradley.

As for Waterman, I knew a lot about him. I knew about his criminal record as well as some of the scum he was known to associate with. I had a pretty good idea where he lived and that he was married. However, I had no idea if he had any children.

As for the others at the meeting last night, I would have to rely on what my pictures would tell me. Jennifer could help me find out who the yuppie was in the Beamer. I had a picture of his license plate. The others I would have to find some other way to identify them.

After I finished with my breakfast, I went into my dark room, gathered all the photos I had taken last night and took them to the kitchen table. I spread them out and started looking them over.

Using a magnifying glass, I carefully studied the photos of the three men that were all dressed alike. I was unable to find anything in the photo that would help me identify them. There was nothing to set them apart except for their size. One was a bit shorter and built on a smaller frame than the other two. He was the one I wanted to know about. He didn't look hardly big enough to be an enforcer. The other two were certainly big enough.

The next photo was of the limo in the alley. I didn't have much better luck there. The only things I could see in the photo were two of the license plate numbers. The numbers were four and seven, and they weren't in consecutive order. I couldn't make out anything else except the car was black or very dark blue. I could only guess as to the make of it.

I started going through the photos of the two "janitors". I still kept thinking I should know the one wearing the shiny dress shoes, but I couldn't place him. It wasn't until I got to the photo I had taken just before I ducked behind the seats of my car.

It was a rather poor picture of the one coming across the street toward me. The photo was a bit out of focus. I still had the feeling I should know who it was.

As luck would have it, I could easily make out the one with the shiny dress shoes in the background. By sheer accident, I had taken a good photo of him just as he glanced up the street. By turning his head, he had inadvertently let the light from a streetlight shine on his face. It occurred as I was taking the shot of his bodyguard. With the help of my magnifying glass I was able to identify him. It was Joseph Angilara.

Angilara owned a string of Italian restaurants from Fort Collins all the way down the Front Range to Colorado Springs. But more importantly he was one of the biggest, if not the biggest, mobster along the Front Range. The word on the street was he was into drugs, prostitution, money laundering and loan sharking. There was also talk that he controlled several local unions in the construction business, which might help explain why he was at the Ace Diamond Building last night.

Over the years the police had not been able to pin anything on him and make it stick. He had a network of thugs, enforcers, and other lowlifes who would do his dirty work for him. As a result, he had been able to keep his hands clean. There was no doubt in my mind that he had his hands in the pockets of the Ace Diamond Construction Company.

I leaned back in my chair to think. I was pretty sure that Williams would not like it if he knew Angilara had anything to do with any of his projects. Williams would not want any connections to the mob. If Williams had found out Angilara had anything to do with something he was involved in, Williams would most likely pull out and take as much of his money as possible with him. If he did that, the Ace Diamond Building could be in serious trouble of losing any financial backing from Williams's friends who had invested in the project.

There was also the possibility the project would lose its anchor firm as well, if it hadn't already lost it. The loss of an anchor firm could kill the entire project and cost the remaining investors millions. It was certainly a motive for killing Williams.

I wondered if killing Williams was such a good move for people like Angilara. If Williams were dead, what would happen to the money he had promised to support the project?

There was also another possibility. He may not have been killed because he threatened to pull his money out. Williams's word carried a lot of weight. If he thought there was something crooked going on, he would not want his reputation tarnished. If he were to make public what was going on at the Ace Diamond Building, that the building had been built with inferior materials, the entire project could go down the tubes. If that happened, all the investors stood to lose millions of dollars and the Ace Diamond Construction Company would most likely collapse. I wonder if the Wednesday night meetings were with some of Williams's friends who had invested in the project and were to discuss what they should do.

If Williams came out and told the world the building was unsafe, he would lose a great deal of money, but his reputation would still be intact. It might even make him look like a hero. From what I knew about Williams, he would probably be willing to lose the money. He had plenty of it and was making more every day from his other ventures.

On the other hand, Frank Waterman and Joseph Angilara stood to not only lose a lot of money, but to have some serious investigations into their part in the use of inferior materials. That would certainly give them motive enough to have Williams killed before the news could be leaked out to the press. The last thing those two would want would be to have the local, state and Federal authorities investigating them.

I knew I had been doing a lot of speculating and guessing, but I had little solid information to go on. I had no proof that anything involving the Ace Diamond Building was illegal. However, if Angilara was involved in the building, it would be a good indication something was not on the up and up.

The one thing that I had become convinced of was that Arnold was not meeting at the Ace Diamond Building on

Wednesday evenings. He would never meet with the likes of Angilara, in private or in public.

I was not getting any closer to what I had been hired to do by Mrs. Williams. In fact, finding out what Arnold had been doing on Wednesday evenings, and where he had been going, seemed to be unimportant any more. As far as I was concerned, people like Angilara and Waterman made it necessary to look into Williams's death and find out how he was associated with them. There were just too many secrets for me to let it go. My curiosity was getting the best of me.

SUDDENLY MY PHONE started to ring. I glanced over at the phone trying to decide if I really wanted to answer it. I thought about letting the answering machine take the call. I hesitated long enough for the answering machine to get it.

"Hi. You have reached Peter Blackstone. I'm unable to come to the phone at this time. Leave me a message and I'll get back to you," the machine droned on for a second more before a tone sounded.

"Hi. Ah, this is Samantha Williams. I would appreciate it if you would call me as soon as possible."

I reached out and grabbed the phone.

"Hi, this is Peter. Hang on while I shut off the answering machine."

I quickly shut it off and returned to the call.

"Okay."

"Mr. Blackstone, I think we need to get together and talk as soon as possible," she said, her voice sounding urgent.

"I agree. Would you prefer to talk in person or on the phone?"

"I don't want to talk on the phone. I'm afraid there might be somebody listening in."

"Do you think your phone is bugged?"

"I don't really know, but it could be."

The tone of her voice and the way she said it gave me reason to believe she was afraid of someone. If her phone was bugged, it was not going to be easy to tell her where to meet me without someone knowing. Then I came up with an idea.

"Listen very carefully. I want you to meet me at City Park next to the statue of Christopher Columbus."

"Why there?" she asked, her voice sounding like she was confused by my request.

"It's in an open place and it will be hard for anyone to hear what you have to say to me."

"Okay."

"How long will it take you to get there?"

"About forty-five minutes, I guess."

"Okay. Leave as soon as you can."

"I'll get there a few minutes before you do to make sure it's safe."

"Okay."

"Be careful," I said and hung up.

I gathered up the photos and put them in a large manila envelope. The last thing I wanted was for someone to come into my apartment and find them. If Samantha's phone was bugged, whoever was listening in would know I was involved. It would not take them long to find my apartment and take it apart for any information they think I might have.

AFTER HIDING THE NEGATIVES in a secure place, I grabbed my jacket off the chair and headed out the door with the envelope in hand. As I went to the garage, I looked around for anything that didn't seem to belong there. There was nothing out of the ordinary.

I got in my car and slipped the envelope under the seat. I headed for City Park where I was lucky enough to find a parking place not far from the statue of Christopher Columbus. From where I parked I could see a good part of the park. I carefully watched everything that was going on from my car. It was important for me to know as much about what was going on in the park as I could. It could make the difference between getting out of the park alive or dying there.

The people I was dealing with would stop at nothing to get what they wanted. If Samantha's phone was bugged, it was because they felt she had something they wanted, or they thought she knew something that might cause them a problem.

I had a problem. My problem was a simple one, one that is often the most serious and hardest to deal with. It was the fact that I had no idea who "they" were. It could be any of those I had seen at the Ace Diamond Building last night, or it could be someone else.

I also had no idea what "they" were up to and how Samantha was involved. The first thing I had to do was to find out what Samantha might know. From the sound of her voice she was scared, but of what? It could be she knew she was in danger. There was also the possibility that whoever had killed Williams had not gotten what he was there for, and thought Samantha might have it. Whatever "it" was, she was worried and had every right to be. The people I had seen last night were not the type of people anyone should mess with.

While watching the park, I saw a man in a dark suit casually walk up to the statue of Christopher Columbus. There was something about the way he walked and the way he looked around that caught my attention. For one thing he wasn't dressed like a tourist. It was interesting that he didn't seem to be looking at the statue even though he walked up to it as if he was interested in reading the plaque at the base. He seemed to be more interested in looking around the park. He was playing it cool, but not cool enough.

He looked around for a little bit, and then he bent down and pretended to tie his shoe. While he was bent over, his coat fell open. I could see part of a gun tucked under his left arm in a shoulder holster. I only got a glimpse of it, but it was enough to alert me to possible trouble. The question racing through my mind was, is he a cop or an enforcer? I studied him closely. I couldn't be sure which he was, but I was sure that either way I didn't want to have anything to do with him.

A quick check of my watch told me that Samantha should be here at any minute. I kept one eye on the guy with the gun while looking for Samantha. I was armed, but I didn't want to use a gun in the park. There were too many people around. An innocent bystander could get hurt.

It wasn't very long before I caught a glimpse of movement in the passenger's outside rearview mirror. It was Samantha. She had apparently parked somewhere behind me.

A quick look at the man near the statue was all I needed to know. He had seen her, too. He had straightened up and looked around as if he might be looking for me. He started to move toward her. As Samantha started to walk past my car, I rolled down the window on the passenger's side and called her.

"Samantha, get in," I yelled.

She hesitated for only a second.

"Get in," I yelled again.

She glanced up and saw the man coming toward her. He was almost running. She quickly opened the door and jumped in. I slammed the car into gear. As the car jumped to life, the door slammed shut. I was out in the traffic before Samantha had a chance to buckle her seat belt.

As I sped down the street, I could see the man in my rearview mirror. He had run out into the street and was watching us. I hoped he had not gotten my license plate number, but I couldn't take the chance. If he had any connections at all, it would not take him long to find out who I was and where I lived.

As far as I was concerned, there were only two people the man could have been. He was either a cop, which I seriously doubted, or he was a hit man to make sure Samantha never got a chance to talk to anyone about what she might know. The only question I had at the moment was what do they think she knows?

I GLANCED OVER AT SAMATHA and could see her chest rise and fall with each breath she took. The look on her face told me that she was scared to death. She turned her head and looked at me.

"Was that one of them?"

"I don't know, but I wasn't planning to stick around to find out. What was it you wanted to talk to me about?" I asked as I slowed down to the legal speed limit.

"Can it wait until I catch my breath? I've never been so scared."

I glanced over at her before I replied, "Sure."

I drove south along Broadway to Littleton. I had no idea where I was going, but I needed time to think. As long as we were moving, we were relatively safe.

"Let me ask you, do you have any place you can go where you would feel safe?"

Samantha looked at me. The expression on her face gave me the impression she had no idea what to say. When she looked down, I realized she probably didn't have very many friends outside of the circle her husband had circulated in. With Arnold dead, she probably didn't have anyone she could look to for help.

Samantha didn't look like the rest of the high society women. She was different, more like a model than someone who had been raised with money. The fact that she was very sexy looking must have played a part in how she was treated by the upper crust of Denver society. It was one thing to be beautiful, but quite another to be sexy as well.

I was beginning to understand her a little better. She was not from a wealthy family, which might have been the reason I had seen nothing about her in the newspapers except with Arnold. My guess would be that he had been able to protect her from gossip from those who were jealous of her good looks. She was a poor little girl who had used her good looks to marry well. I was sure some of her so called friends in high society talked about her behind her back for that very reason.

"Mr. Blackstone, I don't have any place to go. I don't have any money, or a home to go to. I have nothing," she said her voice showing she meant what she said.

"You're the widow of Arnold P. Williams. That alone should set you up for the rest of your life."

"Well, it doesn't," she said rather sharply.

"How so?" I asked, curious about what she was saying.

"Arnold and I had an agreement," she said, then stopped and looked down at her hands folded in her lap.

"What sort of an agreement?"

She looked up and turned to me.

"I get nothing if Arnold died any other way than by natural causes. If he died of natural causes, I would get an allowance that would keep me for the rest of my life and the house in the foothills. Most of the rest of his estate would go to his pet projects like the Performing Arts."

"But you had nothing to do with his death, did you?"

She looked at me, her eyes narrowed slightly. She obviously didn't like my question and what it implied, but I didn't care. I not only wanted answers, I wanted a very good reason to help her. She took a deep breath before she replied.

"No. I had nothing to do with Arnold's death."

"Was this agreement in writing?"

"Yes."

"Did you have a lawyer look at it?"

"No, I loved Arnold. I only signed the agreement because I wanted him to know that I wanted him, not his money."

"I think we need to find a safe place for you until we can get this all sorted out."

"I don't have any money, but would you help me find out who killed Arnold and why?"

I glanced over at her for a second before I replied. I had to ask myself if it really made any difference what direction my investigation took. Did it really matter if I was looking for Williams's killer, or if I was looking into why he was going out on Wednesday evenings without Samantha? I didn't think so.

"You retained me. You are my client even if the direction of the investigation has changed. Let's start by finding you a safe place to hold up for now."

"Thank you," she said with a faint smile.

"You're welcome," I replied. "I've got a friend that has a little motel in Lakewood. I'll take you there. You'll be safe there until I can find out what is going on and what the police know."

"Thank you," she said again as she reached over and put her hand on my arm.

IT WAS ONLY ABOUT a twenty-minute drive to my friend's motel, but I took a lot of detours to make sure there was no one following us. It was past noon by the time we arrived at the motel.

After explaining what I needed to Alex Tindell, my friend, I got Samantha a room. As soon as she was settled in, I went out alone to get us something to eat and took it back to the motel. We sat in her room and talked while we ate.

She talked mostly about Arnold and all the things he was involved in. She never mentioned the Ace Diamond Building. That sort of puzzled me. I wasn't sure if it was because she didn't know about it, or because she did know and hoped I didn't.

As soon as we finished eating, I thought it was best if I got out of there. I had no desire to be seen in the area. Besides, my car was parked out in front. Whoever had been in the park would be looking for it. It could only bring attention to her.

I wanted to get hold of Jennifer and see what she could tell me about the owner of the Beamer. I also thought about getting hold of one of my friends in the police department and see if I could find out anything about the investigation of Arnold's death. I still wasn't sure it was a good idea to contact the police just yet. I needed more information about what was going on.

CHAPTER SEVEN

I LEFT THE MOTEL after giving Samantha strict instructions not to stick her head out the door of her room, to keep the shades drawn and not to even peek out. If she needed anything, she could call the office and have my friend get it for her. It was the only way I could think of to keep her safe until I had a better idea of why her husband had been murdered.

On my way back to the downtown area, I decided I would make a stop at the Ace Diamond Building to see if I could find out anything about Hamilton. It took me only forty minutes to get to a parking place near the front of the building.

Before getting out of the car, I took a minute to look around. I was half expecting to see the police swarming all over the building looking for Hamilton. I didn't see any policemen or police cars around at all. That meant only one of two things. Either no one had found Hamilton's body, or he wasn't dead. I needed to know which.

I got out of my car and walked to the front door of the building. Taking a moment to glance inside, I could see the door to the rental office was open. Ms Bradley was sitting behind the desk. There did not seem to be anything out of place. I decided to go in and talk to her.

Once inside the lobby, I stopped and listened for anything that might seem out of place. It was quiet. The only thing I could hear was the hum of the copier coming from inside the rental office door. It made me think it was Sunday since it was so quiet.

I went to the rental office and stuck my head in the door. When Ms Bradley looked up, I smiled and stepped into her office.

"Hi," I said as I moved closer to her desk.

"Hi," she replied with a pleasant smile.

I could tell she was not expecting to see me again so soon. There was nothing in the way she looked that would indicate there was anything wrong. It was obvious she wondered why I had returned, but she didn't let on she was going to ask.

"Does Mr. Hamilton happen to be in?"

"Not at the moment. I did tell him that you had stopped in and would probably be calling him for an appointment."

"Have you seen him this morning?"

"No. He had a late meeting last night. He doesn't usually come in until after lunch when he works late, unless he has an appointment, of course."

"Of course."

Her voice was pleasant and straightforward. If there was anything wrong, she didn't have a clue. The fact Hamilton had not come to work yet didn't seem to bother Ms Bradley, but then why would it if it was his usual routine not to come in early after a late night meeting.

"When do you expect him in?"

"I'm not sure. There was a message on my answering machine this morning saying he might not be in all day."

"I see. Did he leave the message personally?" I asked as if it was a normal question.

She looked at me sort of funny. The pleasant smile faded away before she spoke.

"No, as a matter of fact it was left for me by someone else," she replied as she looked at me. "How would you know that?"

"Just a wild hunch."

I could tell by the expression on her face she was confused. So was I. Why would someone leave her a message saying Hamilton would not be in today? The only answer was to keep anyone from looking for him for a little longer. Maybe his body had been hidden until it could be removed from the building without anyone knowing.

Then again, maybe it was my suspicious nature along with what I had seen last night that made me think what I was thinking. Hamilton had not returned to his office after everyone else had left last night. That was enough to make me wonder what had happened to him.

It was time for me to leave before Ms Bradley started asking too many questions I wasn't prepared to answer. I bid her a quick good day and left the building. I had left her with a lot to think about and probably a lot to worry about.

I RETURNED TO MY CAR and left for my office. As I drove by the front entrance, I saw a police car parked in front of the building. It made me think the police were in the building to see me.

I turned the corner toward the entrance to the underground parking garage, but decided to drive on down the street. It was time to find out who the man in the Beamer was. I wanted that information before I paid a visit to the police even if I didn't know what value it would be.

I found a parking place on one of the side streets and parked. I placed a call to the Motor Vehicle Department and asked for Jennifer. It didn't take long before Jennifer answered the phone.

"This is Jennifer, how may I help you?" she said in her most professional voice.

"Hi, it's me."

"Hi, me. How are you?"

"I need another favor. I need you to run another license plate for me."

"Is that all you need me for, to run license plate numbers for you?"

"I need you for a lot more than that, I can assure you."

"That's sweet. In that case, I'll try to help you. What's the number?

I gave her the license plate number and waited while she typed it in the computer. I was feeling a little guilty about using her that way, but I didn't see that I had much choice. I didn't know anyone else who could help me.

"Well, let's see what we have here," she said. "It seems the plate belongs to Jeffery M. Mosser. Oh my, he lives in one of those fancy lofts in LoDo."

I knew what she was talking about. The area of LoDo, as they liked to call it, was an area where a bunch of old warehouses and freight buildings in the lower downtown section of Denver had been renovated and converted into condos and loft style apartments. It was *the* place to live if you were a preppy or a Yuppie.

The well-to-do young executive types liked the area. It was close to Larimer Square Historic District with places like the Wolfgang Puck Café, The Penalty Box, the Rock Bottom Brewery and several other microbreweries that were also sports bars. It was *the* in place to be on Friday and Saturday nights.

I had been to several of the establishments in the square. Most of them were full of loud music, loud sports games on big screen TV's and plenty of women. Most of them were not to my taste, but some people like it.

Jennifer gave me Mr. Mosser's address and described the kind of car he drove. It matched perfectly with the car I saw the license plates on, so I was sure I had the right man this time. He fit the profile of a young man who would live in LoDo.

"Thanks."

"We still on for tonight?"

I could hear a hint of hope in her voice. The last thing I wanted was to disappoint her.

"Sure, but it might be a little later than seven."

"How much later?"

"Would ten be too late?" I asked hoping she would be agreeable.

"No, I guess not."

"How about if I bring something to eat and we stay at your place?"

"Are you trying to get out of taking me out to dinner?"

"Well, yes and no. I don't think I will be able to take you out to dinner tonight, but I really do want to see you. Maybe we could go out to dinner later in the week? Maybe make two nights of it?"

"That sounds good, but I know you. What's going on, Peter?"

"I'm working on a case and it's getting a little, shall we say, interesting."

"You mean it's getting dangerous. Peter, what have you gotten yourself into now?"

The sound of her voice gave me a clue to what she was thinking. She was the one person in my life I found it very hard to tell even a little white lie. I knew it would be far more than a little white lie if I didn't at least clue her in on what I was up against, but not now.

"I'll explain everything tonight. I promise."

"Peter," she said with that tone that insisted on a response.

"Honey, it has to do with the death of Arnold P. Williams, and that's all I can say about it right now. But I do have a request."

"What is it?"

"Can I stay overnight with you tonight?"

"Only if you tell me what's going on, and only if you stay with me all night," the tone of her voice telling me that she meant what she said.

"You've got a deal. I'll see you around ten, okay?"

"Okay. And Peter, take care of yourself. I really do need you."

"I will, and I need you, too," I replied, then hung up.

I sat in my car for a few minutes to think about my call to Jennifer. It was hard for me to get a picture of her out of my mind. She was the one person in my life who seemed to understand me. I could talk to her without having to hold anything back.

I TOOK A DEEP BREATH and decided it was time to go to my office and see if there were any policemen waiting for me. The more I thought about it, the more I began to think it might be best if I went to the police station where I could turn myself over to one of my friends. It might prove to be less of a problem.

As I reached down to turn the ignition key, a dark blue sedan with a flashing red light on the dash pulled up behind me. There was no doubt in my mind it was too late. The police had found me. They would have a lot of questions. After all, they knew I had been in the area of the Williams house, and I had been looking into Arnold Williams at the library. Those two things alone would make me one of their prime suspects.

I took my fingers off the ignition key and put both hands on top of the steering wheel. The last thing I wanted was for some badge happy rookie cop to get nervous and shoot me. I watched in my rearview mirror as the officer in the sedan placed a call on his radio. He was checking the license plate to make sure he had the right car. While he was on the radio, he was watching me.

After several minutes, the officer put the radio down and started to get out of his car. With the glare on the windshield, I could not identify the officer while he was in the car. It wasn't until he got out that I saw who it was. I let out a sigh of disgust and disappointment. Of all the officers to pick me up for questioning, it had to be him.

The officer was Lieutenant Daniel Royal, better known as "Royal Ass", as in the "King of Asses". We had had several run-ins over the past few years, and most of them had left him with egg on his face. How he had gotten to the rank of Lieutenant was beyond me.

I looked up as he approached my car. It was not going to be a pleasant experience. He had it in for me. I was sure he was thinking this was his chance to get even for all the times I had made him look bad.

"Well, well, well. If it isn't the great Peter "wise-ass" Blackstone," he said with a nasty grin. "I've been waiting for the time when I could arrest you."

"I'll just bet you have. What am I being arrested for?"

"Murder," he replied with a stupid grin.

"I believe you're mistaken, again. I'm wanted only for questioning about a murder."

"It's the same thing to me," he said as he pulled the door open. "Get out and put your hands behind your head."

As much as I dislike the man, and as many opportunities as he had given me to knock him on his ass, I did as he instructed. I really didn't need any more trouble, and certainly didn't need any trouble with the police.

If I kept my mouth shut, there wasn't much Royal could do except to rough me up a little. The thought of that made me smile. If he did, it wouldn't take much to have him fired. That would give me far more satisfaction than knocking him on his ass. Although knocking him on his ass would make me feel pretty good right about now.

"Well, what do we have here," he said as he reached inside my coat and took my .38 caliber pistol out of my holster.

"It's a gun. You know what a gun is, don't you? By the way, you might be interested to know I have a permit to carry a concealed weapon. But you already know that."

"Well, smart ass, you're on your way to jail."

Royal cuffed me and was none to gentle about it. I didn't say anything as I didn't want to give him the satisfaction. He pushed me into the back seat of his police car, then got in the front.

It was a very uncomfortable ride to the police station, but I wasn't about to let him know it. I would take my time, and when my time came he would be the one who was uncomfortable.

When we got to the police station, he took me to an interrogation room and pushed me down in a chair. Royal had been enjoying tormenting me so much he had failed to read me my rights. I knew that anything I said at this point could not be used against me if I should go to trial on some trumped-up charge. I also knew it was in my best interest not to say anything.

"You just sit there," he snarled as he turned and left the room. "I'll be back in a minute."

The one thing I have always known was there was someone behind the large mirror on the wall watching me. Everything I said would be recorded. So I sat quietly and said nothing. I wasn't sure what time it was because Royal had my hands cuffed behind me. I couldn't raise my hands enough to see my watch.

Unlike most who have been arrested, I didn't sit there looking around. I sat quietly looking at the table directly in front of me and never changed the expression on my face. I was not going to give whoever was behind the mirror the satisfaction of knowing they had me worried.

IT WAS SOME TIME BEFORE Royal came back to the room, maybe an hour. When he came in, I didn't even look up at him.

"I've got you now," Royal said.

I knew he was trying to get a reaction out of me. I was not about to give him the pleasure.

"We know you were parked in the street across from the Williams house about the time he was murdered. What were you doing there?"

I didn't respond to him. His voice indicated he was looking to solve the case by himself, but I doubted he could find a missing Great Dane if it was tied to his ankle.

"Why were you in the library looking up information on Arnold P. Williams?"

Again, I didn't look up or answer him.

"You're going to answer me or I'm going to arrest you."

I turned my head slightly and looked at him. It was probably the slight grin on my face that made him mad as hell.

"We've got a witness that puts you at the scene of the murder. We've got a witness who told us about your interest in Arnold Williams. We've got a bullet that tells us he was shot with a .38 caliber pistol just like the one you carry, and we know the kind of investigator you are. Now, what were you doing at the Williams house?"

I said nothing. I just continued to look at him. I could see he was getting a little impatient with me.

"Damn it, you're going to talk to me," he said as he slammed his fist down on the table.

He reached out, grabbed me by the collar and pulled me up out of the chair just as the door to the interrogation room swung open. He turned sharply as if to say something, but said nothing. I saw his jaw drop open as he quickly let go of me. I turned to see Captain MacDonald walk in the room. I was a little surprised to see Mac show up, but I was not surprised that he was the lead officer in the investigation of Arnold Williams's death. He was a good investigator.

"What's going on here," he demanded as he looked at Royal.

"I'm trying to get him to talk. He refuses to say anything, not a word."

"All I asked you to do was to pick him up so I could talk to him about Williams. I didn't tell you to arrest him unless he refused to come in willingly. I seriously doubt Peter would resist that kind of a request. Take those damn cuffs off him, and do it now."

It was clear MacDonald was mad as hell at Royal. Mac and I go back a long ways. We've known each other for well over fifteen years. I've helped him a time or two, and he's helped me. I wouldn't say we were friends, but we had a healthy respect for each other, and that goes a long way in my book.

Royal reluctantly took the cuffs off me. He had put them on tighter than was allowed by police regulations. I had to rub my wrists to get the circulation back.

"You all right, Pete?"

"Sure Mac, but you better put him on a short leash."

"You son of a .. "

"That's enough, Royal," Captain interrupted. "I suggest you leave before you have more problems than you can handle. You'll be lucky if Blackstone doesn't prefer charges against you. Now, get out."

Royal looked like he wanted to say something, but with the Captain for a witness he thought better of it. I watched as Royal looked at me, then at the Captain. There was some reluctance in his willingness to leave, but to do otherwise would not be good for his career. I wondered what his career would be like once I told Mac what had happened from the time Royal picked me up until he showed up.

"You okay?" Mac asked as soon as Royal had left the room.

"Yeah."

"What did you mean by your comment about keeping a leash on Royal? I already know he doesn't like you."

"That can wait for now. I'll file a formal complaint, in writing, later," I said as I rubbed my wrist.

"Okay, but I expect to see it on my desk within a couple of days."

"Mac, I'm not one of your rookies," I reminded him. "I'll get it to you when I'm ready."

"Okay, Pete. I'm sorry. This Williams thing has got me under the gun," he said as he sat down across the table from me. "Everybody who is anybody is on my neck to get it solved, and I don't have a single lead. So far the CSI people haven't found anything helpful."

I could understand his frustration. It was a high profile case, and I was sure there was a lot of pressure from the top to get it resolved.

"After Williams was killed, we got a call from a local Deputy Sheriff. He said he made contact with you across the street from the Williams house the day he was murdered. Can you tell me what were you doing there?"

"I was doing a little surveillance."

"Of who?"

"Can't tell you that."

"I know there are client privileges you have to protect; so I won't ask who you are working for, but I'm looking for a murderer. Is there anything you can tell me that might help?"

"I can tell you that while I was checking out the Williams house from the road, I saw Arnold P. Williams drive in the driveway only minutes after Mrs. Williams's personal trainer left. I saw no one else come or go."

"Can you tell me when her trainer left?"

"He left about fifteen minutes before Arnold drove in the driveway. If you need the time down to the minute, I'll have to check my notes."

"Can I ask what you are working on?"

"You know I can't tell you that, but I'll tell you this much. You might want to look into the investors of the Ace Diamond Building. That's all I can say for now."

"Has the news story about the inferior material in the Ace Diamond Building got something to do with it?"

"Check into the investors. That's all I can say until I check with my client."

"Okay, I'll do it. By the way, do you happen to know where we might find Mrs. Williams? We would like to have a talk with her. It seems she disappeared shortly after we talked to her at her home right after the shooting."

"Mac, I've said all I can say for the moment. I'll speak to my client. If I'm allowed to tell you more, I will."

"Fair enough. I'll be in touch."

"Me, too. Can I get a ride back to my car? There's probably a ticket on it for overtime parking, that is if it is still there. Royal didn't lock up my car or take the keys out of it."

"I'll get you a ride. If there's a ticket on it, I'll get it voided since we forced you to leave your car there," Mac said.

I nodded that I appreciated his gesture of goodwill. Mac arranged for one of the officers to give me a lift back to my car. My car was still there with the keys in it. There didn't happen to be a ticket on the windshield.

AS I OPENED THE DOOR to my car, I watched the officer drive on down the street and turn at the corner. I glanced around half expecting to see an unmarked police car that was going to be tailing me. I was not going to be disappointed.

Halfway down the block there was a sedan with a man sitting behind the wheel. The interesting thing about it was it didn't look like any kind of car the police would use. It was one of those high-priced BMWs, but not the one I had seen Mosser driving.

At first I couldn't think of anyone other than the police who would be tailing me, that is until I remembered the man in the park who had tried to snatch Samantha off the street. If it was the same guy, he must have some connection with someone who could run my license plate. My car was close to my office, which might explain how he found it so quickly.

He wanted Samantha. There was no doubt I would have to lose him if I wanted to contact Samantha. The last thing I wanted to do was to have him go everywhere I went.

I decided I would let him follow me to my apartment. While he was figuring out what to do, I would slip out the back and grab a cab to some place where I could rent a car of a different make and color than my car.

I got in and pulled away from the curb. A quick glance in my rearview mirror showed he was less than a block behind me. I turned a couple of corners and he was still right there. That certainly confirmed he was tailing me.

When I pulled into the parking lot of my apartment complex, I watched as he drove past the entrance and parked in the street. That made it easier for me. It gave me a few extra seconds to carry out my plan.

I drove to the garage and parked inside, then went in my apartment. I ran through the apartment and out onto the back balcony.

After making sure there was no one out back, I slipped over the railing of the balcony and dropped the eight or so feet to the ground below, then hurried along the back of the building to the corner. A quick look around the corner showed me that the guy was heading to my apartment. He was probably planning to confront me at the door. He must want Samantha pretty bad if he had guts enough to come after me in broad daylight to get to her.

I even thought about waylaying him at my apartment to see what I could get out of him, but that might prove to be the wrong choice. I had Samantha to think about at the moment. He would have to wait. I would have another opportunity to confront him. I would make sure of it.

I ran around behind the garages and out to the street at the end of the apartment complex. I went several blocks before I called a cab. I had the cab take me to an Avis car rental place on South Broadway. I rented a car and drove to the motel where I had left Samantha.

CHAPTER EIGHT

WHEN I ARRIVED BACK at the motel, I found Samantha sitting in front of the television watching the news. There was a deep sadness in her eyes that told me she really did miss her husband. She looked up at me, her eyes pleading for me to understand how she felt.

The anchorman was speaking in low soft tones as he talked about Arnold P. Williams and how much the community would miss his dynamic presence. I was sure Samantha would miss him, too, but I needed to put that aside for the moment and focus on what might happen next.

"You don't need to be watching that right now," I said as I reached over and turned off the television.

"He was a good man. Who would want to do this to him?"

"I don't know, but I intend to find out."

"Do you think you can?"

"I don't know, but I'm going to try."

"Thank you. Thank you for understanding."

"You're welcome, but I have a little problem. I have not been able to figure out what is going on, and why your husband was murdered.

"I don't know what I can do to help."

"Samantha, you don't mind if I call you Samantha, do you?"

"No, of course not. My close friends call me Sam. You can call me Sam if you like.

"All right, Sam. First of all, I need to know that you understand how important it is for you to remain here and stay out of sight at least until I figure out what is going on?"

"I think I do."

"Good. You're a very public figure in this town. Your picture has been in the newspapers and on television enough that almost anyone in the Denver area would recognize you anywhere you go. I can't risk someone seeing you as long as there's a chance that your life is in danger."

"Do you think my life is in danger?"

"Yes, I do. The police picked me up this afternoon for questioning. When I was released and taken back to my car, there was someone staking it out. He followed me to my apartment. It was the same man who tried to grab you in the park. Based on what I heard and saw, I seriously doubt he's a cop."

I could see the concerned look on her face. It was beginning to soak in that she might very well be a target.

"Right now, I need to know everything you know. I have a lot of questions to ask you, and I want you to think about each one very carefully. Do you understand?"

"Yes. I'll do my best to answer them."

"Good. You were in the house when Arnold was shot, weren't you?"

"Yes. Yes I was."

"Did you see who shot your husband?"

"NO. If I had, I would have told the police," she replied sharply as if I had asked her the unthinkable.

"I'm sure you would have. Did you see anyone run from the house or see anyone in the yard that didn't belong there?"

"No," she said thoughtfully.

"I want you to tell me everything you can remember about that morning. I want you to start with what you were doing when Arnold came home. I want every little detail you can think of, even if you think it is not important."

"Okay," she replied, then leaned back in the chair and began to think about that morning.

"I was just stepping into the shower when I heard Arnold come into the house. I had just had a session with my personal trainer, and I needed to take a quick shower before I went to see why Arnold had come home and to find out what was wrong."

"How did you know it was Arnold when he came in the house?"

"He called to me from the front hall when he came in. I told him I would be there after I showered."

"Why would you think there was something wrong when Arnold came home for lunch?

"Arnold almost never came home for lunch. He usually ate lunch in town, usually somewhere near his office."

"Okay. Continue," I said.

"I took a quick shower. Just as I was getting out of the shower, I heard the door to the den close. I had finished drying off and was putting on my robe to go to his den when I heard two shots."

"Are you sure there were two shoots, no more, no less?"

"Yes. I heard just two shots."

"What did you do when you heard them?"

"I hurried to his den. I called out to him, but he didn't answer me. I tried the door, but it was locked."

"Did he often lock the den door?"

"No. He almost never locked it. He didn't keep anything from me," she said.

"He kept something from you. That's why you hired me," I reminded her.

"Well, yes, but he never locked me out of the den, or any other room in the house."

"Go on, please."

"Well, I ran back to our bedroom and got the spare key to the den from his dresser. I returned and unlocked the door," she said, then paused for a moment as she took a deep breath.

There was no doubt it was hard for her.

"When I finally got the door opened and looked in the den, I saw him slumped over his desk. There was blood on his desk and on the wall behind it," her voice cracking as she relived the moment. "I just stood there looking at him. I don't know for how long. I . . I guess somewhere deep inside I knew he was dead. It was about that time I heard what sounded like a motorcycle start up. It might have been an ATV.

"When I heard it start up, I looked out the back. The patio door off the den was wide open."

"Did you see anyone or anything?"

"No. I vaguely remember turning around and going to the phone in the front hall to call the police. I called 9-1-1. I don't remember anything after that until the police arrived. I just sat down outside the den and cried," she said as a tear slowly slid down her cheek.

"I know this is hard, but I need this information. You said you saw the patio door was open. Was it unusual for Arnold to have the patio door in the den open?"

"Yes. Arnold didn't like the breeze blowing in from the hills while he was working. He didn't like any outside distractions."

"Were there often distractions?"

"When the weather's nice, there are almost always kids riding their dirt bikes back in the hills behind our place. It can be very distracting when you're trying to read or concentrate on something."

"Do you know if the police found anything to indicate there had been someone behind your house driving a motorcycle or ATV?"

"No. After I told them what I had seen and heard, they had a policewoman take me to my room. She stayed with me until they were done in the den. They didn't talk to me again accept to ask me if I had someone I could stay with. I don't think they wanted me in the house while they gathered evidence. I did see one policeman walking around behind the pool house, but I don't know if he found anything."

"Where were you calling from when you said you needed to talk to me? Were you at home?"

"Yes. I had returned home for a few minutes to get some things. I've been staying with a friend in Denver. I couldn't stay in the house knowing Arnold had been murdered there. I know I will have to go back sooner or later, but I need time to accept what has happened."

"I understand."

Actually I did understand, but I had a lot of things running through my mind. An ATV or dirt bike type of motorcycle would explain how the killer got away without being seen from the road in front. It would also explain how the killer got to the house without anyone noticing. That area of the hills was heavily wooded and had a lot of trails back behind the houses. The hills behind the houses belonged to the U.S. Forest Service.

I had no idea where any of the trails went, but my guess would be they would make a good escape route for someone who knew them. I felt like it might be a good idea if I went back in there and found out where the trails went for myself.

"Have you had anything to eat?"

"No."

"I'll have Alex get you something."

I called the motel office and had Alex place an order for dinner for Samantha in his name. I reminded him how important it was that he was the only one to see Mrs. Williams, and that no one was to know she was there.

"You ordered dinner for just one. Aren't you going to stay and eat with me?" Samantha asked, her eyes showing her disappointment.

"No. I have a lot to do. I'll get something to eat later."

"I get pretty lonely here all by myself. Will you be coming back later?"

"Not tonight."

She didn't want me to leave her alone, and I couldn't blame her. I think she probably had it in her mind that I would stay all night to protect her. She was a beautiful woman; and if things were different, I might not mind spending the night with her. It was just that I didn't think it was a good idea under the circumstances. Her emotions were running wild and there was too much of a chance things could get a little too personal. I've never been one to mix business with pleasure, and this was no time to start.

"When will I see you again?" she asked, her voice hinting at her concern.

"I'll be back first thing in the morning."

"Okay."

"Goodnight, Sam."

"Goodnight, Peter."

I gave her a quick nod and a smile I hoped would convey the message that everything was going to be all right, then left the motel room. After making sure the room door was closed tightly, I walked directly to the rented car and stood at the door. I looked back at the room for a minute before getting into the car. I wished I could have told her that everything was going to be all right, but I had to be honest with myself. I wasn't sure what was going to happen.

AS I DROVE AWAY from the motel, I got to thinking about what she had told me. I still had a couple of hours before I was to meet Jennifer. The last place I wanted to go was to my home or office. If I went to either of them, I could be picked up and followed again.

It had been twenty-four hours since I had last seen Hamilton. I was growing concerned about him. What I really needed to do was to find out something about him. The best place to do that was at the library.

I drove over to the library and found Lisa was not working. I got a little help from the woman who was at the information desk. She pointed me to the City Directory. I looked up the name Hamilton. It took me almost an hour to sort through all the Hamiltons listed in the book before I found the right one. His name was Russell G. Hamilton. He was married to Julia Hamilton, a corporate lawyer, and they had two children. They lived in Cherry Creek, an area of Denver where a lot of well-to-do people lived.

The City Directory provided me with his address and home phone number. On the off chance he might be alive, a call might verify that. I went out to the entryway of the library and placed a call to the Hamilton residence. The phone rang only three times before it was answered by a woman.

"Hello?"

"Is this the Russell Hamilton residence?"

"Yes," the woman said with a hint of a question in her voice.

"I would like to speak to Mr. Hamilton if I may."

"I'm sorry, but he is not home at the moment. Is there something I can help you with?"

"Do I have the right Mr. Hamilton? The Hamilton I'm looking for works for Ace Diamond Rentals."

"Yes, that is Russell. I'm his wife. May I ask what this is about?"

"I'm not sure, Mrs. Hamilton. I have been trying to get hold of your husband, but he hasn't been at his office all day. Have you seen him today?"

"As a matter of fact, I haven't seen him today. I've been out of town at a conference for the past couple of days. I got home only about an hour ago."

"I'm sorry to have bothered you. I'll try to get in touch with him at his office tomorrow."

"Wait, who are you?"

I quietly hung up the phone. I was not ready to tell her who I was. The only thing I was sure of was if she cared at all about her husband, she would start looking for him. I would have bet the first person she would call would be Ms Bradley. I didn't know if Hamilton was dead or not; but now that someone was missing him, it wouldn't be long before he would be found, dead or alive. I was personally hoping for alive, but had my doubts.

A QUICK CHECK OF MY WATCH told me if I left for Jennifer's apartment now, I would be there about nine. I didn't think she would mind if I got there a little early. Besides, I had to stop and pick up something for dinner.

I didn't know what Jennifer was in the mood for, but I felt it had to be something very special. She liked Cordon Bleu so I stopped at a restaurant that had the best Cordon Bleu in the city. I ordered two meals with asparagus tips, long grain wild rice and raisin bread pudding with a caramel cream sauce for desert. I also picked up a bottle of her favorite wine.

As soon as the dinners were ready, I hurried to Jennifer's apartment. I knocked on the door. When she opened it, I held up the plastic bag with the two dinners safely encased in Styrofoam containers and the bottle of wine.

"What did you bring? I was sure you would pick up a pizza somewhere," she said.

"My fair Lady Jennifer, this is not a night for pizza. This is a night for love," I said with my best English accent.

"Come in, Sir Peter," she said as she stepped back, bowed slightly and smiled.

"Where do we eat this fabulous meal, in front of the television, kind sir?" she asked.

"At the table, my lady. At the table."

I went directly to the kitchen. I got a couple of glasses out of the cupboard and filled them with wine. I don't know if it was the "right" wine for our dinner, but it was the kind I knew she liked.

"Please, sit down."

I got out a couple of plates and put our meals on them. I don't like eating out of a box, unless it's pizza. As soon as I had our meals on plates, I set them on the table.

"Wow, you did go out of your way for this. This is my favorite meal," she said with a grin as she looked at the plate.

"I know, and I have your favorite dessert to go with it."

"Raisin bread pudding with caramel sauce?"

"Nothing less for you. Now dig in."

I found it hard not to watch her as she ate her meal. It was very good and very filling. After dinner, we cleaned up and then sat in the living room in front of the television.

Jennifer curled up next to me on the sofa while I watched the news. She wanted to talk about the case I was working on, but I told her we would after the news. I explained that I needed to know what was going on in regard to the Williams investigation, at least as far as the news media knew.

The anchorman was saying, "It has been reported that Arnold P. Williams was shot to death when he interrupted someone going through some papers in his home office. It seems it was quite by accident that he was even home.

"Mrs. Williams was home at the time of the murder. It was reported she was in another part of the house at the time Arnold Williams was killed. Apparently there was no one else in the house. We have been unable to get in touch with Mrs. Williams for any comment. It seems she has simply disappeared."

"Well, that newsman thinks Mrs. Williams killed her husband," Jennifer said with surprise.

"Do his comments surprise you?"

"No. Not really."

"Me neither. He has no way of knowing if anyone else was in the house. That comment of his implied she killed her husband. People will pick up on that. As far as I'm concerned, if it's worth reporting, it's worth reporting all the facts without the commentary from someone who has no idea what is going on."

"Then why do you listen?"

"Because, in spite of themselves, they will let the world know what they think they know. If they get a hint of something, they will blab it all over even if they don't have it right."

"Do you think Mrs. Williams had anything to do with the death of her husband?"

"To be one hundred percent honest, I don't know. But my gut feeling tells me she had nothing to do with it."

"What makes you so sure?"

"I'm not sure, it's just a feeling. First of all, I have had a chance to see her and visit with her. Secondly, if what I have heard is true, she would be much better off with him alive."

"What did you hear?"

"Unless Arnold died of natural causes, she gets nothing. Now, mind you, I have not had a chance to check that out to make sure it's true. I hope to get that done tomorrow. But if it is true, she would lose everything, and I mean everything."

"I see your point," Jennifer said thoughtfully.

"What I would like to do now is put all this aside and focus my attention on you."

"Now I kind of like that idea. What did you have in mind?" Jennifer asked.

I TOOK HOLD OF JENNIFER'S hand and looked into her beautiful green eyes.

"I recall you phoned me and said you broke up with the guy you were going with. It seems there was something about being too possessive, and you were glad you found out before it got too serious."

"Yes, I did call you and tell you that."

"Is it true then?"

"Yes," she replied softly.

It was easy to see that she was not completely over her feelings for Jason even though I was convinced she was done with him. It was a shame he didn't have the smarts to treat

Jennifer better. She was a great woman, even a passionate woman if she was treated right.

"I'm here to help you get over him."

"Oh, really. And just how do you plan to do that?"

"I plan to lavish you with affection and love like you truly deserve. Now I must warn you that it might take me all night, but I'm sure you will feel loved like you have never felt loved by morning."

"Tell me, is this a good or bad thing?"

"Oh, you cut me deep," I said as I playfully pressed my hands over my heart.

"I suppose I should do something about that," she said with a slight giggle in her voice. "Do you have any idea what it might take to heal your wounded heart?"

"A passionate kiss from my fair lady might help."

"Granted, my lord," she said as she leaned over and gently pressed her lips to mine.

Our kiss started out as a gentle kiss, but soon turned more passionate. As we deepened the kiss, I reached out and pulled her closer to me. Jennifer came to me willingly and easily slipped into my arms.

"Mmmmm," she purred softly as we continued the kiss.

She drew back a little and looked into my eyes.

"You always were a great kisser," she said with a smile.

"I'm good at other things, too," I reminded her.

"Yes, I know. But I would rather work up to them slowly if you don't mind."

"I don't mind at all. We have all night."

"Yes. Yes, we do," she said with a dreamy, sexy look in her eyes.

I drew her against me, and our lips met once more. Only this time it was much more passionate from the very beginning. As we kissed, she pressed her body up against me and purred softly as I gently slid my hands up and down the smooth curve of her back. There was no doubt in my mind that the woman I held in my arms was all woman.

She pulled back and looked at me again. I smiled at her, admiring her slightly flushed face. I knew she was not thinking about what's his name. Neither was I.

"I know a place that is much more comfortable than it is on the couch."

"And where might that be?" I asked.

"The one place we always end up whenever you and I get together."

"And where might that be?"

"In my bed," she said, her eyes revealing what she wanted. "Come with me.

I took hold of her hand. Like two teenagers who were expecting to do "it" for the first time, we walked into her bedroom. She led me to the side of her queen size bed, then turned and stood in front of me. I reached out and put my hands on her narrow waist as she reached up and put her hands on my shoulders. We stood there for a few seconds just looking into each other's eyes.

"You can undress me if you would like," she said in a whisper.

I didn't say a word. I simply took hold of her pullover blouse at her waist and pulled it loose from her slacks. She smiled softly and raised her arms above her head as I pulled her blouse up and over her head. Once I had her blouse off, I tossed it over a chair in the corner.

She again put her arms around my neck and pressed her body against me. I could feel the firmness of her breasts pressing against my chest as she looked into my eyes.

"How about a shower first," she suggested.

"Whatever my lady wants," I managed to say.

She smiled, took her arms from around my neck and stepped back away from me. I watched her as she slipped out of her slacks. I undressed while she removed her bra and panties. As soon as we were naked, I followed her into the bathroom.

The shower was warm and pleasant. We took our time washing and kissing and reacquainting ourselves with each other.

After a while, we dried each other off. I then took her in my arms, picked her up and carried her to the bed. After gently laying her down on the bed, I slipped in beside her.

"Peter, make love to me."

Jennifer's voice was soft, yet demanding. I wanted her, too. I gently rolled over her. Taking our time, we made passionate love. When we were satisfied, she curled up against me. She put her head on my shoulder and slid a leg over mine. It was not long before she was asleep. It wasn't much longer before I fell asleep, too.

CHAPTER NINE

Morning came much too early to suit me. I would have preferred sleeping for a bit longer. On the other hand, the way I woke was not all bad, either. I found myself lying against Jennifer's smooth warm back with one arm under her head and the other around her with one of her full firm breasts resting gently in my hand. I couldn't help but remember the passionate lovemaking we had shared before we drifted off to sleep.

As I gently caressed her breast in my hand, she pushed back against me. I lightly kissed her on the back of the neck. The warmth of her body against me was enough to make me want her again.

"Are you ready to get up?" she asked in a soft whisper.

"Not yet. I like the way you feel."

She rolled over on her back and looked at me. I raised myself up and rested my head on my hand as I looked at her. There was a warm pleasant smile on her face and a sparkle in her eyes. She had the glow of love about her.

I reached out and gently slid my hand across her flat stomach and up over one of her breasts. She closed her eyes and let out a soft sigh that told me she liked the way I was touching her. I leaned over and kissed her gently on the lips.

She reached up and slipped a hand behind my head pulling me to her. After a short but rather passionate kiss, I rose up a bit and looked down at her again. She was looking into my eyes.

"I really need to go," I said reluctantly.

"I understand."

She may have said she understood, but I could tell by the way she looked at me that she didn't want me to leave. I didn't want to leave, either, but I had things that needed to be done.

I rolled over and sat up on the edge of the bed, then turned my head and looked at her. She was lying with the sheet covering her from the waist down. As I looked at her, I realized there was more to her than her body. She was a loving and sensitive woman who could make a man very happy. I also realized she was vulnerable. She had just ended a relationship with a man who had hurt her deeply. I felt very lucky that I was the one she came to, but then we had always had a very special kind of relationship.

Gathering my clothes off the floor, I went into the bathroom. I took a quick shower and shaved. As soon as I was dressed, I returned to the bedroom to find the bed empty.

I found Jennifer in the kitchen fixing breakfast. She was barefoot and wearing a terry cloth robe that tied in the front at her waist and came down to about mid thigh. I couldn't help but think how sexy she looked.

I walked up behind her and slipped my arms around her waist. I leaned down and kissed her on the neck.

"Mmmmm, that's nice," she whispered.

"Very nice," I said as I pulled her back against me and held her tightly.

"All you have to do is untie my robe and I'll return to bed with you."

"I know."

She had no idea how much I wanted to untie her robe, drop it on the floor and carry her back to bed. In fact, I would have liked to spend all day in bed with her, but I couldn't.

"You have to go, don't you?" she asked softly as she turned in my arms and looked up at me.

"Yes."

"Will you stay long enough for breakfast?"

Her eyes seemed to be pleading with me to stay just a little longer. Since I liked having breakfast before I start my day, I agreed to have breakfast with her.

Jennifer knew me well enough to know what I liked. She set breakfast out on the table. We didn't talk much. I had gotten into something that was very dangerous and she knew it.

After breakfast, Jennifer gave me a deep passionate kiss before I left. It was almost enough to get me to stay.

I DROVE TO ONE of the large office buildings in downtown Denver. It didn't take me long to find the offices of Tucker, Wade and Jones, a prominent law firm I knew from the newspapers had done legal work for Arnold P. Williams. It was a long shot at best because I wasn't even sure if it was the law firm that had drawn up the agreement between Samantha and her husband. I was hoping to find out if what Samantha had told me was true.

After I explained to one of the secretaries what I was interested in, she directed me to Mr. Charles Wade's secretary. She buzzed Mr. Wade, then stood up and led me to the door of his office.

Mr. Charles Wade was a fairly tall and distinguished looking man in his early sixties. He looked every bit the successful attorney in his dark pin striped suit with red tie and white shirt.

"Come in, Mr. Blackstone," he said as he stood up and directed me to a chair in front of his desk. "How may I be of help?"

"I'm looking into a matter for Mrs. Arnold P. Williams," I said.

"Oh. And what matter might that be?"

"I'm looking into what she might inherit since her husband has been murdered. She told me that she will inherit nothing since her husband didn't have the option of dying of natural causes. I know she will not inherit anything except a jail cell if she had anything to do with Mr. Williams's death. What I would like to know is, will she inherit anything if she had nothing to do with his death?"

"I'm afraid I cannot tell you what the will actually says, but I can confirm there was an agreement that mentioned natural death along with the will."

"Does that mean she will not inherit anything even if she had absolutely nothing to do with his death?"

"I would like to answer your question, Mr. Blackstone, but I would have to know what it is you're looking for?"

"I'm looking for a motive for Mr. Williams's death."

"I see. You're wondering if Samantha might have had something to do with Arnold's death in order to gain his money?"

"Not really. I guess you would have to say I'm trying to make sure she had no motive to kill him."

"I take it she is a suspect?"

"Yes."

I got the impression Mr. Wade might have thought I was a police officer investigating Arnold's death. Apparently the police had not checked to find out if Samantha might have a very big motive to kill him.

"Well, I think you can eliminate Samantha as a suspect."

"Why's that?"

"She signed an agreement before they were married that if Arnold died of anything other than natural causes, she would get nothing."

"So what she told me was true."

"Well, not entirely, if that was what she told you."

"Would you mind explaining that?"

"I was present when Samantha signed the agreement. She never read it. She took our word for what it said. What she doesn't know, is she will get a substantial lifetime income as long as she had nothing to do with his death, no matter what the cause of death," Mr. Wade explained.

"That means we have to prove she had nothing to do with Arnold's death in order for her to get her inheritance?"

"It would seem that way."

"What do you mean," I asked.

"Since you have not been able to find her to talk to her, it might look like she had something to hide. Wouldn't you think?"

"I see what you mean. One more thing, would she have had a chance to read what she signed at a later date?" I asked.

"No. The form she signed has always been kept here in my safe. And before you ask, I'm sure Arnold would not have told her about what the form really said."

"What makes you so sure?"

"I knew Arnold for a good many years and knew that his word was as good a gold. He told me that he never wanted the agreement mentioned again. He didn't like the idea of the agreement in the first place. It was my idea as a way to find out if Samantha really loved him, or if she was just interested in his money."

"I see. And what did you decide?"

"Samantha proved to be the best thing to ever happen to Arnold. She was truly devoted to him, and him to her."

"Thank you for your help," I said as I stood up and shook Mr. Wade's hand.

As I left the law offices, I had a lot to think about. It may have been time to take her to the police and let them interview her, but there was a problem. Samantha needed protection. There was someone out there who wanted to get to her and I wanted to know why. I had no idea what he was after. I didn't want to expose her to the press, either. It was time to go and have another talk with her.

I STARTED FOR LITTLETON. I was thinking about what Mr. Wade had said. I decided to keep it to myself, at least for a little while. If that information leaked out, the news media would have a field day. Once something is hinted at in the papers, some people tend to think it's the gospel truth.

If the police got wind of the fact that she would inherit a tidy sum, she would likely become their only suspect. If that happened, it would make it much harder to keep her whereabouts a secret. It would also force me to prove there was someone else they needed to look at as a suspect. That was never easy.

There was another thing I felt warranted some investigation. I needed to know where the trails behind the Williams house went and how someone might get in and out of the area without being seen.

I TOOK A ROUNDABOUT way back to the motel where Samantha was hiding just to make sure that I was not followed. When I pulled up in front of the motel room, I noticed the drapes were pulled back slightly and I could see someone looking out. I figured Samantha was impatiently waiting for me.

I went to the door and looked around before I knocked. Samantha opened the door. I ducked inside and quickly closed the door.

Samantha was wearing a thin cotton wraparound dress that was held together by a tie in the front at the waist. My first thought was that for such a simple dress, she sure made it look expensive. But it was my second thought that concerned me.

"Where did you get the dress?"

"Alex picked it up for me. He's such a nice man. I hadn't brought anything with me and I needed something to wear."

"Oh," I said with a sigh of relief.

"You didn't think I went out to get it, did you?"

"No. If you had gone out to get a dress it would have been something far more, shall we say, upscale."

"I used to wear dresses like this all the time before I met Arnold."

"I'm sure you did. Listen, I need to talk to you about the trails behind your house."

"What about them?"

"Do you know where they go?"

"No. Not really. Arnold and I have only gone for walks on them a few times. We never went far enough to find out where they come out. Why? Is it important?"

"I don't know. I was thinking about going there to find out."

"Can I go with you? I'm getting tired of being cooped up. Alex is nice, but I need some air."

I looked at her. I could understand her feelings, but it didn't make a whole lot of sense to take her outside. It would be risky at best.

"I don't think that's a good idea."

"I could use some different clothes. We could go to my house and I could get a few things. Honest, I wouldn't be any problem, and I'd do whatever you say. I promise."

She did have a point. It would be a chance to get her some fresh clothes. Plus it was not likely anyone would be expecting her to go back to the house so soon after Arnold's death. The police were probably done searching the home and gathering evidence.

"Is there some place not too far from your house where we could leave the car and come in from behind the house?"

"Well, we could stop in at Mrs. Holcombe's home and go behind her house to get to mine."

"Is Mrs. Holcombe someone you can trust?"

"Oh, yes. She's ninety years old and lives alone. She is still a very active woman. She plays Bridge every Friday afternoon down the road from her place. She wouldn't even be there. We could park your car behind her house. No one would be able to see it from the road."

"Well, I'm not very fond of the idea, but we'll go out there this afternoon."

"Great," she said excitedly. "What do we do until then?"

"WE don't do anything. I need to have a talk with the police."

"What about?"

"About you. I've got to go. You stay here. I'll be back about noon. I'll bring lunch."

"Okay," she said reluctantly.

I LEFT THE MOTEL and headed for the police station where Mac worked. I felt if I could talk to him, he might be able to tell me if he had any more evidence.

On my way to the police station, I would have to pass the Ace Diamond Building. It caused me to wonder if Hamilton had ever returned. I decided to drive around in front of the building. The thought passed through my mind that I should stop and see if Ms Bradley had been in contact with him.

As I started to turn the corner in front of the building, I saw a lot of commotion going on. There was an ambulance, a rescue vehicle from the Fire Department and several patrol cars. There were police all over the place.

I wanted to pull over and find out what was going on. It was really a case of I wanted to know if they had found Hamilton or not. As I attempted to pull over and park, an officer flagged me to keep going.

While passing the front of the building, I could see Mac talking to Ms Bradley in the lobby. I wondered why he was there. I would have thought someone else would have been put on this. With the murder of Arnold Williams being such a high profile case, I would have expected Mac to be too busy to look into anything else.

I pulled over and parked in the next block. I walked back to the building. With all the police standing around, it might be difficult for me to get to talk to Mac for a while. I stopped near one of the officers. The officer was busy watching some people with cameras trying to get pictures of the stretcher being wheeled to an ambulance. There was a body bag on it. I had a feeling it was Hamilton in the body bag, but I wasn't sure.

The fact that Mac was there led me to believe he must think there was a connection between Hamilton's and Williams's deaths. If that were the case, then we were on the same track.

"Officer," I said to the young officer who was keeping the crowd back.

"What?" he said sharply.

It was clear he was tired of the on-lookers. A killing brought out the curiosity seekers.

"I'm Peter Blackstone. I need to talk to Captain MacDonald as soon as possible. I may have some information he might want."

"He's busy."

"I know, but it's important. Just tell him I'm here. You can bet your badge he'll want to hear what I have to say," I said looking him straight in the eyes.

The young officer looked at me as if he were trying to decide if what I said was true, or if I just wanted to get closer to what was going on. He must have decided what I had to say to Mac might be important, and it might be a bad decision not to at least let the captain know I was there. He turned and called out to one of the other officers at the scene.

I couldn't hear what he was saying to the other officer, but I could tell he was relaying my message. The other officer looked over at me for a second, then turned and walked into the building. I could see through the glass window that the officer went directly to Mac and spoke to him.

I was glad to see Mac acknowledge my presence. I watched him as he continued to talk to Ms Bradley. When he was done, he glanced at me to make sure I was still there. He then motioned to an officer to come get me.

I followed the officer into the building. Mac met me at the door.

"What's up, Pete?"

"Was that Hamilton in the body bag?"

"Yeah. What do you know about this?"

I looked around the lobby. There were a number of people sitting and standing around, some of them police officers, some of them people who worked in the building. The last thing I wanted was for outsiders to hear what I had to say.

"I think we need to talk, in private."

Mac looked at me for a second. The expression on his face indicated he was wondering how much I knew about Hamilton's death. He must have decided that what I had to say might be of interest. He reached out, touched my arm and then started toward Hamilton's office. Once inside the office, he closed the door and leaned back against the desk.

"What do you know about this, Pete?"

I sat down and told him about the meeting that had taken place the other night in the Ace Diamond Building. He listened very carefully.

"What makes you so sure they were here to meet? There are several businesses in the building. Even mobsters invest in stocks, bonds and mutual funds. They could have had a meeting with one of their investment counselors, or with one of their accountants."

"You might be right, but I have a hard time believing they all had meetings with their investment counselors at the same time. The fact they arrived here within minutes of each other, and they left within minutes of each other would indicate to me they were meeting together."

"I agree, but it's going to be hard to prove."

"Maybe not. I took pictures of them coming and going."

"I want those pictures," he said with a degree of interest in his voice that hadn't been there before.

"Okay. How was Hamilton killed?"

"Keep this under your hat. We don't want the press to get hold of this, but he was shot with a small caliber pistol behind the left ear. Probably a .22 caliber pistol."

"It could be a mob hit."

"Yes. It could, and from what you've told me, it's beginning to look that way."

"I was wondering why you're in on this investigation when the Williams murder is such a high priority case? I would've thought they would put someone else on this so you could work on the Williams case."

"I was close by when the call came in."

"I think you should consider this along with the murder of Williams. I think there's a connection."

"How so?"

"I think if you look into the financial records of the Ace Diamond Construction Company you will find a very strong connection to several members of the mob. If the allegation that the building is unsafe is proven to be correct, Williams would almost surely have pulled his financial support. That alone would be enough to cause the project to fail.

"Add to that the possibility Williams had found out about the involvement of the mob in the project, there would be no doubt in my mind Williams would pull out and let the whole world know about it. The mob doesn't like it when they are looking at losing millions of dollars and having an investigation into the finances of the project."

"What makes you so sure Williams would have pulled out?"

"It's really just a guess on my part."

"It wouldn't be because of your interest in Mrs. Williams, would it?"

"She's just a client. I've done a lot of research on Arnold P. Williams. I'd lay money that he was squeaky clean, and he would do almost anything to keep his reputation that way."

"But what does Hamilton have to do with this?" Mac asked.

"I'm not sure, but I hope to find out."

"I'll keep in mind what you've told me. I'll get right on the financial records. I want you to keep me posted, and I want those pictures."

"No problem. You'll know what I know," I said.

"One other thing. Do you know where Mrs. Williams is?"

"Yes, but I can't tell you right now."

"Why? I need to talk to her."

"I promise I will bring her in for you to question. Right now, I need to find out who else is trying to find her."

"What do you mean?"

"She was almost grabbed at City Park when I went to meet her there, and it was not a cop. Someone has been trying to tail me to find her. I would bet if you went to my apartment, you would find someone has ransacked it. They were probably looking for a clue as to where she is."

"You want me to go to your apartment and find out?"

"Sure. Here's my key. See what you can find," I said as I took my apartment key off my key ring and gave it to him.

"Do you think he might have found the pictures you took?"

"No. I have them safely hidden away, but I will get them to you this afternoon."

"Great. Will you bring Mrs. Williams with you?"

"Maybe. I'll see you later."

Mac nodded, but didn't move. As I left the office, he remained behind leaning against the desk. I could tell by the look on his face that he was thinking very hard about what I had told him. There was no doubt in my mind he would follow up on looking into the financial records of the Ace Diamond Construction Company. And I was also sure that if he looked hard enough and deep enough he would find the connection.

AS I LEFT THE ACE DIAMOND BUILDING, I saw Lieutenant Daniel Royal arrive on the scene. He must have been assigned the job of finding out who had killed Hamilton. If that was the case, I wasn't so sure I wanted to share what I knew with him.

I hurried on down the sidewalk to my rented car. The last thing I wanted was a confrontation with Royal. He didn't like me and I had no respect for him.

"Hey, Blackstone."

The tone of Royal's voice told me that he was looking for another encounter with me. I made it a point to ignore him, and continued on down the street as if I had not heard him. Even if he thought I had heard him, I was not about to be pestered by the likes of him.

When I got to my car, I glanced over the top of it. I could see Royal standing in front of the building watching me. He had apparently decided that to pursue me would gain him nothing, and he would have been right. I smiled to myself as I got in the car.

As I pulled away from the curb, I glanced back in my rearview mirror. I saw someone else watching me. It was the same guy who had tried to grab Samantha in the park, and the same guy who had followed me to my apartment.

My first thought was to stop and have a little discussion with him, but I doubted I would get anything out of it except maybe the satisfaction of beating the hell out of him. It was in my best interest, and my client's best interest to do nothing at the moment. There was no question in my mind I would run into him again.

As I drove away, it occurred to me that he probably got my license number. If he did, it wouldn't take him long to track down the car and find out where I rented it. That probably wouldn't help him find me, but the fact he had seen the car might make it easier for him to spot it. That could prove to be a problem since I had no idea how many eyes he might have out on the street. I decided it would be best if I rented another car of a different color and make from some place else. At least that way he wouldn't have any idea what I was driving.

After making sure I was not being followed, I returned the car. I went down the street a couple of blocks before I called for a cab. I had the cabby take me to another one of Denver's suburbs where I rented a completely different car, and then I headed back to Littleton.

CHAPTER TEN

When I arrived back at the motel, I found Samantha sitting on the edge of the bed. The television was on a local news channel, again. The reporter was talking about the body found at the Ace Diamond Building. She was shaking her head in disbelief. I couldn't understand what difference it could make to her.

"What's the matter, Sam?"

"First they say the building is unsafe, now someone was found dead in the building. I doubt the building will ever be used to its full potential," she said with a sigh.

"What do you know about the building?"

"Arnold was so proud of it. He had a lot to do with the design, the interior decoration, the financing, and getting people to invest in it. It was his dream."

The way she talked about the building gave me the impression there was more to it than Arnold's dream. There was something else.

"Can you tell me if the building had an anchor firm scheduled to take a large part of the building?"

"Yes. At least it did until the report leaked out that the building was unsafe."

"Is the building unsafe?"

"No. Of course not. That was the ramblings of a foreman who had been fired because he was always late for work and was using drugs on the job. If there was anything unsafe about the building, it was the foreman making it unsafe for the men to work with him."

"Why wasn't this ever brought to light?"

"Because there was no proof that would hold up in court. If it were brought out he was on drugs, he would have sued. That would have been as damaging as the report of an unsafe building. At least the allegation of the building being unsafe could be proven to be false, which would make the foreman the bad guy."

"How do you know all this?"

"Arnold and I would sit up for hours in his den and talk about the building and his dreams for it."

"So you're telling me that you knew a lot about what he was doing?"

"Yes, I guess so."

"Do you know the name of the company that was to anchor the whole project?"

"Not really. All I know was that it was some big eastern credit card company that was planning on moving their western headquarters to Denver. They were going to take about twelve of the sixteen floors of the building. With the tenants that are already there, it would have given it an eighty three percent occupancy rate. That's very good in the current market place."

"Can you tell me when things started to fall apart?"

Samantha looked at me as she tried to think while I sat in a chair and looked at her. She was a beautiful woman. I couldn't help but think how sexy she looked in the simple cotton wraparound dress. It was easy to see why Arnold had been attracted to her. But there was more to her, so much more.

I was slowly discovering that she had a head on her shoulders as well. Arnold must have discovered it, too. She was both sexy and smart. That was probably why Arnold had married her.

"I think I told you it was about six or seven months ago."

"Yes, you did. You said it was about the time he started having meetings on Wednesday evenings. But could you be closer to the time, like the week or possibly even a date."

"I don't know, but I'll try to remember when he first talked to me about troubles with the building, but I really need to get out of here for awhile. Maybe I could remember if I got a chance to look at his appointment calendar."

"Okay. I forgot to get something for lunch. We can grab something at a drive-thru on our way to your place."

"We can get something to eat at my house if you think it would be better?"

"Good idea. Let's get out of here."

Samantha didn't need any further instructions. She was ready to get out of the motel room even if for only a little while.

I went to the door and checked to see if there was anyone around that looked like they didn't belong there. I saw no one except Alex. I motioned Samantha to hurry out of the motel room and immediately get in the car. I hopped in behind the wheel. Within seconds we were pulling out on the street and headed for the interstate.

"This is a much nicer car than the one you had before," Samantha said with a smile.

"Yes it is. I decided a Chrysler would not be as out of place in your neighborhood. If one of your neighbors should see it, they might not call the cops."

"You're pretty smart," she said as she put her hand on my knee.

I glanced over and smiled at her, but quickly turned my attention to my driving. It wasn't that I minded a beautiful woman wanting to put her hand on my knee. It was simply not the time or the place. I needed to keep my concentration on what was around and who might be following us.

AS I DROVE, Samantha tipped her head back and closed her eyes. I glanced over at her every once in a while. I could tell that she wasn't sleeping. It was more like she was thinking, or maybe remembering something she wasn't ready to share with me.

As soon as I turned off the interstate, Samantha sat up. She took a quick look around, and then looked at me.

"If you drive past my house and turn into the first drive on the same side of the street, that would be Mrs. Holcombe's driveway."

"Okay."

"Take the drive around behind the house. If you park next to the horse barn no one will be able to see the car."

"Will there be anyone around the barn?"

"No. There shouldn't be. Mrs. Holcombe doesn't have any horses any more."

I followed Samantha's instruction and parked the car behind the small barn. It was the perfect place to hide the car, as it could not be seen unless someone walked behind the barn.

We got out of the car and walked along a row of thick bushes and trees to the area behind Samantha's pool house. I had her stay out of sight while I crept to the side of the pool house to take a look. I needed to know if anyone else was around.

From next to the pool house, I could see into Arnold's den. The curtains on the sliding glass patio door were open. I checked out the back of the house, then went across the lawn to the house. Looking back at the pool house, I could see Samantha. I motioned for her to stay there while I checked out the rest of the house.

I worked my way around the house looking in any window I could see in. I avoided the front of the house because I didn't want anyone to see me stalking around and call the cops. I did get close enough to the front of the house to make sure there was no one there. I returned to the back of the house and motioned for Samantha to join me. She hurried across the lawn and ran up next to me.

"Do you have a key?" I asked.

"No, but the keypad on the backdoor of the garage will let us in the garage. We have a key to the house in the garage."

"Let's go in."

She smiled and led the way. She punched in a series of numbers in the keypad, and then opened the door. I followed her to a workbench. She opened a small metal box on the back of the workbench and removed a silver key. She held it up and smiled.

There was a bright green Mercedes-Benz convertible next to the Lincoln I had seen Arnold drive home the day he was killed. I didn't have to ask. I knew the convertible belonged to Samantha. The third space in the garage was empty. That car was probably the one she had driven to the City Park and was most likely in the Police Impound Lot by now.

I stood next to her while she unlocked the door. As she was about to reach for the doorknob, I grabbed her arm. Samantha turned and looked at me, but didn't say anything. I reached under my coat and removed my gun. She looked at me, then stepped out of the way. I reached around and slowly opened the door. It opened into a laundry room off the kitchen. Samantha followed me into the kitchen then waited in the kitchen while I went from room to room, checking to make sure we were the only ones there. When I was satisfied the house was empty, I returned to the kitchen.

"All clear," I said.

"How about something to eat?" she asked.

"Sounds good. Sam, I don't want you going into any room where the drapes are open."

"Can't we just close them?"

"No. If we do that, someone might notice they are closed when they had been open."

"I see. I'll fix us a salad and sandwich. Would that be okay?"

"Sure. I'm going to look around your husband's den, if you don't mind."

She looked at me with sadness in her eyes. I had the feeling she was uncomfortable with the thought of going into Arnold's den.

"I don't mind, but I don't think I'm ready to go in there."

"I understand. Can you tell me where he kept his appointment book?"

"It should be in the credenza behind the desk. The second drawer on the left."

"Thank you," I said, then turned and headed for Arnold's den.

AS I ENTERED ARNOLD'S DEN, I reached inside my coat and pulled a pair of rubber gloves out of my inside pocket. I had no desire to leave anything behind, including fingerprints. I didn't want to contaminate the crime scene in case the forensic people came back to look for more evidence.

As I walked up to the desk, I could see the dried blood on the desktop indicating Arnold had slumped over the desk after he was shot. There was also a small pool of blood on the floor behind the desk where the desk chair would have been if Arnold had been sitting at his desk when he was shot.

Although I had not seen any photos of the crime scene, the blood evidence indicated Arnold had been sitting at his desk when he was shot. That seemed to confirm what Samantha had told me.

The desk chair was off to one side. I assumed it had been moved when they removed Arnold's body from the house.

The credenza was directly behind where Arnold's chair would have been. The blood splatter on the credenza, bookshelves and books indicated that whoever shot him was directly in front of him. The killer had not been standing near the patio door, nor near the door leading into the den from the front hallway.

Looking at the arrangement of the furniture in front of the desk along with the blood splatter, it would have been my guess that whoever shot Arnold had been sitting down when he or she pulled the trigger. The blood splatter looked to be too high on the bookshelves for Arnold's killer to have been standing up when he shot him, especially if Arnold was sitting down at the desk.

I wasn't sure if it proved anything or not. If the assassin's intent was to simply kill Arnold, why bother to sit down? It would be quicker and less risky to get in, kill him and get out. It got me to thinking that whoever shot Arnold had been in the den long enough to have talked with him. The real question was what did they talk about.

I was just about to open the drawer to the credenza when I heard Samantha call out.

"Lunch is ready."

I didn't reply. I simply opened the drawer and looked inside. There was Arnold's appointment book right where Samantha said it would be. There was also something else next to it. Half hidden under a notepad was the barrel of a small caliber pistol.

I picked up the appointment book and set it on the floor, and then moved the notepad off the pistol. I retrieved the pistol and looked it over. It was a .22 caliber semi automatic pistol. I smelled the barrel. It smelled as if it had been fired recently. I dropped the clip out of it and found it was one bullet short of being full.

I put the clip back in the gun then put the gun back where I found it. I picked up the appointment calendar and headed to the kitchen.

Samantha was sitting at the small kitchen table waiting for me. On the table were two plates, each one with a sandwich neatly cut in half. There was a cup of coffee sitting in front of each plate next to a small bowl of salad.

"Looks good," I said as I pulled the chair back.

I sat down at the table across from her. As soon as I was seated, I set Arnold's appointment book on the floor next to my chair.

"I see you found it," Samantha said.

"Yes. We can look at it after we eat."

Nothing more was said about it while we ate our lunch. As soon as we were finished, Samantha got up and took the dishes to the sink. I retrieved the appointment book and started looking through it. I had only a hint of what I was looking for. I wanted more information on when the problems with the building started to emerge.

"Do you think it will tell you anything?"

I had not realized Samantha was standing next to me looking down at the book. I looked up at her. She had a sad look in her eyes.

"I don't know. Would you prefer I look at this some place else?" I asked, not sure if it was upsetting to her.

"No. If it's okay with you, I would like to take a shower and change clothes. Do we have time for that?"

"I think so."

She smiled, then turned and left the kitchen. I quickly returned to the appointment book.

AS I SCANNED THE APPOINTMENT BOOK, I read where Arnold had an appointment scheduled with Russell Hamilton for the very afternoon he was killed. It was the same day the meeting was held that Hamilton never returned from. I had no idea what it meant, but I was sure there had to be a connection.

Was it possible Hamilton was going to spill what he knew to Arnold? Was it possible Arnold already knew what Hamilton was going to tell him? Why had Arnold come home for lunch when according to Samantha he had not been expected?

That last question gave me cause for concern. Did he catch someone in his den like the police suspected? Since Arnold had not been expected home, whoever shot him must have been there for some other reason. It seemed logical that the individual was in the act of trying to find something.

The puzzling thing was the fact Samantha was in the house. There was no mistake that the house was big. It would not be too difficult to have someone in the house without knowing it. On the other hand, it would have to have been very important for someone to enter the house and risk being seen.

What could be so important that someone would be willing to take such a risk? To take the risk when it would have been so easy to find out when the Williamses would be away for the evening seemed to indicate there was a time frame of some kind involved. Whatever the intruder wanted, he must have needed it in a hurry. I had to think that what the assassin was looking for was extremely important to the Wednesday night meeting where Hamilton was murdered.

Again I started going through the appointment book. The one thing that seemed to stand out was all the Wednesdays in the book had no appointments, they were blank. It was as if Wednesday had been set aside to do absolutely nothing.

I don't know how long I spent looking at the book, but I had gone back six and a half months before I came upon anything different. I found a Wednesday that had appointments scheduled on it, but they had been cancelled. The time corresponded closely with when he began going out alone on Wednesday evenings, and with when the board of the Ace Diamond Building would have gotten the letter about the building being unsafe.

"What would you like me to wear?" Samantha asked, interrupting my thoughts.

I turned and looked at her. She was standing in the doorway to the kitchen. She was standing there in nothing but a white towel wrapped around her shapely body. She also had a towel wrapped around her head, but I hardly noticed it. I almost said she was wearing a bit too much, but I thought better of it.

"Ah, I think something fitting for a walk in the woods would be appropriate. Maybe slacks and a comfortable blouse," I replied when I finally got my mouth working.

"Okay," she replied with a smile.

It was easy to see why Arnold had chosen her for his wife.

I watched her turn and walk back toward the bedrooms.

As soon as she was out of sight, I turned my attention back to the book. I began to realize the book was an important piece of evidence.

My thoughts returned to the gun in the drawer. Why hadn't the police found it? Maybe they didn't search the credenza. There was always the possibility it wasn't there when they looked.

I turned and looked toward the bedrooms. I wondered if Sam knew about the gun. It was clear Arnold had not been shot with such a small caliber gun, but Hamilton had. Had the gun been left behind to incriminate Arnold or possibly Samantha in the death of Hamilton? It hardly seemed likely. It would not be too difficult for the forensic people to figure out Arnold was murdered hours before Hamilton. That alone would clear Arnold from suspicion of killing Hamilton, but it wouldn't clear Samantha.

I GOT UP AND WALKED down the hall. I found the door to Samantha's bedroom open. She was sitting in front of a vanity combing her hair. She was still wearing the towel. I stood there in the doorway looking at her. I wondered what she really knew.

She looked up at me. The expression on her face was one that seemed to ask if I wanted something.

"I have a couple of questions I would like to ask."

"Okay. What are they?"

"Did Arnold have any guns in the house?"

She stopped combing her hair and looked at me in the mirror.

"Why do you ask?"

"Did he have any guns in the house?"

"No, not that I know of," she replied as she seemed to regain her composure.

"Not that you know of? You have been married to him for how many years? Twelve, I believe, and you don't know if he had any guns in the house."

"What are you saying? You don't believe me?"

"Let's just say I find it very hard to believe you have lived with a man that long and don't know if he has any guns."

I could see she was beginning to think about my question. When someone takes that long to think of an answer to such a simple question, I have to wonder what's going on.

"Yes," she finally admitted softly. "Arnold had two guns."

"What kind of guns?"

"I don't know what kind they are."

"Pistols, rifles, shotguns?"

"Both of them are pistols."

"Where did he keep them?"

"He kept them locked up in a cabinet in his den."

"He didn't keep one in the credenza?"

"No. There's no lock on the credenza. I insisted they be kept locked up. He kept them in the cabinet next to his reading chair in the corner. It has a lock."

"Do you have the key for it?"

"Yes, of course. Why do you want to know?"

"I found a gun in the credenza behind his desk. It had been fired recently."

"Arnold liked to go out and pistol shoot with a couple of his friends once in a while. He has two target pistols in the cabinet. He only takes them out when he's going target shooting. He hasn't done that for several months."

The gun I found in the credenza was certainly not a target pistol. It was something one might use for protection. I wondered if he might have gotten it for that very reason and had not told Samantha about it.

"I would like to see his guns."

Samantha looked at me in the mirror for a second before she stood up. She walked across the room to a dresser and opened a man's jewelry box. She took out a small key on a short gold chain and held it out to me.

"Here," she said flatly.

She turned sharply and stormed off toward the bathroom. Just as she was getting to the door, her towel slipped off her body and fell to the floor. She never missed a step. She strolled on into the bathroom without so much as a glance back. I smiled at the sight of her naked backside as she disappeared into the bathroom.

AS SOON AS SHE WAS out of sight, I went down the hall to the den. I found the cabinet next to Arnold's reading chair and opened it. Inside were two very expensive and very nice target pistols. These guns were not your everyday Saturday Night Specials. These guns were designed for one thing and one thing only, target shooting. Each one was in a hand finished hardwood box with a gold name plate on the top that told me the guns had belonged to Arnold.

I checked both guns and found that neither of them had been fired recently, and they were clean. That left me with the question of how did the gun get into his credenza?

I was sitting in the chair thinking when I heard Samantha at the door to the den. I looked up and found her looking at me. I had to admit she knew how to dress for a walk in the woods. She was wearing a pair of tailored slacks and a blouse that showed off her assets very nicely. But it was the look on her face that grabbed my attention. She didn't want to come into the room.

I got up and walked out of the den, closing the door behind me. I took her gently by the arm and led her back to the kitchen.

"Are you ready to leave?"

"Yes," she replied softly. "Did you find the guns?"

"Yes, right were you said they would be."

"Can we leave now?"

"Yes. If you would rather not go back on the trail, I can come back some other time."

"No. I'll go back there with you. I'm sorry about earlier. I miss Arnold. I miss having him around. I miss having him touch me, and having his arms around me," she said softly, a tear sliding down her cheek.

"I understand."

"Peter, I need to find out who killed Arnold and why."

"So do I."

I took her hand and led her out into the garage. After locking the door to the house, I checked outside to make sure it was clear. We locked the garage and walked off behind the house and into the woods.

CHAPTER ELEVEN

Samantha held my hand as we worked our way into the woods. We had gone only about fifty yards before we came to the trail. It wasn't much of a trail, but dirt bikes and ATV's had traveled on it enough to make it easy to follow. People riding horses had also used the trail. It was not going to be easy figuring out which set of tracks the killer had made. The only way to find out was to find where the killer had left his transportation.

I looked around. From where I was standing I could not see the Williams house, or where the trails went. The killer would not have been able to see the house from the trail either.

"I think this is a mistake," I said.

"What's a mistake?"

"We are looking for tracks on the trail, right?"

"Sure, but I don't understand what you're getting at."

"Look around. You can't see your house from here, the trees are too thick."

"So?"

"Let's assume the person who killed your husband was no more familiar with the trails than I am. And let's say all he knew was it went behind your house. How would he know where to stop on the trail to get to the back of your house?"

"I see what you're getting at. He wouldn't be able to use the trail to find the house."

"Right. We're looking in the wrong place. We need to start looking for tracks closer to the house, probably from the back of the pool house since it is as close to the house as anyone can get without being in the open. Come on."

I led Samantha back through the trees. I thought the place where the lawn stopped and the forest began would be the best place to start looking. The forest floor had a layer of pine needles on it, which made it hard to find tracks. It was generally smooth and undisturbed. I began looking for places where the pine needles had been disturbed.

I found several places where the pine needles had been disturbed, but it was easy to see the tracks of deer. It wasn't until I was directly behind the pool house that I found places where the pine needles had been disturbed, but only on the surface. That indicated deer had not caused it. Deer with their small sharp hooves tended to leave deeper and smaller impressions than those left by a man's boot or shoe.

"Sam."

"Did you find something?"

"I think so."

I waited for Samantha to join me. Looking at the faint tracks left in the needles, I could see it went back deeper into the woods. The trail turned and ran parallel to the tree line. The tracks were not so far back in the woods that I couldn't see the houses enough to identify them.

"I may have found where Arnold's killer came from."

Samantha looked at the tracks, and then looked at me. I wasn't sure if she was ready for this, but I needed to find out where the killer had come into the woods. I wasn't about to leave her behind unprotected.

"You ready?" I asked as I looked at her.

"Yes," she replied softly.

We began walking along side the tracks I believed had been left by the killer. I didn't walk on the tracks but a little off to the side of them. I didn't want to damage any evidence. From the looks of the tracks, whoever had made them had apparently been in a bit of a hurry which would eliminate anyone out for a casual walk. It also made the tracks easier to follow.

As we moved along through the woods, I noticed there were several places where a good shoeprint had been left in the dirt where the pine needles failed to cover the ground completely. We must have followed the shoeprints for a good hundred feet or more before we came to a place where the shoeprints stopped and ATV tire tracks began. The tracks went out onto the trail. Whoever had come in had started out on an ATV and returned to it to make his escape.

I looked down the trail in the direction the ATV had gone. I wondered how far down the trail the tracks would go. There was no way of knowing without following them.

"What do we do now," Samantha asked.

"I think it would be a good idea if we got hold of the police and had them make castings of the shoeprints and the tire tracks. There's no telling if they will be of value, but they might.

"Then what?"

"Then we wait. Since we are this far along the trail, I want to follow the tracks a little further. You game?"

Samantha didn't say anything, she simply nodded. I took her hand and we began walking along the trail. To anyone who might come along, we looked like a couple enjoying an afternoon stroll in the woods.

It wasn't long before we came to where the trail split off. One trail went on down a hill while the other turned and went off in the direction of the road. It took a minute for me to figure out which way the ATV had gone.

The ATV had gone off to the right. Since it had gone to the right, we were going to the right.

It wasn't long before we rounded a curve in the trail where we found a small parking area. As I looked through the woods, I could see a paved road. It had to be where the ATV had been brought in.

I let go of Samantha's hand and very carefully followed the ATV tracks until they disappeared. At the very end of the tracks were two deep impressions in the soil. The tracks didn't continue past the impressions. There was no doubt the impressions were made by the ramps used to load the ATV onto a trailer or into the back of a pickup.

I immediately began looking for clues as to what was used to take the ATV out of the woods. Only a few feet in front of the impression I found a set of wide tire tracks. As I examined the area, I came to the conclusion the ATV had been loaded onto a large pickup truck with off-road type tires.

It took me a minute to get my thoughts together. I needed to get hold of the police to make castings of the tire tracks. Next, I needed them to check around and see if anyone had seen a truck in the area carrying an ATV in the back. The time had come for us to pay a visit to the police.

"Let's go back," I suggested to Samantha.

She didn't say anything. She simply took hold of my hand and walked beside me. It was good she didn't say anything because I was busy thinking. All I could think about was that someone had gone to a great deal of trouble to find their way to the back of the Williams house without being seen.

There was no doubt in my mind that the killing of Arnold had been carefully planned out. If that was the case, how did they know Arnold was going to be home at that time? The logical explanation was someone had to get him to go home. There was no way anyone could have pulled it off if Arnold had simply forgotten something. He had to have gone home to get something he needed, something he would not have taken to the office under normal circumstances. I was having a hard time thinking of what that might be.

MY THOUGHTS WERE INTERRUPTED when Samantha stopped. I looked at her face. She seemed nervous, almost frightened.

"What is it?"

"There's someone at the house," she said in almost a whisper.

I looked toward the house. She was right. There was someone at the back of the house. He was looking in the patio door.

After pushing Samantha behind a large tree, I motioned for her to stay there. Ducking behind a tree in front of her, I drew my gun from under my jacket. I couldn't see who was snooping around, but I had a feeling I knew him. I was almost sure I would recognize him if he would turn around.

I watched and waited, but he seemed very interested in what was inside the den. It didn't look like he was going to turn around. He had his hands cupped against the patio door and his head pressed against his hands in an effort to see inside.

I could see the pool from the tree. There were several pinecones floating in the pool. That gave me an idea. I picked up a pinecone and tossed it into the pool. The sound of the splash in the water caused the man to turn his head and look. I got a good look at him. It was Lieutenant Daniel Royal.

What was Royal doing at the house? It didn't make sense that he would be peeking in the window. If he was working on the investigation, why didn't he simply go inside through the front door? I knew the police had keys to the house since it was still an active crime scene.

It made sense he would be here if he had been told about what I had told Mac earlier. But then came the real question, did Mac tell him? I knew from experience that Mac didn't like Royal any more than I did. Why would he let Royal snoop around the Williams house? It was time to talk to Mac about Royal and why he was there.

I looked back at Samantha. She was staying well hidden behind the big tree. I again looked toward the back of the house and saw Royal start to move on around the house.

When he disappeared around the corner, I dropped back to where Samantha was hiding.

"Come on. We need to get out of here."

"Who was that?"

"A cop we don't want to run into right now," I said as I grabbed her hand and started leading her back deeper into the woods where we could not be seen.

WE MOVED THROUGH THE WOODS until we were directly behind Mrs. Holcombe's house. We headed for the car behind the barn when I noticed a dark blue sedan pull away from the front of the Williams house. From where I was, I could only see one person in the car. It was Royal. Whatever he was looking for, he had either found it or decided it wasn't there.

Just as we got to the car, an old woman came around the corner. She had a garbage bag in her hands. I think we surprised each other as we both froze in our tracks.

"Who are you, and what are you doing behind my barn?" the woman demanded to know.

Just then Samantha stepped out where the woman could see her.

"Oh, it's you, my dear. What are you doing sneaking around here?"

"I'm sorry, Agnes," Samantha said.

"Oh, I'm the one who should be sorry. I'm so sorry about Arnold. He was such a nice man. What is this world coming to?"

"Mrs. Holcombe, I'm Peter Blackstone. I'm a private investigator. I'm trying to find out who killed Arnold."

"Please call me, Agnes. I'm not one of the stuffed shirts you find around here. But aren't the police doing that?"

"Yes they are, but we think there are some pretty dangerous people who don't want the police, or anyone else, to find out why Arnold was murdered."

"This is no place to be talking about this. Come inside."

The tone of Agnes's voice gave me the impression she expected me to do as she said. The fact that she simply turned around and started back toward the house made it even more convincing that she meant what she said. I could see no reason not to accommodate her.

Samantha smiled as I shrugged my shoulders and began following Agnes to the house. Once inside we were led into a sitting room. Agnes motioned for us to sit down, and then she sat down in a high backed chair.

"Now, what is this all about?"

There was no reason to keep some of what we knew from her. There was always the possibility she might have seen someone snooping around behind the Williams house. I decided it would be best to keep what I knew about the Ace Diamond Building to myself, at least for now.

Agnes listened to what I told her very carefully. She seemed to understand.

"That's very interesting, young man, but the news on television seems to want to point the finger at Samantha. Can you tell me why that is?"

"I had nothing to do with it," Samantha countered.

"Now, dear, I didn't say you did. I said the newscasters seem to think you did."

"The newscasters don't have anything to go on except that someone told them there was no one in the house except Samantha," I said.

"I see, but we know there was someone else, don't we?" Agnes asked.

"What do you know about that afternoon?" I asked.

"I know there were several young boys out on the trail in the woods. I heard their, oh I don't know what they call those things."

"ATV's?"

"Yes. I think that's it."

"Did you see them?"

"No, not really, but I heard them. I was taking the garbage out to the trash containers behind the barn. I heard several of them back in the woods. From what I understand, it was about the time poor Arnold was murdered."

"Did you happen to see anyone?"

"No. No, I didn't," she said, disappointment showed in her voice.

I looked at Samantha. She looked disappointed, too. I was a bit disappointed myself. It would have been nice to have a witness. It would have given us something to work with.

"Where are you staying, my dear?" Agnes asked.

"Mr. Blackstone is hiding me out in a small motel in Lakewood. He feels it's safer for me there."

"I'm sure it is, but wouldn't you feel more comfortable if you were here with me?"

"I don't think it's a good idea," I objected.

"Why? I rarely have any company and its back off the road. I could still go to my activities like I normally do. Besides, I don't have anything planned for the next couple of days. I also doubt anyone would think to look for her here. Who would even guess she was hiding right next door to her own house?"

She had a few good points. I looked at Samantha. The expression on her face told me that she would like to stay with Agnes.

"I could keep an eye on the house and let you know who comes by while you're out looking for evidence that would show I didn't do it," Samantha suggested.

"I also have a number of places where she can hide if someone does come to call. Besides, I would like to have the company," Agnes said.

"You can stay here," I said to Samantha. "I have to have a talk with the police. I need to know what they know, and I need to fill them in on a few things."

"Okay," Samantha said.

"When you come back, you can park your car in the barn. No one will be able to see it there. I have plenty of room here for you, too. You could stay the night if you want," Agnes suggested.

Samantha smiled at the suggestion that I stay the night at Agnes's. I wasn't sure how it made me feel, but with the way things were at my place, it seemed like it might not be a bad idea."

"Sam, you need to stay away from open windows and keep out of sight. And Agnes, don't close drapes that are normally open, and don't open curtains that are normally closed"

"I understand," Sam replied, while Agnes responded with a nod of her head.

"I have to go, but I'll be back this evening."

"Okay," Samantha said.

"You be careful, young man," Agnes said.

I nodded to Agnes, and then headed for the backdoor. After making sure there was no one else around, I left the house for the car behind the barn.

I DROVE OUT FROM BEHIND the barn and headed toward town. Once I was in town, I placed a call to Mac and made arrangements to meet with him. Since I had some time, I swung by my apartment to see if it was still being watched. The same car that had followed me home the other day was there, but no one was inside the car.

After parking the car around the corner and part way down a side street, I got out and looked toward the apartment complex. There was no one around and the street was quiet. It was about dinnertime.

I headed toward the apartment complex. Once I was near the buildings, I moved to the corner. The nice landscaping made it easy to peek around the corners without being seen. I could see all the way along the front of the building. About half way down the front of the building I saw a man standing behind a large flowery bush. It wasn't until he looked in my direction that I recognized him. It was the same guy who had followed me the other day. He had been keeping a close eye on my place. I wondered why. I also wanted to know who had hired him, but I decided this was not the time to try to find out.

Pulling back, I went to my garage and retrieved the envelope with the photos and then returned to my rental car. I sat there for a while before I started the car and headed for the downtown area. I decided I had time to stop by my office and see if someone was watching it.

WHEN I GOT TO WHERE I normally pulled into the underground parking, I drove on by and parked about a block away on a side street. I walked to the back of the building. Getting into the building without being seen had proven to be rather easy.

I went directly to the service elevator, pressed the button, then stepped back in the shadows while I waited for the elevator to show up. When the doors finally opened, I waited to make sure no one was on the elevator before I got on. I pressed the button for the floor two levels below my office. I would walk up the last two flights using the stairway at the end of the hall, the one farthest from my office. There was one closer, but it might be watched.

When the elevator stopped, I reached inside my coat and put my hand on my gun. I slowly peeked out and checked the hallway. It was empty.

I stepped out of the elevator just as the door began to close. The closing of the door made me feel a bit exposed. I had nowhere to go if I was discovered.

I walked at a good pace to the end of the hall, then peeked through the window. I had no idea if there was anyone in the stairwell, but I knew it would be one place where a person could watch my office door without being seen.

After entering the stairwell as quietly as possible, I stood on the landing close to the door and listened. Although the door had opened and closed quietly, I still wasn't sure if it had been heard.

I heard nothing to indicate there was anyone else in the stairwell, either above or below me. I carefully moved over next to the stair rail and looked up. I could see all the way up to the top, but could see nothing. I glanced down and saw nothing below me, either.

With my gun in hand, I started to move up the stairs. I stayed close to the wall so if anyone was up above me, they would not be able to see me. I covered the two flights of stairs without making a sound.

I moved close to the door with my back against the wall. I peeked through the window, but saw no one in the hall. The doorways to the offices along the hall were recessed slightly. If I went out into the hall, they would provide only minimal protection, and were not likely to prevent someone from seeing me. The only thing I had going for me as far as cover was concerned were the restrooms. They were located about half way between the stairwell and my office. It occurred to me that if I got caught in a crossfire, the restrooms might prove to be a trap. Once in the restroom, there was no way out except for the door I went in.

I decided it would not be in my best interest to risk being caught in a shootout in the hall. The fact there might be someone in my office was not important enough to take the risk.

Then I came up with an idea. I would simply place a call to the police and tell them there was someone in my office. If nothing else, it would clear them out. I took my cell phone and dialed the police.

"Nine-one-one emergency, what is your emergency?"

"There's a man in the office of the Bricker Building. That office is supposed to be closed. It's not the man who rents the office. I think it's being ransacked."

"What is the office number?"

"Nine-thirty-two. It's on the ninth floor."

"What is your name, sir?"

I quickly hung up. I knew it wasn't proper to use 9-1-1 like that, but I couldn't think of any other way to make sure there was no one in my office. I leaned back and waited to see what happened.

It wasn't more than about ten minutes before two uniformed police officers and a security guard from the building got off the elevator. They looked both ways before they moved carefully down the hall to my office.

I waited until they tried the door and found it to be locked. I stepped out of the stairwell and started down the hall. The sound of my shoes on the hard marble floor caught their attention and they turned toward me.

"What's going on, officer?"

"We got a call there was someone in your office that didn't belong there," the security guard said.

"Are you Peter Blackstone?" one of the officers asked.

"Yes. Here's the key. Let's go in and check."

The officer took the key from me and unlocked the door. I waited while they went inside and looked around. As soon as they had finished with the outer office, I went inside. It didn't take them long before they had looked around and were satisfied that there was no one there.

"All clear, Mr. Blackstone," one of the officers said.

"Did you place the call to nine-one-one?" the other officer asked.

"Me? Why would I place the call? I have a gun. I could have checked it out myself. And before you ask, I have a permit to carry a concealed weapon."

I watched as one of the officers took hold of his mike on his shoulder and reported back that all was clear and that the owner had shown up. I thanked them for checking it out and watched them as they left the office. I checked out my office for any signs that someone had been in it. I found nothing to indicate it had been searched. I locked up my office, and took the elevator down to the ground floor and walked out the front door.

I returned to my car and drove to the police station to talk to Mac. I had a lot to talk to him about, and I was sure he had a lot of questions to ask me.

It didn't take me long to get to the police precinct. I parked in the parking lot for visitors and went directly to Captain MacDonald's office. He was waiting for me.

I WALKED INTO Captain MacDonald's office and sat down in front of his desk. The look on his face caused me to wonder what was going on. He looked distressed and irritated. He was more than likely getting a lot of heat from the upper brass, but I had a feeling there was more to it. After all, he was an experienced detective with many years on the force.

"What's up, Mac?"

"I'm not having a lot of luck with this one. There's very little evidence to go on. We couldn't find any fingerprints other than Mr. and Mrs. Williams. There was no fiber evidence that didn't match up with what was already in the house. There wasn't even a footprint in the yard or near the pool. We didn't find anything left behind that shouldn't have been there. I usually have all kinds of things that lead me to some sort of conclusion, but not this time."

"What about the blood evidence? Didn't that tell you anything?"

"Nothing that would be conclusive. It looked like whoever shot Williams was sitting right in front of him when he was shot. About all it tells me is there's a possibility the killer was someone Mr. Williams knew. It doesn't help me determine the height of the killer, how long he was there, or anything else that would help me find him.

"There hasn't been anything so far that would give us any indication as to who shot him. Plus, we haven't found a single piece of evidence that would indicate there was anyone in the house at the time of the killing except Mrs. Williams," Mac added, the tone of his voice showing his frustration.

"I might be able to help you out on that."

"How? Do you have a witness?"

"Yes and no."

"Okay, I'll bite," Mac said with a sigh. "Explain yourself."

"We found some tracks behind the pool house that would indicate someone had been back there."

"Wait a minute. You said "we". Who is "we"?"

"Samantha Williams and I."

"You took her to an active crime scene?"

"Yeah, but it was worth it."

"I thought you were smarter than that."

The tone of his voice and way he said it immediately pissed me off. I was there to help him, and all I was getting was an ass chewing.

"Hell, I'm sorry to disappoint you, but your people didn't find anything. It didn't take a genius to figure out someone other than Samantha might have gotten into the house and killed Arnold. We not only found the tracks from an ATV, we found shoeprints behind the pool house at the edge of the woods. The ATV tracks led us to where it had been loaded onto a pickup truck."

"We thought of that. We found all kinds of tracks on those trails, but nothing that would prove they were made by someone who had been at the Williams house. We didn't find anything to indicate there was anyone else around," Mac said raising his voice in anger.

"Maybe you should hire a few Boy Scouts. They'd do a damn sight better job. Hell, I found the tracks, but then your people didn't look all that hard, did they?"

"They found the trail, but there was no way to figure out which tracks were which."

"That's because they didn't start where the trail began. Now I admit the tracks from the edge of the woods to where the ATV was parked were not easy to find, but the tracks were there and your people should have found them. I might also suggest you get someone out there to make castings of the tracks and shoeprints before they get ruined and you lose what little evidence there is."

Mac sat there and looked at me for a minute or so before he said anything more. I think he was beginning to realize I had come to help him, but at the same time I wasn't going to put up with him yelling at me and calling me stupid. It had not been my intention to make him angry, only to help.

"I'll do that," he said, his voice taking on a quieter tone. "But what I want to know is where is Mrs. Williams now?"

"I'm sorry, Mac, but I'm not at liberty to answer that."

"I need to talk to her."

"I need to think about it."

Mac let out a long sigh. Although we were not friends, we did have a fairly healthy respect for each other. He knew me well enough to know he was not going to get anything out of me by bullying me, or that I didn't want to tell him.

"Did you get anything out of the lead I gave you on the Ace Diamond Building?"

"Not yet, but we have people going over the books. Did you get me those pictures you said you took?"

Since Mac had settled down, I decided I would try to keep my cool as well. Even so, I was feeling like I might want to be cautious.

"Yeah. They're under the seat in my car."

"Are you sure they have something to do with Williams's death?"

"Not a hundred percent sure, but there has to be a connection somewhere. I just haven't found it, yet."

"I'll want Royal to see them as soon as possible."

"Wait a minute. I didn't take them to help Royal file charges against some mob hood for killing a rental agent. I took them because I think there is a chance to get the one behind the killing of Williams."

"You don't like Royal, do you?"

"No kidding. I suppose he thinks I helped Samantha kill her husband."

"You're not far off."

"What do you think?"

"I doubt you had anything to do with it, but if you keep hiding her that may change."

"I'll have another talk with her about coming in to see you. I can assure you it will be with her attorney. In the meantime, I think I'll keep the pictures to myself."

"I could take them from you as evidence in a murder investigation," Mac threatened.

"You could, but without me to authenticate them, you couldn't use them in court. And you know it."

Mac didn't say anything more. He simply sat there and watched as I stood up and walked out of his office. If I knew Mac, he would have a tail on me before I hit the street.

I went directly to my car and pulled the envelope out from under the seat. I took a pen and wrote "*Attention: Captain MacDonald*" on the outside of the envelope. I decided that I would get the envelope of pictures to Mac as more or less a peace offering. I wanted to let him know that I wasn't going to keep them from him.

After starting the car, I drove to the entrance of the parking lot. Two uniformed officers were walking toward me. They looked like they were coming to work. I rolled down the window and called one of them over. Both officers walked up to the car. One stood back and watched with his hand on his gun while the other leaned down to talk to me.

"Do you know Captain MacDonald?"

"Yeah, sure."

"Would you do me a favor?"

"Depends."

"My name's Peter Blackstone."

"Yeah. I've heard of you. You're a PI."

"Right. Would you be so kind as to see he gets this envelope? It's something he has been waiting for."

The officer hesitated for a moment before he reached out and took hold of the envelope.

"Yeah, sure. I'm going by his office anyway."

"Thank you very much."

The officer stepped back away from the car and I drove out onto the street. I no more than hit the corner of the block when I saw a dark colored sedan pull out of the parking lot and turn in behind me. I smiled and thought to myself how nice it was that Mac was so predictable. The only thing I didn't know was whether he would follow up on what I had told him.

I turned at the next corner. I kept one eye on the rearview mirror. Sure enough, the same dark sedan turned again and was about a half block behind me. I wondered who was in the car and how much experience he had tailing someone. It really didn't matter, because I was about to find out.

I turned at the next corner and hit the gas. I raced to the middle of the block and made a quick turn into an alley. I drove fast down the alley and onto the next street. It wasn't long before I had zigzagged enough to leave my tail far behind.

Once again, it was time to get a different car. The police would have the license number. They would be putting an APB out with a "find but do not apprehend" order. With all the police on the streets, it would not take them long to locate the car.

I returned the car to where I had rented it, and then walked down the street and around the corner. I grabbed a ride on one of the RTD buses and rode it to a different suburb where I rented a Lincoln Town Car. I felt I needed a little class if I was going back to Mrs. Holcombe's in the foothills.

CHAPTER TWELVE

It was getting dark when I arrived back at Agnes's house. I parked the Lincoln in the barn and went into the house. I was greeted at the backdoor by Agnes. She directed me into the kitchen.

"I thought you might be hungry, so I kept your dinner warm. Please, sit down and eat. While you're eating, I'll get Sam."

"Thank you."

I sat down in the breakfast nook while Agnes put my dinner on the table. She motioned for me to go ahead and eat, and then left the room. Agnes returned in a few minutes with Samantha. They slid into the nook and sat down across from me.

"Hi. How did things go with the police?" Samantha asked.

It was clear she was expecting me to have some good news for her. She seemed so bubbly I found it difficult to bust her bubble.

"Not as well as I had hoped."

The grin disappeared from her face and her eyes showed her disappointment.

"What do you mean? Do they still think I killed Arnold?"

"Well, they don't have any evidence to prove otherwise."

"Didn't you tell them about the tracks we found behind the pool house?"

"Yes, I did. The only question now is will they follow up on it. For the answer to that we will have to wait and see.

Captain MacDonald wants me to bring you in to answer some questions."

"What do you think, Agnes?" Samantha asked.

"I don't think you should go in yet, my dear," Agnes said.

Both Samantha and I looked at her. We were puzzled by her remark. Up to now she had remained silent on that subject. I needed to know what was on her mind.

"What are you thinking?"

"Mind you, it's just a thought. If Sam hides out here, she can keep an eye on her house. If the police return and start looking for tracks in the woods, we will know they have started looking for someone other than Sam as the murderer. If they don't, we will know she is their only suspect and they are not interested in looking for anyone else," Agnes said.

I took a minute to think about what she had said. She made a good point. However, there were some flaws in her thinking. Even if they did come out and look for tracks, they might still think of her as their prime suspect. But on the other hand it would give us some idea of how serious they were about looking at the possibility that someone else could have murdered Arnold.

"What do you think, Peter?" Samantha asked.

I found them both looking to me for answers. I wasn't sure I had any, but it was better than nothing. And nothing was what I had at the moment.

"Okay, you stay here for the time being. Sam, the rules are the same. Stay away from open windows, make sure you are not seen, and don't make any phone calls.

"As for you, Agnes, you go about your business as usual. Don't open curtains or drapes you normally don't open and don't close ones you normally have opened. If anyone comes by, don't answer the door until you have given Sam a chance to hide in a safe place."

"I understand, Peter," Agnes replied.

"Now what do we do?" Samantha asked.

"What time do you normally shut off the lights and go to bed?" I asked Agnes.

"Oh, about eleven."

"Then eleven is when we will go to bed, but I want no lights on in any room that normally doesn't have lights on in the evening."

"I have black out curtains on the two bedrooms facing east so my company will not be awakened by the early morning sun. You can use those rooms tonight. That way you could at least have small night lights on without them being seen from outside."

"That's perfect. Now I would like to find a place where we can sit and have a talk. I want to find out how much you saw the other day even if it seems unimportant to you," I said to Agnes. "I also want to see if you can remember anything that you might have forgotten or overlooked the last time we talked."

"As soon as you finish your dinner, Peter."

I had to smile at the old lady. She reminded me of my grandmother. Always fussing over me and making sure I ate well.

AS SOON AS I FINISHED dinner, we went into the den at the back of the house. It was a nice room with lots of bookshelves and pictures. It looked very comfortable.

"This was my late husband's den. I read a lot in this room. It makes me feel close to him. As you may have noticed, I do keep the drapes closed. I'm often here until I go to bed."

"It's a very nice room," I said as I walked over to a comfortable looking chair.

"Agnes, I want you to relax and think back to the day Arnold was murdered. I want you to try to recall everything you saw and everything you heard."

Agnes sat in her chair and closed her eyes. When she began to talk, I listened very carefully. I didn't want to miss the smallest clue that might come out of what she had to say.

Her day had started out being pretty routine. She had her breakfast as she usually did, and then puttered around the kitchen cleaning up. She had the kitchen window open and could hear several dirt bikes running around in the forest, but couldn't remember seeing any of them.

"When I finished in the kitchen," she continued. "I went outside to work in my garden. After awhile I realized it was quiet. I remember glancing at my watch and thought the kids must have gone home for lunch."

"Do you remember what time it was?"

"Shortly before noon, I think. It could have been closer to eleven than to twelve."

"Okay."

"I went inside to have my lunch. While I was cleaning up, I saw a man behind the Williams pool house. He was walking toward the woods."

"You saw him from the kitchen window?" I asked.

"Yes."

"Did you get a good look at him?"

"Not really. He was walking away from me and seemed to be in a hurry."

"Think about him. What was he wearing? How tall was he? Could you see anything that might set him apart from anyone else?"

"He was wearing jeans and a dark colored shirt. At the time I thought he was just the pool man. He was fairly tall, maybe a little taller than you."

"I'm six-two."

"He was at least as tall as you and a little stockier than you. He had dark brown hair that sat on his collar."

"Is there anything that would distinguish him from someone else?" I asked since her description of the man could have fit a large number of men.

"He walked with a slight limp. I noticed it because my husband walked like that. My husband had been shot in the knee in France during the war," she explained.

I thought about everything she had said. I was able to pull out of the back of my mind someone who fit her description. It was one of Joseph Angilara's henchmen. He was the big enforcer who tried to open my car door the night Hamilton was murdered. I only wished I had gotten a better picture of him.

"Peter, what's the matter?" Samantha asked.

I turned and looked at Samantha, then at Agnes. They were staring at me. I had been lost in my own thoughts. I turned back to look at Samantha before I answered her question.

"I think I know who the man is. I don't know his name, but I know who he works for. I think it's one of Joseph Angilara's enforcers. I saw him at the Ace Diamond Building the same night Russell Hamilton was killed."

"That means we have a witness that someone was in my house. The police will have to believe me now," Samantha said with a sigh of relief.

"Not so fast. Agnes didn't see his face or see him come out of the house. It would be hard to prove he was actually in the house."

"But just the fact she saw someone will support my story that there could have been someone else in the house. Won't it?"

"It will do that," I assured Samantha. "If nothing else it will provide another direction for the police to look, but it doesn't mean you will no longer be a suspect."

"What do we do now, Peter?" Agnes asked.

"We keep what you've said a secret for the time being. If it gets out that there is a witness who saw someone behind the Williams house near the time Arnold was killed, it might not take long for someone to figure out who saw him. That could put you in danger."

"I see what you mean," Agnes said thoughtfully. "But I'm not afraid."

"I still don't want anything to happen to you."

"Will I still be able to stay here with Agnes?"

"Yes, I think so. Besides, I want you to keep an eye on the house when I'm not here."

"Okay. I can do that. What do we do now?"

"It's almost eleven o'clock. It's time for you ladies to turn in and get some rest."

"That sounds like a good idea," Agnes said. "Samantha, you take the room on the left at the top of the stairs. Peter, you can have the one on the right."

"Thank you," I replied as I stood up.

Samantha and Agnes started for the stairs, but I sat back down. Samantha stopped at the door and looked back over her shoulder at me.

"Aren't you coming, Peter?"

"No. I have a couple of things I need to work out in my head."

"Oh."

"Goodnight, Sam."

"Goodnight, Peter."

AS SOON AS THEY WERE GONE, I went into the living room. The lights were off and I could see the Williams house from the bay window in Agnes's living room. I sat down in a chair and stared out into the darkness. I wasn't really watching anything in particular, I was thinking.

I wondered what was Angilara's interest in Williams? Did he know Williams was going to pull out of the deal and leave them high and dry? There was no evidence to indicate that was the case.

My thoughts continued to bounce around in my head. I wanted to know what had been found out in Mac's investigation into Ace Diamond's financial situation, and the results of the investigation into the allegation that the building was unsafe.

Suddenly, my thoughts were interrupted by a set of headlights turning into the drive at the Williams house. The headlights went out almost immediately. There was a night light over the garage that gave off enough light so I could make out the car as it drove up to the house. The car stopped in front of the garage. There was enough light to see the car was a non-descript car, much like the unmarked cars used by the police.

I'd seen the binoculars on a table near the bay window. Agnes probably kept a pretty good eye on the neighborhood with them. I smiled at the thought that she was probably the one who had reported me to the police.

I picked up the binoculars and looked toward the car in time to see someone get out of it. As he turned to look around, I saw who it was. It was Lieutenant Daniel Royal.

From what I could see, he was alone. I wondered what he was doing there in the middle of the night. It was hard enough to find evidence in broad daylight, but at night it would be impossible. Besides, he was supposed to be working on the death of Hamilton. I could think of nothing he would have found that would lead him here. It occurred to me that Mac might have shown him the pictures I had taken in front of the Ace Diamond Building. Why I thought of that now, I didn't know.

I watched as Royal disappeared around the corner of the house. It looked as if he was going around to the back of the house. From where I was, I could not see the back of the house. However, I could see most of the pool house.

The security light on the corner of the pool house came on. I waited, but didn't see anything until I saw Royal go behind the pool house. He had a flashlight in one hand and something else in the other that I couldn't make out. The only thing I could think of was that Royal was there to find the tracks I had reported to Mac. But why was he looking for the tracks at night? The only answer was he was there to destroy them.

It was only a minute or so before I saw Royal return to his car. I had no idea what he had hoped to find in the dark, but the tracks seemed to provide the most logical answer. As I watched him return to his car, I wondered how he could find the tracks in the dark. The answer was simple, he couldn't. There was only one other conclusion open to me, he was there for some other reason. I decided I would go over there first thing in the morning and take a look around.

As soon as Royal left, I decided it was time for me to try to get some sleep. I had a feeling tomorrow was going to be a long day.

I PUT THE BINOCULARS back on the table and went upstairs. There was a night light in the hall, which made it easy to find my room. I opened the door and went in. A small light on the table next to the bed was on. I must have been deep in thought because I was in the room for a minute or more before I realized Samantha was lying in the bed.

"I guess I have the wrong room," I said in a whisper.

"No, you don't. I've been waiting for you," she said softly.

"Do you think this is a good idea?"

"Probably not, but I saw the car at my house and I got scared."

"The car is gone now," I told her.

"I know, but I'm still scared. Can I stay here for the night? I promise I won't do anything inappropriate."

Even in the dim light I could see the look in her eyes. I found it hard to refuse her request.

"You can stay, but you have to behave," I said.

"That depends on your definition of "behave". I can behave very well if I have the right incentive."

"If you don't behave, I'll see to it that you go to your room. Is that the right incentive?"

"I like a man that takes charge," she said as she held up the blanket for me.

Samantha was wearing a little shorty nightgown with a plunging neckline. The nightgown was one of those that left little to the imagination.

I sat down on the edge of the bed and took off my shirt, shoes and sox. I stood and took off my pants, before I slipped in under the covers.

After lying down, Samantha lifted my arm up and then rolled over against me as she laid her head on my shoulder. I wrapped my arm around her while she slid one of her shapely legs over my leg. She rested her hand on my chest and let out a soft sigh.

I laid there without moving for sometime. The feel of her warm body through the flimsy nightgown was making it hard for me to sleep. Having her lying against me was almost more than I could stand until I realized that she had fallen asleep.

She had fallen asleep quickly. If this had been Jennifer next to me, we would have been enjoying the feel of each other's body. We wouldn't have gotten any sleep at all.

I couldn't help but smile to myself. Samantha was a lovely woman with all the equipment to keep a man up all night. Yet, she was lying up against me and I wasn't even touching her except where her body touched me. I began to realize she really was scared, and what she really needed right now was someone to make her feel safe. I guess I could do that. It wasn't long before I drifted off to sleep, too.

CHAPTER THIRTEEN

I COULDN'T TELL WHAT TIME it was when I woke. The blackout drapes did a good job of keeping the morning sun out, but there was enough light for me to see Samantha. She was lying on her side with her back to me. She seemed to be sleeping very peacefully.

The last thing I wanted to do was to wake her. I rolled over to the edge of the bed and sat up quietly. I grabbed my clothes off the chair and tiptoed into the bathroom.

As soon as I was dressed and ready to face the day, I snuck out the door and down the hall. The house was quiet. The sun was up and it looked like it was going to be a nice day.

When I reached the bottom of the stairs, I could hear the sounds of someone making breakfast. I wandered out to the kitchen and found Agnes fixing a breakfast of waffles, bacon, eggs and coffee. I hadn't seen a breakfast like that in years. I was used to a bowl of cereal with fruit, a cup of coffee and a glass of juice, but I had to admit it smelled good.

"Good morning, Agnes."

"Good morning, Peter. Did you sleep well?"

"Yes, very well. Breakfast sure smells good."

"Sit down. It's all ready."

I sat down in the breakfast nook. My watch showed it was later than I had planned to be up, but there was nothing that required my immediate attention.

"There you go," she said as she set a plate loaded with waffles, bacon and eggs in front of me. "It's been a long time since I've had the chance to prepare such a breakfast."

I noticed the sad tone of her voice. She had probably fixed breakfasts like this for her husband. It was probably why he was dead. The fats and cholesterol had to be pretty high. I decided I would eat it just the same. One time in about five years shouldn't hurt me too much.

Agnes stood next to the table looking down at me with a big smile on her face. She was waiting for me to try the meal and let her know how it tasted. I tried the waffles that were smothered in melted butter and real maple syrup. I had to admit it tasted great.

"This is really good, very good."

"I'm so glad you like it."

I smiled and nodded my head, then returned to eating the meal she had set before me.

"Is Sam up?"

"I don't know. She wasn't when I left the bedroom."

"I know the two of you slept together. I'm sure she needed a man close by last night," she said as she smiled that knowing kind of smile like my grandmother used on me.

"She said she was scared and needed to have someone with her."

"Oh, I'm sure she did. What is on the agenda for this morning?"

"I want you to do the same things you would normally do. I don't want you to make any changes in your routine."

"I usually have breakfast and then I work in my garden before it gets too warm."

"Then that is what you should do. You might keep an eye out to see if the police come by the Williams house."

"I'll do that. Samantha can watch the house from inside."

"I'm going over to see what Lieutenant Royal was doing behind the pool house last night."

"When was that?"

"It was after you went to bed. Anyway, I want to find out what he was up to."

I finished my breakfast, which was not easy. I wasn't used to eating such a heavy meal for breakfast. I left by way of the backdoor and walked into the woods. I worked my way over toward the Williams house. As I came up behind the pool house, I noticed a small place at the back of the pool house were the grass had obviously been pulled up. I hadn't seen it yesterday morning. I was sure that I would have noticed it when Samantha and I were looking for tracks. Someone had disturbed the ground on purpose, but for what reason?

Royal had been snooping around behind the pool house last night. What had he been doing? I decided to find out.

I knelt down beside the area. I pulled back the lose patch of grass and pushed the loose dirt aside. I discovered a plastic sandwich bag with a gun inside. Taking hold of the plastic bag with my finger and thumb on the bottom corner of the bag, I pulled the bag out of the dirt and held it up to get a better look. There was a .38 caliber pistol inside the bag. My instincts told me it was the gun that had been used to kill Arnold.

My gut feeling was Royal had planted it there to make Samantha look guilty. I wondered how he got hold of it. The thought occurred to me that he shot Arnold, or he knew who did. Either way, it would make Royal a dirty cop.

I stood up and looked around. I didn't want the gun to fall into the wrong hands, yet to keep it would put me at risk of being charged with tampering with evidence or concealing evidence, maybe both.

Finding the gun put me between a rock and a hard place. There was no way I could be sure Mac would believe me if I gave it to him. I knew if I told him Royal had planted the gun, it would be my word against his. Even though Mac didn't like Royal, he was a fellow cop.

This whole thing also brought up another interesting point. What was Royal's connection to all this? Who was he really working for? It certainly wasn't the police.

After giving it some thought, I realized I had little choice but to keep the gun and hide it until I had a good reason to turn it over to Mac. I replaced the dirt and the grass and tapped it down. I slid the plastic bag under my jacket and started back to Agnes's house. I had no desire to try to explain what I had found to Samantha or Agnes so I took the gun into the barn. I found a corner in the barn that looked like it hadn't been used for a very long time and hid it in the corner under some old straw. Once it was hidden to my satisfaction, I went back to the house.

AS I WALKED INTO THE KITCHEN, I saw Samantha sitting at the table eating breakfast. She looked up and smiled at me.

"Good morning, Peter."

"Good morning, Sam."

"Where have you been?"

"I went over to your place and had a look around. I hope the police follow up on the lead I gave them."

"So do I."

"Sam, do you have an attorney?" I asked.

"Arnold had one."

"No. Do you have one that handles your affairs?"

"No, not really. But I trust Mr. Wade."

"I'm sure you do, but I think it would be better if you had a criminal attorney, one who defends people accused of murder."

"Am I going to need a criminal attorney?" she asked, the look in her eyes indicating she was afraid of what my answer would be.

"Most likely. I can't keep you hidden forever. Sooner or later, they're going to arrest you. When they do, I don't want you to say anything unless you have an attorney with you."

"I remember Arnold saying Mr. Tucker was a criminal attorney and a very good one. He knew Arnold and liked him. I think I could trust him."

"Good. I don't want you to do anything at the moment, but keep him in mind if you should be arrested. And if you are arrested when I'm not around, don't say anything, not even your name until he is present. Do you understand?"

"Yes, Peter. I understand."

"Good. I have to leave for a little while. I should be back by lunch time, but don't wait for me."

"Where are you going?"

"I'm going to see a man about a gun."

There was a puzzled look on her face, but she didn't say anything. I simply nodded and headed out the backdoor.

I WAS ON MY WAY to the barn when I saw two vehicles turn into the driveway of the Williams place. One was a sedan and the other a van with a light bar on the roof. Painted on the side of the van was "Criminal Investigation Unit". I sort of smiled to myself thinking that the reason they were there was a result of my conversation with Captain MacDonald.

I watched from the barn as the vehicles stopped near the garage. Mac got out of the car and waited for two men and a woman from the van to join him. They all went around to the rear of the house.

In order to get a better view of what they were doing, I moved around to the back of the barn. I still couldn't see very well, so I moved along the trees. I got to a position where I could see the open space between the back of the pool house and the edge of the forest. They went directly to the back of the pool house and began looking along the foundation of the pool house. It was obvious they were not looking for tracks. They were looking for the buried gun.

If it hadn't been clear to begin with, it was now. Someone wanted Samantha charged with murder. Someone had told the police where to find the gun. The only question I had was who? Royal would not have told the police about the gun and where it was hidden. That might cause Mac to wonder how he found out about it. Mac probably found out through an anonymous tip, which Royal, or one of his associates, directed to Mac's office.

For me to move from my position was probably not a good idea. If I moved, they might see me. Instead, I settled in to watch. Two of the investigators were poking around in the dirt along the foundation of the pool house, but that was all.

"Captain, there's nothing here," I overheard one of the investigators say. "It looks like someone has been pulling up weeds. There's definitely no gun buried here."

I watched Mac as he rubbed his chin. He was probably feeling like he had been sent on a wild goose chase and from the look on his face he didn't like it. He turned and looked toward the woods for a couple of minutes.

"I want you to see if you can find any tracks just inside the woods back here. They might be hard to see. If you do find any tracks, I want you to follow them to wherever they lead. You got that?"

The investigators looked at each other, nodded their heads and started toward the woods. Mac joined them in the search for the tracks. I smiled to myself, but there really wasn't anything to smile about. It was apparent Samantha was still their prime suspect, if not their only suspect.

I was about to sneak back to the barn when I heard one of the investigators call out. They had found the tracks I had told Mac would be there.

It was time for me to get out of there. I returned to the house where I found Agnes watching the Williams house from the kitchen window. She seemed to be very concerned with what was going on.

"Are they looking for something?" Agnes asked without turning to look at me.

"Yeah. I think they found the tracks I told them about. Samantha's still not in the clear yet, but at least there is some doubt about whether there was someone else in the house when Arnold was murdered."

"That's good, isn't it?" Agnes asked.

"Yes. It gives reasonable doubt. By the way, where is Samantha?"

"She's upstairs."

I STARTED UP THE STAIRS. When I walked into the bedroom, she was standing at the window looking toward her home.

"What's going on over there?" she asked without turning around.

"They were looking for something behind the pool house."

"Do you know what they were looking for?"

"Yes. They were looking for a gun that was buried there."

"What gun?" she asked sharply as she turned toward me.

"I don't know, but I think it's the gun that was used to kill your husband."

"You mean the killer buried it behind my pool house?"

"Not exactly. The gun was planted there last night."

"Last night? The police are going to think I planted it. I'll be arrested for murder."

"First of all, they already think you killed your husband. All that was going to do was to help make them sure of it. But they didn't find the gun."

"How come. Did you get it before they got there?"

"Yes. I'm sure it's not the best decision I've ever made. I could be in a lot of trouble."

"Then why did you take it? Are you trying to protect me?"

"Not really. I'm more interested in the truth. If the police had gotten hold of the gun, it might not be as carefully tested as I would like. I'm going to take it to the State Crime Lab and have it checked inside and out for fingerprints, residue, and ballistics. I have a friend in the State Crime Lab. I'm sure he will do a good job on it."

"What do you hope to find?"

"I hope to find some evidence that will show you never handled the gun."

"Oh," she said, the tone of her voice showing a hint of disappointment.

Her reaction was not what I had expected. I had hoped she would be a little more upbeat about it. It caused me to wonder what she was keeping from me.

"Sam, have you ever handled a .38 caliber revolver before?"

"Yes."

"When and where?"

"Arnold took me to a pistol range about a year ago. We met someone he knew there who was shooting one. He let me try it out. I didn't like it as well as the .22 caliber pistols Arnold used to target shoot."

"Who was the friend? What was his name?"

"I don't remember his name, but he was an accountant Arnold worked with sometimes. He was a rather nice looking young man, drove a fancy BMW."

It didn't take a genius to figure out who she was talking about. She was describing Jeffrey Mosser.

"I have to go. I want you to stay out of sight. I'll be back as soon as I can."

"Okay."

I left her in the bedroom and immediately left the house. I went out to the barn and retrieved the gun. After carefully placing it under the seat of the Lincoln, I headed for town.

IT DIDN'T TAKE LONG to get to the State Crime Lab. I took the gun in the bag to the forensic lab and asked for

John Farrell, a long time friend of mine. I only had to wait for a few minutes before he came out to the waiting area.

"Say, Pete, what brings you all the way out here?"

"I need a really big favor."

"Come to my office. We can talk there."

I nodded and followed him down a long almost sterile looking hall. We went into his office and closed the door. He motioned for me to sit down as he moved around behind his desk.

"Now, what's this big favor you want from me?"

I explained about the case I was working on. I also explained how I came to have the gun. He listened intently while I explained what I knew for a fact and what I thought I knew.

"Okay, about this gun. What exactly do you want from me?"

"I would like you to go over the gun with a fine tooth comb," I said as I put the gun on his desk. "I would like you to examine it for fingerprints, any residue that might be important in finding out who used it, who owned the gun last, and I would like you to find out if it is the gun that killed Arnold Williams."

"That's asking for a hell of a lot."

"I know."

"You said a cop buried the gun behind the Williams pool house? Are you sure a cop buried it there?"

"To be honest, no. I'm reasonably sure that it was. I'm hoping you can prove it, one way or the other."

"You say the cop's name is Daniel Royal, and he's a detective on the Denver Police Department."

"Yes."

"Have you touched the gun or the bag, other than by the corner where you held it when you set it on my desk?"

"I've been very careful to touch the bag as little as possible. I have held the bag only by the one corner. I never touched the gun."

"Okay. I'm not sure how much information I can get off the gun or the bag, but I'll try."

"That's all I'm asking."

"Pete, what happens if it proves your client killed Williams?"

"John, I'm interested in the truth. That's all."

"Okay. I'll see what I can do. Where can I call you?"

I gave John my cell phone number, thanked him and left the gun in his possession. As I walked to my car, I began questioning the wisdom of turning the gun over to the lab. I didn't have much choice if I really wanted to know the truth.

If Samantha's fingerprints were on the gun, she could say she had held it and fired the gun at the shooting range. However, it wouldn't be hard for the DA to make a convincing argument that she knew where to get the gun, she had fired the gun so she knew how to use it, and she used it to kill her husband to gain control of her husband's wealth. I needed something that might help me find the truth.

I STILL HAD HIDDEN in my apartment the negatives of the pictures I had taken at the Ace Diamond Building. Since I had given my copies of the photos to Captain MacDonald, I needed to make a set of prints to show Samantha. I didn't know if she would recognize anyone. If she recognized Mosser as the man she met at the pistol range, it might help. Just how, I wasn't sure.

I drove across town to my apartment. I didn't see anyone hanging around, but that didn't mean my apartment was not being watched. Whoever had been watching it might have given up and figured I was holding up in a secure place.

I parked the Lincoln on one of the side streets. I'd been switching cars so often it was beginning to get hard for me to remember what kind of a car I had. I had no desire to switch cars again, but I would if I thought it necessary. I walked along the side street toward my apartment. I kept an eye out for anyone who looked like they didn't belong there.

As I came to the front of the building, I checked out the parking lot. There was a sedan parked near the back of the parking lot with two men sitting in it. I had no trouble figuring out it was the police. They were there for one of two reasons. Either to keep an eye on my place because of what I told Mac about the guy following me, or I was about to be picked up for questioning. Yet, there was a third possibility that crossed my mind. They might want to follow me to find out where I had hidden Samantha. I guess I would have to wait and see what the two officers did when I was ready to leave.

The one comforting thing about the police being out front was there was less of a chance I would run into the guy who had been after Samantha. But the fact they were there didn't necessarily eliminate the possibility someone was in my apartment.

I stuck my key in the lock and turned it. As I reached for the doorknob, I also reached inside my jacket for my gun. I pushed open the door and rushed in. I figured anyone close to the door would have a harder time catching me off guard.

No one was in my apartment, but I did find my apartment had been trashed. I wondered what Mac thought about it. At least it would give credence to my claim of being followed.

Looking out at the parking lot, I could see the two cops watching my apartment had not moved. They were still sitting there as if they didn't have a care in the world. That thought caused me to wonder if they were there to keep an eye on my apartment.

I closed the door and went into my dark room. It had been searched, but nothing was missing and the room had not been trashed. I immediately began processing a second set of photos. It must have taken me a little over an hour to get them done. Now all I needed was time for them to dry.

A quick glance out the front window allowed me to breathe a bit easier. The two cops were still sitting there. They were most likely there to simply report my whereabouts to someone else. The only question was, were they there to report to Mac, or to Royal?

Since I knew Mac had been to my apartment, I began picking up my bedroom. I put things back where they belonged. When I was finished, I went onto the living room. As I was picking up the cushions to the sofa, I found a book of matches under one of them. It was a book of matches from a local club, a club I have never been to. Even if I had, I would not have picked up a book of matches.

After I finished straightening up my apartment, I checked on the photos. They were dry. It was time to return to Agnes's home and find out if Samantha could identify any of those in the photos.

I WAS JUST ABOUT TO LEAVE when my cell phone rang. I answered it hoping that it was good news.

"Hello."

"Pete, it's John."

"What did you find out?"

"First of all, it is the gun that killed Williams."

"That's something. You said "first of all". Do you have something else for me?"

"I found two sets of prints on the gun. They are just partials, but I think I can identify who they belong to. I also found two sets of partial prints on the outside of the bag. I'm assuming the ones on the bottom corner of the bag are yours. The others are smudged thumb and fingerprints along the top of the bag. It looks like it was from whoever closed and sealed the bag. It's one of those zip-lock bags for sandwiches. However, at the one end I've got a partial I might be able to identify, but not with enough points to hold up in court."

"That's great. Anything to connect the gun to Samantha Williams?"

"No. Not so far, but I'm not done. The gun was empty, so there were no cartridges in the cylinder to get prints off. Someone had wiped the gun clean, but didn't do a very good job of it. I was able to get several partial prints off the gun.

"I'm in the process of checking out all the prints now. I'll get back to you when I have something more to tell you."

"The prints on the gun might belong to a guy by the name of Jeffrey Mosser. It might help make it go faster."

"Thanks. You know I don't like looking into a fellow cop?"

"I know. But you don't want a dirty cop out there any more than I do."

"You're right about that. I'll get back to you."

"Thanks."

As I hung up the phone, I began to think it was time to find out what Mac had found out on his little outing in the woods. A glance at my watch told me it was early afternoon. If I was lucky, John might have something for me before the day was done.

I gathered up the photos and started for the door, but stopped. I knew the cops were right out front. Since they had not come in to arrest me, I figured they were there to follow me. That was the last thing I wanted right now.

I went out on the balcony and looked around. I didn't see anyone hanging around. I swung my legs over the balcony railing and dropped down the back. It was only a short dash to the back of the garages. After ducking behind the garages, I worked my way to the side street and back to the car.

CHAPTER FOURTEEN

I DROVE BACK TO AGNES'S home the long way to make sure I was not being followed. I arrived there shortly after two. I parked the car in the barn again and went into the house.

When I stepped into the kitchen, Samantha was waiting for me. She was sitting at the table in the nook. The look on her face almost demanded to know what I had been up to and what I had found out. I walked over to the table and dropped the envelope on it, then sat down across from her.

"I want you to take a close look at each of these photos. I want to know if you recognize any of them," I said, then leaned back in the chair.

Samantha looked at me for a second before looking at the envelope. She hesitated as if she was afraid of what she might see. Slowly and carefully, she opened the envelope and let the photos cascaded onto the table.

Agnes came into the kitchen and saw the photos scattered on the table. She sat down next to Samantha.

"What are we looking at?" Agnes asked without looking up at me.

"We are looking at photos I took the day Arnold was murdered. I want to know if either of you recognize anyone."

"I recognize this man," Agnes said as she picked up a photo. "This is Russell Hamilton. He's the rental agent at the Ace Diamond Building."

"What can you tell me about him?"

"Not much really. My husband knew him from the country club. They played golf together a few times, as I recall. My husband didn't like him very much."

"Why was that?"

"I'm not sure, but if I remember correctly my husband didn't think much of him as a businessman, and he certainly didn't like some of the people he associated with at the country club."

"Anyone in particular?"

"The only one I can remember my husband mentioning was a man by the name of Angilena, Angilara, or something like that."

"Was it possibly Joseph, or Joe Angilara?" I asked as I picked out the picture of Angilara and handed it to her.

"That's him. My husband said he was into all sorts of criminal activity, but the police had not been able to get enough evidence to put in him jail."

"That is Angilara," I assured her.

Samantha looked at the picture I had handed to Agnes. Her mouth fell open and her eyes got big.

"Peter, I know this man," she said, a hint of excitement in her voice.

"Where do you know him from?"

"I met him at the Performing Arts Center, well sort of. We ran into him in the lobby of The Buell Theater. He pulled Arnold off to the side and talked to him for a few minutes. It didn't look like it was a very friendly conversation.

"When Arnold came back to me, he was visibly upset. He sat through the play, but didn't seem to enjoy it. He was upset the rest of the evening, but he wouldn't talk about it."

"Do you think Angilara threatened Arnold?"

"I have no idea why he would threaten Arnold, but if he did it didn't scare him. If anything, it made Arnold mad."

"When was this? Do you remember?"

"It was about a week before I came to see you."

I leaned back in my chair to think about what she told me. I found it interesting that it had only been about seven or eight days before Arnold was killed that he had the conversation with Angilara. I had no idea what significance that had, but it had something to do with his death and probably the death of Hamilton. I was convinced of it.

I hadn't been watching Samantha while I was thinking about what she told me. My thoughts were suddenly interrupted when she spoke again.

"I know this man, too," she said as she looked up at me.

I must have had a puzzled look on my face as she was looking at the same photo.

"You know the other guy in that photo?"

"Yes. It's not a very good picture of him, but I saw him with Mr. Angilara at The Buell Theater, too."

So, Angilara went everywhere with his enforcer. It was obvious the guy was Angilara's personal bodyguard. And if there was anyone who would know what his name was, it had to be Mac.

"Peter, this man was at the house," Samantha said as she showed me the photo of Mosser, the accountant who liked to flash his money around and drive expensive cars.

"Do you know why he was at the house?"

"He's the accountant for Ace Diamond Construction Company and the Ace Diamond building. He came by the house to give Arnold some information."

"Do you know what that information was?"

"I believe it was cost analysis, projected income from the rental of space in the building, and projected profit and loss statements. It was the kind of financial information needed to make an informed decision on investing in the project. I'm not sure what was included, but I know Arnold always studied the financial records and projections of any project before he invested in it. He was very good at that, you know."

"Mr. Mosser brought them by personally?"

"Yes."

"Did he stay very long?"

"Not as I recall. Arnold wanted to go over the information without the company's accountant standing over his shoulder. I remember Arnold telling Mr. Mosser if he had any questions he would contact him then walked him to the door."

"How was Mosser with that?"

"I don't think he liked it very much, but he left without a fuss."

"I take it his visit was in the evening."

"Yes, how did you know that?"

"I've done a little background work on your husband. For the most part, he kept his work confined to his office."

"That's right. He actually did very little work at home. He liked to keep work separate from his home life. In order to make sure, he avoided bringing his work home."

"Yet, he did do some work at home. Didn't he?"

"Yes, but only during the last few months."

If Arnold was so set on not bringing work home that he maintained an office downtown, why did he suddenly start bringing work home? There had to be a reason, and I was beginning to think the reason was to keep what he found more secure.

I vaguely remembered reading something about a break-in at the same building where Arnold maintained an office. And if my memory served me right, it was about three months ago. I couldn't remember anything to indicate Arnold's office was one of them broken into, but it probably made him cautious about what he kept there.

"Samantha, do you have a key to your husband's office?"

"Sure. It's in my purse. Are you going there?"

"I think it would be a good idea."

"Can I go?"

"No. The last thing I want is for anyone to see you before I get more information on the gun. Once I get that, it will be time for us to get you a lawyer and pay a visit to the police."

"Okay."

I could tell by the look on her face and the tone of her voice that she was either disappointed because I wouldn't take her with me, or she had no desire to talk to the police. It might have been a little of both.

I was hoping the gun would help lead the police away from Samantha. If it didn't, we would still have to let the police interview her. To keep her hidden away much longer would do more harm to her case than we needed.

Samantha gave me the key to her husband's office while I put the photos back in the envelope. We talked about getting an attorney lined up for Samantha while Agnes prepared dinner.

After dinner, I went out to the barn and got in the Lincoln. I headed for Arnold's office.

I DROVE DIRECTLY DOWNTOWN and pulled into the underground parking at the building where Arnold had his office. I took the elevator to the fourteenth floor where Arnold's office was located. When I stepped off the elevator, I saw someone at the door. He was picking the lock. I slipped into a doorway where he couldn't see me and waited. As soon as the door opened and the man went inside, I hurried down the hall before he could get the door completely closed.

I slammed my shoulder into the door, pushing it open hard. It hit the man and knocked him off balance. Unfortunately, I was off balance, too. Before I could recover, he was standing there ready to take me on. I didn't like the idea of taking a beating if the guy was trained in hand-to-hand combat so I reached for my gun. The moment I moved for it, he gave me one of those fancy karate kicks. It sent my gun off in the corner of the room. Before I could react, he smacked me in the chest with the heel of his hand.

I went down like a ton of bricks and found myself gasping for air. By the time I was in any condition to know what was going on, he was making a beeline out the door.

I pulled myself up off the floor and leaned against the desk. While I was trying to catch my breath, I remembered where I had seen him before. He was the same guy that had tried to catch Samantha in City Park, and the same guy that followed me to my apartment.

There was no doubt in my mind I had underestimated his ability. The most irritating part was he hardly broke a sweat taking me out. I would be better prepared if we should meet again, and we would meet again. I would see to it.

I sat down behind the desk to lick my wounds, so to speak, and to think about what it was he had come here to find. It was probably the same thing I was looking for, but I didn't know what it was. If I had done nothing else, I had prevented him from finding whatever he had come there to get.

Since I was sitting at Arnold's desk, I pulled open the center drawer and shuffled through the papers. There was nothing of interest so I pressed on to the drawers on the sides.

During my search of the desk, I dropped a file on the floor. Several pages slid out of the folder and under the desk. I got down on my hands and knees to retrieve them. As I was gathering them up, I bumped my head on the bottom of the center drawer. I hit something with the back of my head. I turned and looked up to find a thin tin box that was designed to hold keys, maybe one or two keys at the most. It was not the best place to hide a key, but I doubted Arnold had been an expert at hiding things.

I reached up and opened the box. Inside I found two keys. One of the keys looked like it was to a file cabinet while the other was a typical key to a safe. If that was the case, then there was probably a safe in the office somewhere.

I crawled out from under the desk and stood up. There were two file cabinets in the office, but only one of them had a lock. I looked around the room for a place where a safe, such as a wall safe, might be hidden. Since there were three fairly large paintings on the walls, it only made sense that the safe would be behind one of them.

I tried the key in the file cabinet first. It immediately unlocked the cabinet. I took it one file drawer at a time. The only things I found that might be of interest were the projections of how the Ace Diamond Building might do once it was occupied.

Once I was finished with the file cabinet, I started looking behind the paintings on the walls for a safe and found nothing. I thought the safe might be some place other than here, but that didn't make a lot of sense. Why would you keep a key hidden in an office if the safe was somewhere else? The logical answer I came up with was you wouldn't. That meant the safe was here. I just hadn't found it.

I stood there looking around the room. It seemed logical the safe might have been put in the wall behind the bookshelves, but that was a very common hiding place.

I sat down on the corner of the desk to think. It happened I was looking at the floor while thinking. I wasn't looking at anything in particular, but I noticed a bit of loose carpet in a corner behind a floor lamp. I looked around the room before looking back at the corner. It struck me as strange that there would be loose carpet in an office that was otherwise in perfect condition. The dawn came when I realized Arnold might have a floor safe.

I knelt down on the floor and lifted up the piece of loose carpet. The lamp had set over the carpet to hide the fact it was loose. It apparently had gotten moved when I got knocked on my ass. Like they say, a little good comes out of every setback.

Under the carpet was the safe. I slipped the key into the lock, turned it and opened the safe. I found several items in it. There was a blue folder like the lawyers use to hold important documents, an envelope with no name on it, and a paper with several names on it. There was nothing else in the safe.

I took everything out, sat down at the desk and began looking through the papers. I started with the blue folder. I found a Last Will and Testament along with a letter. The will was dated only three days before Arnold was murdered. A quick scan of the will showed Arnold had left everything to Samantha. This was not a good thing to find at this time. It gave the police a good motive to point the finger at Samantha. I wondered if Samantha knew about it.

The letter to Samantha was in Arnold's own handwriting. It was an apology to Samantha for making her sign the agreement that was with the old will. After that it got very personal and was really none of my business. The letter made me think that Arnold had not told Samantha about the change in his will, but I couldn't be sure. I folded it back up and put it back in the safe.

I opened the envelope and found a letter from Hamilton telling Arnold that Angilara and another mobster by the name of Stan Rickett were heavy investors in the Ace Companies. It went on to say they were concerned that Arnold might pull his money out of the Ace Diamond Building project if he ever found out about them. It also stated Rickett and Angilara were siphoning money off the project by using less expensive material and charging for the expensive ones. However, the letter didn't indicate the less expensive material was causing the building to be unsafe.

The reason Hamilton let Arnold know the names of the secret investors was not clear. However, Hamilton had expressed his concern for Arnold's safety by suggesting it might be wise if he played dumb and acted as if he didn't know who the big investors were.

From what I had learned about Arnold, he didn't strike me as the kind of person who would try to hide something that might come out later. He was more the kind of a guy who would get it out in the open so it didn't come back and bite him in the ass.

Arnold knew what would happen if he made public who was involved in the project. He undoubtedly would lose a lot of money, but at the same time he would probably save his reputation.

I was holding in my hand the best motive I could think of for Angilara and Rickett to want Arnold dead. If I turned this letter over to Mac, it would force him to look at someone other than Samantha as Arnold's murderer. It would also show there was a likely connection between Arnold and Hamilton's murders.

I folded the letter up and put it back in the envelope. After slipping it into my coat pocket, I took a look at the list. It had the names of several people on it. Beside each name was something about that person. I recognized several of the names. Three or four of them were enforcers for Angilara and a couple of them were enforcers for Rickett. One of the enforcers for Rickett was Brad Sims.

I knew I should have known the guy who tried to grab Samantha in the park, and who had knocked me on my butt just minutes ago. It was Brad Sims. He was well known by the police as a very violent man.

It suddenly occurred to me that the black limo I had seen parked alongside the Ace Diamond Building the other night belonged to Stan Rickett. I would also bet Brad Sims was one of the men with him. I remembered the guy in the middle was short. Rickett was short, but he had a criminal record as long as your arm. He had been in and out of jail from the time he was ten. From what I knew about him, he was as mean, if not meaner, than Angilara or any of his enforcers.

Now that I had all this information, I had to decide how to best use it. The envelope with the letter from Hamilton would be best used by giving it to Mac. The list of enforcers and others might best be kept safe for a while. As for the will, I thought it would be best left in the safe where I found it.

Now, what to do with the key to the safe? Where would be a good place to keep it? Since I was connected to Samantha, it was probably best hidden some place away from me.

I remembered one of the pictures on the wall had a heavy paper backing. I went to the picture and took it off the wall. I laid it on the desk, then took my pocketknife and loosened a small area of the backing along the top. I opened it just enough to slip the safe key in behind it. I pressed the paper backing back in place and examined it. It was almost impossible to see where I had dropped the key in behind the backing. I returned the picture to its place on the wall.

The list of enforcers was a different matter. It might best be hidden in one of the many books on the bookshelves. It was not so important if it was found. After all, it wouldn't take a genius for the police to figure out who did the dirty work for Angilara and Rickett. The police already knew most of their enforcers.

Before I was ready to leave Arnold's office, I made copies of the letter and the list of enforcers. I hide them in different books and on different shelves of the bookcase.

It was time to pay a visit to Mac. I looked around the room to make sure everything was back in place. The floor lamp was once again setting over the loose carpet making it impossible to see. There was no longer anything out of place. It was time for me to leave.

I went to the door and checked out the hall. There was no one in the hall. I stepped out of the office and locked the door.

AS I STARTED DOWN THE HALL, the bell rang and the elevator door opened. I mentally prepared myself for a confrontation. I let out a sigh of relief when I saw Mac step off the elevator. I smiled at him as he approached me.

"What are you doing here?" Mac asked.

"I might ask you the same thing."

"Don't get smart with me. Have you been in Mr. Williams's office?"

"As a matter of fact, yes I have."

I figured I might as well admit it. If he had his team of forensic people go over the room and found my fingerprints, it would not look good for me if I had told him that I hadn't been in the office.

"What were you doing in there?"

"I was looking for something that might indicate someone other than Mrs. Williams murdered Arnold."

"Did you find anything? You'll be in a lot of trouble if you found something and don't tell me."

"Yes, I know. And yes, I found something that might very well interest you," I said as I reached into my inside coat pocket and took out the envelope.

"What's this?"

"It's a letter from Hamilton to Arnold Williams warning him to be careful. Who's your partner?" I asked.

There was something about the guy with Mac that told me he was not a cop. He looked more like a maintenance worker.

"He's a locksmith. I have a warrant to search Mr. Williams' office. Since I don't have a key and I don't have contact with Mrs. Williams, it seemed to be the thing to do," Mac replied.

"Will this help," I said as I held up the key Samantha had given me. "It's the key to Arnold's office."

Mac looked at me with suspicious eyes, but then he always looked at me that way. He reached out and took the key. I followed him to Arnold's office door then stood back as he slipped the key in the door and turned it. He looked at me again before he turned the knob and opened the door.

He told the locksmith he could go. Mac looked at me for a second before handing back the key.

"Are you coming in?"

I guess I hadn't expected him to invite me into the office. He never seemed to want me around, but then I had already been in the office. I was sure he was thinking I might be able to save him some time.

"If you insist."

"I insist," he said.

I guess it really didn't make any difference since I had been planning on paying him a visit anyway. I followed Mac into the office. I stood off to the side while I watched him look around.

"Pretty nice place. Where did you find the letter?"

I wasn't ready to tell him. I figured if he had his lab people go over the place he would find a lot of my fingerprints on the desk. It would make sense to him if I told him that I found the letter in the desk.

"I found it in the desk hidden under some papers."

Mac glanced over at me. The look on his face gave me the impression he wasn't sure I was telling the truth. I was far more interested in what he could prove than in what he thought.

Mac moved around behind the desk and sat down in the chair. I walked across the room and sat down in the chair next to the floor lamp. I watched Mac as he opened the letter and began reading it. By the look on his face there was no doubt it proved to him just what I thought it would. There was a connection between Hamilton's and Williams's murders.

"It seems you were right about Hamilton and Williams. The only real question is why were they both murdered?"

"The way I figure it, someone found out Hamilton told Williams about the other investors. That's why Hamilton was killed. The fact Williams knew about the mob being part of the controlling investors was why Williams was killed."

"Why kill Williams? Williams stood to lose a great deal of money. He wasn't likely to bail out and lose probably three to five million dollars."

"Williams was a man of very high principles. I'm sure the way he saw it was that he could afford to lose the money more than he could afford the damage to his reputation. After all, three to five million dollars was not all that much to him."

"Are you sure?"

"I've spent a lot of time looking into Arnold's background. Everything I've seen on him would indicate he was not the type of man to allow his reputation to be tarnished by some scandal if he could prevent it."

"What about the allegation the building was unsafe?"

"My guess is, but I haven't been able to prove it, he might have found out the allegation was true. He may even have found out who was responsible for it."

I watched as Mac looked off into space. I was sure he was thinking about what I had told him. If he had as much sense as I thought he had, he would be seeing the same picture I was seeing.

"We got a tip there was a gun hidden next to the foundation of the Williams pool house. When we got there, we found nothing. You wouldn't happen to know anything about that, would you?"

"That depends on two things," I replied.

"If you're keeping evidence from me, you're in big trouble, Pete."

"It still depends on two things."

"Okay. What are they?"

"First of all, I will bring Mrs. Williams in to have a private talk with you, and only you, on Monday. You will not place her under arrest."

"That would depend on what she has to say."

"I see we don't have a deal right from the get go," I said as I stood up.

"You know I can put an APB out for her. Anyone hiding her could be charged with aiding and abetting."

"You could, but you won't."

"And why is that?"

"Because you want to solve this murder as quickly as possible. But more than that, you want the right people going to jail."

Mac looked at me for a moment or two. I wasn't sure if he was going to listen to me, or arrest me for hindering a murder investigation.

"Okay. I'll agree with your first request, but if you're playing me for a sucker it will be a long time before you see the light of day except from a jail cell."

"That's fair enough. The second thing I'm not ready to tell you about. I might be by the time you interview Samantha, Mrs. Williams."

"You expect me to agree to your second request without telling me what it is? You've got to be crazy."

"You're not the first person to call me crazy, but yes. I'm asking you to do something that runs totally against your grain, but I assure you that you will not be disappointed. If you are, I'll give myself up to you and you can lock me up."

"I can lock you up now."

"Yes, you can. But I don't think you want to do that. It wouldn't help your case any."

Mac looked at me as if he thought I had gone off the deep end. He may not have been far off. I was sticking my neck out, and he had every right to cut it off.

"Okay, but you better not make me sorry."

"I won't. I'll meet you at your office at ten in the morning on Monday with Mrs. Williams. She needs to have time to talk to her attorney. I assure you that she will be ready to talk to you."

Mac reluctantly nodded that he agreed. I decided it was time to get the hell out of there before he changed his mind. I left Mac in Arnold's office and quickly retreated to the elevators.

CHAPTER FIFTEEN

As soon as I got to the underground parking, I started for my rental car. I looked around to see if there was anyone that might be watching. As luck would have it, I saw the same car that had followed me to my apartment a few days ago. It was parked back in the corner next to a cement pillar. I couldn't see who was in the car, but there was no doubt it was Brad Sims. He was planning to follow me until he found out where I was hiding Samantha. I had no intentions of letting him. Besides, I had a score to settle with him.

I was tempted to go over to the car, drag him out of it and beat the shit out of him. He had caught me off guard with his karate kick. It still hurt a lot more than I wanted to admit, but it didn't stop me from wanting to do him harm. I couldn't think of anything that would make me feel better than to return the favor.

Just as I was about to turn and go over to him, I saw two police cars. One was inside the garage near the far elevator. The two officers in the car were watching me. The other was outside the garage next to the street. My guess was they were here as back up for Mac. This was not a good time to get into a fight. Win or lose, I would probably end up in jail. I couldn't afford that right now.

I walked over to the Lincoln and got in. I looked in my rearview mirror and watched Sims. It only took me a couple of minutes to come up with a plan on how to deal with him.

A smile came over my face as I reached down and started the car. It was my turn to show him how to take someone out. I backed out of the parking space and drove to the exit.

A quick glance in the rearview mirror showed me that Sims was planning to follow me. I couldn't have asked for more. I was pretty pleased with myself.

I casually pulled out onto the street and headed east. I had to stop at a traffic light, which gave me a chance to make sure he was still following me. We had tangled once, so I was thinking he was probably feeling pretty superior. I was hoping to use it to my advantage.

My plan was simple. I would lead Sims around town for a little while as if I was trying to lose him. I had lost him once before, and I doubted he wanted to lose me again. The difference between then and now was simple. I didn't want him to lose me. I wanted him right on my tail.

I had good knowledge of the back alleys and deadend streets in the downtown area. In order to get him to stay fairly close, I took a few sharp turns without using my turn signals and turning rather quickly or at the last minute. Those types of maneuvers were commonly used to lose a tail, but I did them much slower so he would think I was trying to lose him.

WHEN I GOT TO WHERE I wanted to carry out my plan, I sped up after making a sharp turn down a side street. He was making the turn at the corner when I turned into an alley and hit the brakes. I threw the car into park, jumped out and ducked behind a Dumpster. Turning into the alley, he suddenly found the Lincoln stopped directly in front of him. He hit the brakes and squealed to a stop only a foot or so from my car.

There was no doubt he was surprised. Sims sat in his car and stared at the Lincoln. All he could see was an empty car. Cautiously, he looked around, then turned and looked at the Lincoln again. He was confused. I was sure he was wondering where I had gone.

Slowly, Sims opened his car door. He got out and stood behind the door for a couple of minutes as he again looked around. I had to give him credit, he was a cautious man.

The alley was the perfect place to set up an ambush. It was not the perfect place to be the one being ambushed. The alley was narrow, especially where the Dumpsters were setting. For Sims, there was only one way out of the alley and that was behind him. For a minute or so I thought he might be thinking about backing out of the alley and let it go this time.

He still had no idea where I was. I could have left the car and ducked into one of the buildings, or I could have gone done to the end of the alley on foot. From the looks of him, he had another thought. He was probably thinking I was lying down in the Lincoln waiting for him to approach the car.

Sims took a step back and closed the door to his car. He reached inside his coat and drew out his gun. He slowly moved closer to the Lincoln. His concentration was fixed on the Lincoln.

As he started to move past the Dumpster, I lunged out at him. Using all my weight, I planted a hard right to his jaw. His head twisted sharply to the side and he slammed hard against the car. He didn't fall to the ground, but his gun fell from his hand. It hit the ground and slid under the Lincoln. He was now disarmed, which made things a lot better for me.

"I owed you that," I said as I waited for him to turn and look at me.

Sims looked at me with hate in his eyes. He didn't like the idea I had surprised him. He shook off the effects of my punch, straightened up, and took a karate stance. It was like before when he kicked me, only this time I was ready for him.

"You're going to be sorry you hit me," Sims said angrily. "I'm going to beat you within an inch of your life."

"Not this time."

I put my hands up and took a stance as if I was ready for a good old fashion boxing match. He smiled, and then he threw a karate jab at me. I was able to duck the full force of it, but he caught me on the side of the face and it set me back a bit. He followed it with another quick jab to my mouth that sent me back against the building and then to the ground.

He backed off a step or two and smiled. He waited for it to soak in that I might have taken on more than I was able to handle. He was sure he had the best of me, and at the moment I would have agreed with him.

"Where's the Williams woman?" he demanded.

"You'll never know," I replied as I wiped the blood off my mouth and stood up.

"You'll tell me before this is over," he said with a sinister grin.

The smile left his face and he attacked me again. I blocked another of his karate punches and delivered a hard right hook to his left eye followed by a quick jab to his gut. Blood splattered from a cut above his eye and he doubled over. I had cut him deep and almost closed his eye, and I had taken the wind out of him. It was at that moment he must have realized it was not going to be as easy to take me as he thought. He backed off a couple of steps and looked at me. There was a hint of caution in his eyes now, something that had not been there before.

He started to shift his weight on his feet, and then suddenly came up with a swinging leg kick. His leg caught me in the side and spun me around. I crashed into the side of the Dumpster, flattening my face against it. It dazed me for a moment and I slid to the ground again. He stepped up to me and kicked me in the upper leg causing me to grab my leg and curl up in pain. He moved up closer. Taking his time now, he leaned over me and put his hands on the Dumpster. I knew what was coming next. He planned to hold onto the Dumpster while he kicked me into submission.

As he reared back to take a good hard kick at me, I prepared myself for the kick. He hit me in the ribs, but I somehow managed to catch hold of his leg at the ankle. With all the strength I could muster, I quickly twisted his leg putting him off balance. Although the kick to my ribs had hurt like hell, I didn't let go of him. With all his weight on his opposite leg, I quickly twisted his leg again putting a great deal of pressure on the knee.

As he fought to maintain balance, I quickly twisted his leg in the opposite direction he was falling. The sudden sound of his knee snapping assured me that I had achieved the desired effect, that of putting him down. He went down with a cry of pain.

Experience had taught me that no matter how big the man, if you snap his knee he will go down like a ton of bricks. Sims was no different. He collapsed on the ground next to me. I quickly hit him in the knee to make sure the pain would keep him down and keep him from kicking or hitting me again.

I stood up and hung onto the Dumpster as I backed away from him. I was having difficulty standing up and my breathing was coming in short painful gasps. He had worked me over pretty good, but he was in no position to fight me any more. I had won the fight, but not without paying dearly for it.

As I stood leaning against the Dumpster, I tried to catch my breath and get control of the pain while keeping an eye on Sims. I doubted I could handle any more surprises. I hurt all over.

Sims was still lying on the ground in pain. I knew by snapping his knee he would not be able to stand or walk for sometime without crutches. He was trying to straighten out. It soaked into my clouded brain that he was trying to reach under the car for his gun. I drew my leg back and planted the tip of my shoe hard on the point of his chin. His head rose slightly from the impact then his eyes rolled back and he collapsed on the ground. He was out cold.

I looked around, but didn't see anyone. It was time to get out of there. If one of his cronies caught me now, I would not be in any shape to defend myself. Sims was part way under my car. I didn't think it would be a good idea to run over him, although I was tempted. I reached down and grabbed him by the hair. I dragged him out from under the car and over to the Dumpster.

With a great deal of pain and effort on my part, I pulled him to his feet and rolled him over the side of the Dumpster. There seemed to be a bit of poetic justice in unceremoniously dumping him in it. I wanted to laugh, but to laugh would have been too painful. My ribs hurt like hell and my head was throbbing as if someone was hitting me with a club. I had not gotten my satisfaction as easily as I had hoped. I would probably hurt for several days.

I stumbled over to Sims's car, shut off the engine and removed the keys. I returned to my car and got in rather slowly, I admit. I drove down the alley to another Dumpster, stopped and tossed his keys in it. I then drove out the end of the alley.

I was reasonably sure Sims would know the car I was driving if he saw it. However, I was in no condition to take it back to the rental agency and rent another car. I was sure my face looked pretty bad at the moment. I could feel my lip was cut and swollen, I could hardly stand up straight, my clothes were a mess from the fight and I was in pain. All I wanted was to find a place to lie down and rest.

It wasn't easy to drive in my condition, but I had to get to somewhere I could hide out for a day or two. At the moment, I could think of no better place to go than Agnes's house. I doubted anyone would look for me there. It was a longer drive than to my own apartment, but it would be safer.

I drove directly back to the foothills. I kept an eye out behind me for a tail, but no one seemed to be following me.

I didn't think Mac would even try. I had already shown him that I could ditch a tail anytime. Besides, he was going to get what he wanted on Monday, namely Samantha to question.

WHEN I GOT BACK TO AGNES'S, I drove directly into the barn. Once inside, I shut off the engine and sat there for a few minutes. I was feeling like I had been run over by a Mack truck. The last thing I wanted to do was move.

After a brief period of rest, I slowly got out of the car. I leaned against it for a moment to catch my breath. The beating I had taken was beginning to cause my muscles to stiffen up. I started to make my way to the house. It seemed like a long ways. When I opened the backdoor Samantha and Agnes greeted me.

"What happened to you?" Samantha said with a worried look on her face.

"I had a little skirmish with one of Stan Rickett's enforcers."

Samantha slipped an arm around me to help me through the kitchen. As her hand pressed against my side, a sharp pain shot through me causing me to flinch. I was beginning to realize how hard I had been kicked.

"Take him to the bathroom upstairs. A good soaking in a warm tub will help," Agnes said.

Samantha carefully led me to the stairway to the second floor. I took it one step at a time, but even with her help I found myself out of breath when we finally got to the top of the stairs. She gently guided me into the large bathroom and sat me down on the toilet seat. It was getting hard to move.

"We have to get you out of your clothes."

"I can handle it," I assured her.

She smiled, and then started filling the tub with warm water. When she turned back, she found me still struggling to get my sport coat off. It didn't seem to matter how I moved, it was painful. And no matter how hard I tried, I couldn't get my sport coat off.

"Let me help you," she said as she stepped up to me.

I let her help. She managed to get me out of my sport coat. She took my shoulder holster and gun off and hung it over a nearby chair. I think the real shock for her came when she removed my shirt and saw all the bruises on my chest and sides.

"My God," she gasped.

Being careful not to cause me any more pain than necessary, she finished undressing me. As soon as I was naked, she helped me into the tub. I have to admit the warm water felt good on my body. It didn't take me very long to settle in and do what I could to relax.

"Would you like me to stay with you?" Samantha asked.

"If you like."

"I'll get a washcloth and wash the blood off your face. You look like you could use a bandage or two, maybe a few stitches. Should I call a doctor?"

"No. We can't let anyone know where you are, or where I am."

"Okay. I'll fix you up as best I can."

"Thank you," I said as I leaned back, closed my eyes and rested my head on the end of the tub.

Samantha was as gentle as she could be while wiping the blood and dirt off my face. It stung like hell when she cleaned the open cuts on my face and applied dressings to my cheek and to the abrasion on the side of my face.

"That's about all I can do for you," she said.

"Thank you."

"Is there anything you want?"

"Just to lie here for a little while."

She reached in and touched the water.

"I'll warm it up a little for you before I go and leave you alone."

"Thank you."

She ran a little more hot water in the tub, and then left me alone with my thoughts. It seemed funny that something as hard as a tub could feel so good on an aching body. I closed my eyes and let the feel of the warm water gently wrap around my hurting body.

WHILE I LAY THERE IN THE TUB, I began to wonder what Sims had gone to Arnold's office to find. I had found the list that included Sims's boss's name on it, but I didn't know how it would connect him to the death of Arnold.

I was sure there had to be something else. It could be the letter from Hamilton warning Arnold. Now that could connect Rickett to Arnold's death if in no other way than to provide a motive. It would be enough to get the police looking at him. I doubted he would want the police looking too closely.

I also wondered what his interest in Samantha was. Did he know that Samantha knew Arnold had planned to pull out of the project and leave Angilara and Rickett holding the bag? It was certainly a possibility. Or was it possible he just thought she knew and couldn't take the chance that she would keep quiet? Was it possible Rickett thought Samantha knew about the letter and the list, and where they were hidden?

All this would make sense if it had been proven that the building was unsafe. It could cost a fortune to repair the building since it was almost completed. But as far as I knew there had been no proof the building was unsafe. That would be something to look into.

The thought crossed my mind that if the state inspectors were on Rickett's or Angilara's payroll, then there might never be any proof the building was unsafe. I wondered if Arnold had thought of that. Who would he get to inspect the building? In order to get a creditable inspection, Arnold might have to go out of town to find someone he could trust.

If Arnold had decided to hire an independent inspector, had he told anyone about it? If he was planning to hire an independent inspector, and Rickett or Angilara had found out about it; there was another good motive for either Angilara or Rickett to murder Arnold.

I needed to find Arnold's appointment book again. It would probably require me to check out every name in it, as I doubted Arnold would have listed the independent inspector by the company name. That would draw too much attention to what he was doing. He would have had to keep that very quiet. If he hadn't written it down in his appointment book, where would he have kept the information? That thought brought up the idea he may have kept the information in his head. If that were the case, no one would know unless he told someone. I realized the one person he would have told was Samantha, which could be the reason Rickett wanted her.

If Samantha didn't know, then it became a question of whether he had already hired someone to inspect the building, or whether he had not had the chance to do it. If he had hired someone, he would have had to pay him a retainer and that person's name or the company name might be found in Arnold's checkbook.

There was nothing I could do while I was in the tub, but I didn't really want to get out. It was still warm and felt good. I seriously doubted there would be anything I could do now, anyway. For the moment, I would rest. I tipped my head back, closed my eyes and let myself drift off to sleep.

I DON'T KNOW HOW LONG I slept, but I was awakened by a gentle touch to my arm. I opened my eyes to find Samantha kneeling next to the tub. There was a look of concern on her face, which quickly turned to a soft smile.

"You ready to get out?" she asked softly.

"I think so."

"I think it would be a good idea if you went right to bed. The rest will do you good."

"You're probably right, but I need to talk to you for a few minutes."

"Okay, but after I get you into bed."

I nodded in agreement. Samantha helped me out of the tub. She took a large soft towel and carefully patted me dry. It felt good except when she patted my bruised ribs. When she was done, she wrapped the towel around me and led me to the bedroom. As soon as I was comfortable in the bed, she sat down beside me.

"Okay, what is it you want to talk to me about?"

"Did Arnold ever talk to you about hiring an independent inspector to look over the building to make sure it was safe?"

"Yes, he did."

"Did he actually do anything about it?"

"Yes. He hired a guy from a large firm in Los Angeles to come here and inspect the building."

"Do you know if he ever came?"

"I don't think so. Arnold told me that he was due this weekend. Arnold thought if he came on the weekend, there would be less chance of the inspector being discovered while he inspected the building."

"That makes sense, but I wonder if he is here yet."

"I don't know," Samantha replied.

"Do you know the name of the firm?"

"No, but it would be in Arnold's checkbook. I know he sent a retainer to them."

"Where would his checkbook be?"

"Behind his desk."

"Would that be at home or in his office?"

"At home."

"Do you know where he kept his checkbook?"

"Sure. It's in the bookshelf above the cadenza."

"I didn't see any checkbook there," I said a little puzzled by her reply.

"Of course not. But do you remember seeing a red and gold bound book on the shelf?"

"Vaguely."

"That's his checkbook, the one he uses for investments and business. The title on the end of the checkbook is *Gold Mines in the Rockies.*"

"He was rather sneaky wasn't he," I said with a grin.

"Yes, he was," she replied.

I heard a hint of sadness in her voice. I was beginning to understand the relationship between Arnold and her. They were much closer than most people realized.

"Do you want me to get it?" she asked.

"No. I don't want you leaving the house without me. Do you understand that?"

"Yes."

"Tomorrow, we'll get the checkbook. We can go there the same way we did before."

"Okay," she agreed. "You better get some rest. I'll be back up later."

She smiled, turned and left the room. I watched her as she pulled the door closed, leaving it slightly ajar. The more time I spent with her the more fascinated I became with her. She knew how to please a man, and yet she was certainly her own woman.

I dozed off and on until it was getting late. I woke at the sound of someone coming into the room. Samantha walked across the room and turned on a small light on the dresser. I watched her as she took off her clothes and slipped a nightgown on over her head. The soft material gently cascaded down the smooth lines of her body. She looked over her shoulder, saw me watching her and smiled.

She didn't say anything and neither did I. She turned off the light and walked back across the room to the bed. Samantha lifted the covers, sat down on the bed and swung her legs under the covers. She didn't say anything as she lay down and rested her head on the pillow.

"Thanks for taking care of me," I whispered.

"You're welcome," she replied softly, then turned her back to me.

I laid there for some time thinking about her. I had a lot to think about, but she was right. I needed to rest. I closed my eyes and let sleep come to me.

CHAPTER SIXTEEN

WHEN I WOKE there was a little bit of sunshine trying to sneak in around the edges of the drapes. I had no idea what time it was, but I was alone in the bed. I turned to see if Samantha might still be in the room, but she was gone.

The simple act of turning over quickly reminded me of the beating I had taken yesterday. It hurt to move, so I moved as little as possible. I rolled over on my back and settled in to think. There was a lot to be done before Samantha was to be interviewed by the police.

As I lay there looking up at the ceiling, I remembered what I had been thinking about last night. I needed to get hold of Arnold's checkbook. Since it was unlikely anyone would be nosing around the Williams house today, it seemed like a good time to go over there and find it. It would also be a good time to call an attorney for Samantha and brief him on what was coming up.

I lifted the covers off and swung my legs over the side of the bed. Getting up to a sitting position was painful. I was stiff and sore. I hoped I didn't have to move very fast today. I don't think I could have even if I wanted to.

As I was about to attempt to stand up, I heard someone at the door. I turned and looked over my shoulder as Samantha came into the room.

"Morning sleepyhead. You deciding whether or not you should get up?" Samantha asked with a smile as she crossed the room to the bed.

"Not really. I've decided to get up, but it's turning out to be more difficult than I had expected."

"I don't wonder with the way you looked last night. May I help you?"

"Sure. I can use all the help I can get."

Samantha came around to the side of the bed. She pushed the covers off me, and then slipped her arms around me. It took a lot of effort on both our parts, but I soon found myself standing up along side the bed with Samantha's help.

"I think it would be a good idea if we got you some clothes to wear. Your clothes were in pretty bad shape. I doubt it's a good idea for you to run around naked."

"You're probably right. I might scare the wildlife."

"I doubt that. I think you could wear some of my husband's clothes."

"And how do you suggest we get them?"

"I could sneak over to the house like we did before, get a few things and bring them back here."

"I really don't like the idea of you going over there alone."

"And just how are you going to get over there without anything to wear? It would be pretty hard to explain your lack of clothes if you get caught."

"You have a point."

"Good, then I'll go. It won't take me long."

"Help me over to the bench by the window."

Samantha helped me to the window and sat me down on the bench. I pulled back the drapes a little and looked outside while she got a blanket off the bed to wrap around me. I could see her house and most of the yard. I would not be able to see her all the time, but I would be able to see if anyone came around, either from the woods or the road.

"Take my cell phone from the car. It's on the front seat. I'll watch from this window. If I see anyone approach the house, I'll give you a heads up."

"I'll call you as soon as I get the phone. That way we can stay in touch all the time I'm gone."

"Good thinking."

Samantha gave me a light kiss on the cheek, and then left the room. She returned in a couple of minutes with the binoculars that had been in the living room.

"These might help."

"Thanks, and be careful."

"I will."

She moved the phone over next to me before she left the room. I was worried about her being out of my sight, but there was little I could do about it, under the circumstances. I needed something to wear and she was the one person who could get what I needed.

It was only a matter of a minute or so before I caught a glimpse of her as she ran between the house and barn. I knew it would be only a couple of minutes before the phone would ring. The phone began to ring. I quickly grabbed it up.

"You okay?"

"Yes."

"Okay, any time you're ready. It looks clear from here. Be careful," I said.

"I will. I'm a little nervous."

"You don't have to do this. I can wait until later."

"No. I'll do it. I want to do it."

"Okay."

I didn't say anything more. I waited for her to move out from behind the barn where I could see her. I saw her dash from behind the barn to the row of trees we had used for cover before. She worked her way to the back of the pool house.

Samantha would go in and out of my line of sight, but I knew I would not be able to see her all the time. The last sight I had of her was when she ducked behind the pool house.

"Peter?"

"I'm here."

"Anyone around?"

"No. Looks clear at the moment."

"I'm going in."

"Okay," I replied as I watched her dash to the back of the house.

It seemed like it took forever for her to let me know she was in the house. I grew more nervous by the minute.

"I'm in the house. I'm going to the bedroom."

"Okay."

I could picture her in my mind walking through the house and down the hall toward her bedroom. I waited patiently for her to say something.

"What would you like to wear?"

"I don't care. Just get something and get out of there."

"We have that meeting with the police tomorrow. I should find you something that will look good."

"Just get me something causal, yet a little on the dressy side and then get out of there," I insisted.

"Be patient."

As far as I was concerned, every minute she was in the house was a minute closer to getting caught. It would not be too bad if the police caught her because she knew enough to keep her mouth shut until her attorney arrived. If she was caught by anyone else, it could prove disastrous.

"I've got a pair of slacks and a nice dressy sport shirt for you. Do you need anything else?"

"A sport coat to cover my gun."

"Oh. Okay. Would you like a suit?"

"No. Now get out of there."

"What about Arnold's checkbook. Do you still want that?"

"Yes, but we can get it later."

"I'll get it now."

I thought about telling her to forget it, but I really did want to have a chance to study it. I wondered how she would handle being in Arnold's den. The last time we had been in the house, she had not been able to go into the den where Arnold had been murdered. I really didn't want to put her through that right now.

"Are you sure?"

"Is it important for you to have it?" she asked, her voice hinting she would get it if it was.

"Yes, it's important, but not so important you have to go into his den unless you're ready."

"I'll get it," she replied, but I could hear a note of reluctance in her voice.

I didn't know what to say to her. As far as I was concerned she was being very brave. It had not been my intent to put her through this, but if she was willing I would not try to stop her.

Suddenly, I noticed a limo coming up the road. The fact it was a limo in this area was not all that surprising. What was interesting was the fact it was moving rather slowly. I watched the car carefully.

With the binoculars, I could see the license plate. The license was not familiar, but it had two numbers on it that rang a bell. If my memory served me right, it was the same two numbers and in the same order I had seen on the limo in the alley next to the Ace Diamond Building the night Hamilton was murdered. I would only be guessing, but based on what little information I had it was probably Rickett's limo.

"Sam?"

I watched as the limo turned onto the driveway of the Williams house. I needed Samantha to respond to me. It would not take long before Rickett would have one or more of his enforcers in the house.

"Sam? Damn it, Sam, answer me."

"What's the big problem?"

"Rickett is right outside your door. Don't try to run out the back. One of his enforcers just got out of the car and is headed around back. Find a place to hide, and do it now."

"Okay."

Samantha sounded scared. I couldn't blame her for that. I had to do something to get her out of there without being seen.

Another one of Rickett's enforcers got out of the car and stood next to the corner of the garage. He didn't move very far away from the limo. I didn't recognize the enforcer, but I was sure Mac would have a pretty good idea of who he was.

I suddenly heard the sound of glass breaking in the phone. It was a pretty good sign to me that the enforcer was at the backdoor and was breaking into the house.

"Samantha, you've got one coming in the backdoor."

"I know. Is there anyone who can see the bedroom window on the end of the house?"

I took a quick scan of the area before answering her.

"No."

"I'm going out that way," she said, and then the phone went dead.

"Sam! Sam!"

She didn't answer. I dropped the phone on the bench next to me and called Agnes.

"Agnes!"

"What is it, Peter?" she called up from the bottom of the staircase.

"Get me one of Mr. Holcombe's rifles. Bring it up here, and hurry."

I quickly turned back around and looked toward the Williams house. I saw one of the windows on the end of the house open. Out flew some clothes. They were immediately followed by Samantha. The windows were quit large and not far off the ground. I could see Samantha climbing out the window. She had the red book in her hands. She closed the window behind her, grabbed up the clothes and moved around behind some thick bushes at the corner of the house. She had no more than disappeared behind the bushes when the phone began to ring.

"Samantha, don't move from there."

"I got the book," she whispered with a note of excitement in her voice.

"Don't move," I repeated.

Agnes came into the bedroom with one of her husband's rifles. It was a hunting rifle with a scope on it. She handed it to me with a box of ammunition. I took a couple of rounds from the box and slid them into the rifle.

I opened the window, laid the rifle on the window ledge and pointed it toward the window Samantha had escaped from. I waited and watched. I was ready to fire at anyone who looked like they might find her.

It was the waiting that was the hardest. It didn't appear they had heard or seen Samantha. No one showed up at the window. The only danger to her now was if they decided to walk the perimeter of the house, or if she tried to run for it.

It seemed like it took forever before the enforcer that had gone around behind the house returned to the limo. I could see him through the scope as he shrugged his shoulders at the bodyguard standing next to the car. It was clear they had not found what they were looking for. He walked up to the car and leaned over. He talked to whoever was in the back seat of the car, probably Rickett.

After what appeared to be a brief conversation, the enforcer opened the door and got in the car. I watched and kept the rifle pointed at the car in case they changed their minds and decided not to leave.

AS SOON AS THE CAR was going back down the road, I picked up the phone.

"It's all clear. Go around back and come back the same way you went."

"That was close," Samantha said with a sigh.

"Yes, too close. Now get back here."

"Yes, master," she replied with a slight giggle in her voice.

It may have seemed funny now, but at the time she had to have been scared to death. I was sure the giggling and the smart remarks were her way of releasing the tension of the moment and calming her nerves.

I continued to watch as Samantha worked her way back. It wasn't long before she was in the bedroom. Her eyes got big when she saw the rifle leaning against the bench next to me.

"You had me covered all the time. Why didn't you tell me?"

"Because I didn't have you covered all the time. Now, how about some clothes? We have a lot to do."

"Your underwear will be ready in a few minutes. I washed them and your socks," Agnes explained. "I couldn't do much with your dress slacks and sport coat. There was blood all over them. They will have to be dry cleaned."

"Okay. I'll wait here. Samantha, let me see the checkbook."

"Aren't you going to thank me for getting it for you?"

"Yes. Thank you. And thanks for getting me something to wear. You took a hell of a risk. I'm just happy it turned out the way it did."

"Peter, would you have shot one of those men if it looked like he might have found me?"

"I would have tried," I assured her.

She smiled, then handed me the red checkbook. I smiled back at her as I reached out and took it.

I settled onto the bench at the window and began looking over the checkbook. Samantha sat beside me and looked over my shoulder. I don't know if she knew what was in the book, but I didn't think it would hurt any for her to see. Besides, she might be able to explain some of the entries.

I didn't have to go back very far in the checkbook to find an entry showing a check had been written to a large well-known architectural firm in Los Angeles. There was no doubt it was the company Arnold had hired to inspect the Ace Diamond Building.

"Samantha, do you think you could find the phone number for this company?"

"Sure, but it won't do any good to call them today. There won't be anyone in the office."

"You're right. See if you can find a phone number for them. We'll call them first thing Monday morning."

"Okay. What are we going to do now?"

"I want you to call the attorney your husband said was a good criminal attorney."

"You mean Mr. Tucker?"

"Yes. It might be a good idea if you contact him now so we can have a talk with him."

"Don't you think it would be better if you talk to him? You can explain what is going on better than I can."

"You might be right. Right now I'd like something to eat. I'm starving."

"I'll get you something," Agnes said with a smile.

As soon as Agnes left the room, Samantha stood up. I watched her as she walked toward the bedroom door. She stopped, turned around and looked at me. I wasn't sure about the look on her face.

"Peter, thanks for protecting me," she said softly.

"My pleasure," I replied with a smile and a wink.

A smile came over her face before she turned and left the room. I continued to stare at the door long after she left. Her "thank you" may have been premature. I wasn't sure how long I would be able to protect her. There were some pretty nasty people out there who seemed intent on getting to her.

I LOOKED BACK OUT THE WINDOW. There were probably a number of people who wanted to see Arnold dead. Most of them had criminal records, and maybe a few who stood to lose a great deal of money. But I wondered how many were actually involved in murdering him. The most notorious of them who would be a threat to Samantha were Angilara, Rickett and their enforcers.

Then there was Mosser, the accountant. I wondered if he had anything to do with the murder of Arnold or Hamilton, other than having been present when Hamilton was murdered. I felt he was drawn into it by virtue of his accounting practices.

I could remember the look on Mosser's face when he exited the Ace Diamond Building on the night Hamilton had been murdered. When he left with Waterman, he looked almost as if he had had something to eat that didn't set well with him. They seemed very friendly going in, but didn't even look at each other when they left.

The more I thought about it, the more I had to think Mosser might have been drawn into the murder of Hamilton to make sure he didn't talk. My last thought gave me the idea that Mosser might very well be the weakest link in the chain.

Waterman didn't look too happy on his way out of the building, either. He may have had a criminal record, but nothing as serious as murder.

If Mosser and Waterman had been witnesses to the murder of Hamilton, or were part of any related crimes, that would make them accessories to murder. It would make them want to keep quiet. They were undoubtedly witnesses to the murder for the sole purpose of keeping them quiet. If Angilara and Rickett were charged with the crime, they would point fingers at Mosser and Waterman. The real question was, were Mosser and Waterman really only witnesses to the murder, or had they been active participants?

It would be interesting to get Mosser or Waterman out from under the influence of Angilara and Rickett and see if one of them would roll on the others. Waterman had already served time in prison and would probably be a little harder to get to talk against the others. Mosser with his love of money and his lifestyle might be the easier one to get to turn against the others, especially if it meant a shorter time in prison.

There was another question. Who actually killed Arnold? If it was one of Angilara's men, there was little likelihood Angilara would serve a minute in prison for ordering the hit. There was little doubt any of Angilara's men would act without Angilara telling them what to do. The problem was it would be very difficult to prove without an eyewitness to say Angilara gave the order. The loyalty of Angilara's enforcers made that almost impossible.

In Rickett's case, I wouldn't doubt for a minute that Rickett would pull the trigger himself. He came up from the streets. He had a record dating back to his childhood and had been arrested several times for murder. Each time he got off on some technicality. Rickett was one of the most egotistical people I had ever known. It would be just like him to have murdered Arnold himself. The problem was to prove it.

Agnes had seen one of Angilara's enforcers behind the Williams house about the time Arnold was murdered. Yet, Arnold was killed with the violence that fitted Rickett's methods. Was it possible Rickett murdered Arnold with the help of one of Angilara's men? It was possible, especially since it was apparent that both Rickett and Angilara had a lot to lose. The fact they were both involved in the Ace Diamond Building made me think it was more than a possibility.

CHAPTER SEVENTEEN

SUDDENLY, THE DOOR to the bedroom opened distracting me. Samantha entered the room carrying a tray. She set it down on the bench beside me.

"I hope you like it," she said as she took the cover off the plate.

On the plate was a hamburger with all the trimmings and a scoop of potato salad. I was so hungry that it looked like a meal fit for a king.

"Thank you. It looks good."

"Thank you. Dig in."

I picked up the hamburger and took a big bite. It was as good as it looked.

"Very good. Did you make it?"

"Yes. Well, Agnes made the potato salad."

"It's very good."

"Go ahead and eat. I'll be back in a few minutes with the rest of your clothes."

I nodded as I took another mouthful of hamburger. I watched her as she left the room. It wasn't long before Samantha returned with the rest of my clothes. She placed them on the foot of the bed. She had gotten me a dressy sport shirt, a pair of slacks and a sport jacket.

"Would you like me to help you get dressed when you finish eating?" she asked politely, as if it was the most normal thing in the world.

"I'm still a bit stiff and sore. I might like to have a little help, if you don't mind."

"I don't mind," she replied with a pleasant smile.

Samantha sat down on the edge of the bed to wait for me to finish my meal. I found her watching me closely. It made me feel a little uncomfortable, mostly because I didn't know what was going on in her pretty head. The fact I had only a blanket around me might have had something to do with it, too.

"Peter?"

"Yeah?"

"Do you think I will be arrested?"

"I think there's a pretty good chance you will, but you will have the best criminal attorney money can buy. I also think it's a little early to worry about that. We have to talk to Mr. Tucker first."

"I want you to know that no matter what happens I appreciate all you have done for me."

"Now, let's not start that. This isn't over, yet."

"I know. I just want you to know I appreciate what you have done for me no matter how things turn out."

"Don't you worry. I'll stick by you until it's over."

"What do we do now?"

"I get dressed, and then we go downstairs and call Mr. Tucker."

Samantha didn't say anything more. I stood up and she helped me get dressed. It seemed a little strange having such a beautiful woman helping me get dressed.

AS SOON AS I WAS DRESSED, we went downstairs. I was a bit slow on the stairs, but by the time I got to the bottom I was feeling a little better. At least I was able to move a little easier. Some of the stiffness was gone.

We went into the den where Agnes was sitting. I sat down in a large chair and took a deep breath.

"Are you feeling better, Peter?"

"Yes. I was wondering if we might use your phone to call an attorney for Samantha."

"Certainly. Mr. Tucker's number is right next to the phone."

I moved to the desk and dialed the number.

"Mr. Tucker's office, how may I help you?"

"Hello. I'm Peter Blackstone and I would like to speak to Mr. Tucker."

"One moment, please. He's expecting you."

"Thank you." I said then waited for her to transfer my call.

"Mr. Blackstone. I've been expecting a call from you?"

"You have?"

"Yes. Mr. Wade said you might be calling with regard to Mrs. Arnold Williams."

"Well, he was right. I believe Mrs. Williams will be in need of a criminal attorney. She is scheduled to talk to the police about the death of her husband."

"When is that scheduled?"

"Ten a.m. Monday."

"Good. I'll meet you at the police station. Tell her not to say a word to anyone until I'm with her."

"I will. There's a problem."

"What's that?"

"It seems the police have been reluctant to look at anyone else as a possible suspect. I hope to have something for them before Monday morning's meeting that might convince them to look elsewhere."

"Can you tell me what it might be?"

"Yes, sir. The murder weapon. It is currently being examined by the State Crime Lab."

"Will it help her, or cause her harm?"

"I'm hoping it will help her."

"I hope so, too. Will you let me know the results of the examination before you turn it over to the police?"

"I can't do that, but you will have a chance to see the report before you and Mrs. Williams talk to the police."

"I understand."

"I would like to meet with you before you talk to the police, too. I have some information that may be of help in presenting your case to the police."

"I'll meet with you and Mrs. Williams before I let the police talk to her."

"I'll see you on Monday morning."

"Good," he replied, and then the phone went dead.

After I hung up the phone, I looked over at Samantha. She looked like she needed some reassurance that everything was going to be okay.

"Mr. Tucker will take your case and will meet us at the police station on Monday morning."

Samantha smiled and let out a long sigh of relief. I'm sure she felt somewhat relieved, but there was a long way to go before it would be over.

WE SPENT THE REST of Saturday and all of Sunday relaxing. For me it was a time to recover from the beating I had taken. For Samantha it was a time to relax and get some rest. For Agnes, it was a time to pamper her guests, something she seemed to like to do.

On Sunday evening we all turned in early. Samantha went to bed with me. She curled up against me and almost immediately fell asleep. I was sure the past few days had been hard on her. Waiting for something to happen was always hard, usually more mentally than physically.

It took me a while to get to sleep. I had to admit I was a little worried about what the tests on the gun would reveal. If it wasn't in Samantha's favor, it would be hard to prove she was innocent.

I WOKE WITH SAMATHA sleeping beside me. I found myself watching her as she slept. She was a very beautiful woman, and it was easy to see why any normal male would like to be seen with her. However, the thought of her in a prison cell wearing prison clothes did not appeal to me. I was sure it wouldn't appeal to her, either.

That thought caused me to wonder what this day was going to bring. At the moment it was peaceful and quiet, but it would not last much longer. Mac seemed to be convinced that Samantha had killed her husband, and given the evidence he had I could see his point. There was little evidence to point to anyone else, even though most of what he had was circumstantial. Although there were several possible suspects that I felt had good motives for killing Arnold, I still didn't have anything to link them directly to the crime scene.

I had a cop that I was convinced was dirty, but I had no real connection between him and anyone else with a motive, nor could I prove he was dirty. I knew he worked for one of the mobsters that had a connection to the Ace Diamond Building, but which one? There was a big difference between what I knew, and what I thought I knew and what I could prove.

John in the State Crime Lab had told me that he had found several partial prints on the gun Royal had buried behind the pool house, but it was unlikely they would be useable in court. I wondered if the prints would be good enough to find a new suspect for Mac to investigate.

Contacting John about the prints would be the first order of business, but it would have to wait until after breakfast. I think better on a full stomach.

I ROLLED OVER AND sat up on the edge of the bed. Samantha moved slightly, but didn't wake up. It had been a stressful time for her.

I got dressed as quietly as I could and left the bedroom. As I walked into the kitchen, I found Agnes busy salting a large roast. She turned and smiled.

"Good morning. You look better this morning."

"I feel better, thank you."

"Are you hungry?"

"Not hungry enough for a roast for breakfast."

"This isn't for breakfast. Oh, you're kidding," she said with an embarrassing little laugh.

"Yes, I was."

"What would you like for breakfast?"

"A bowl of cereal and some juice would be fine."

She stopped what she was doing and fixed me a breakfast of cereal, milk, and orange juice while I sat down at the table. I ate my breakfast while watching her prepare the roast.

"You planning on company today?"

"No. What makes you ask?"

"That roast looks like its big enough to feed an Army."

"Oh. I guess it is a little big, but I can make a lot of things out of the leftovers."

"Are you planning on having it as the noon meal?"

"It could be ready."

"I might suggest you plan it for the evening meal if you expect Samantha and me to help you eat it."

"Do you think it will take that long with the police?"

"I'm not sure how long it will take, but it might. We still can't ignore the fact that they might arrest her. If she is, she will be arraigned and that could take time."

"Oh, my."

The tone of her voice and the look on her face indicated she had not thought of that possibility. She looked at the roast as if she had started something she should have waited on.

"Now don't you worry. She has a good attorney on her side."

"Will you be with her?"

"Yes. Of course."

I watched Agnes as she turned around and went back to her work. She seemed a little depressed, but that was to be expected. She seemed to like Samantha, and there was plenty for all of us to worry about today.

AFTER I FINISHED BREAKFAST, I went into the den and placed a call to John at the State Crime Lab. The phone only rang a couple of times before he picked it up.

"Hello?"

"Hi, John. It's Peter."

"I've been waiting for your call."

"What did you find out?"

"I found your fingerprints and some partial prints of Royal's on the outside of the bag. Royal's prints clearly show that he closed the bag. Unfortunately, the fingerprints left by Royal do not have enough points to hold up in court, but I'm sure they are his fingerprints."

"Maybe it's enough to get Mac to take a close look at Royal's involvement in all of this."

"It probably would do that. But what I found on the gun itself was much more interesting."

"How so?" I asked, trying to keep an open mind.

"You suggested I check for prints from some guy named Mosser. Well, I did that. On the upper part of the cylinder, under where the frame goes over the cylinder, I found a partial print of Mosser's index finger. I also found the gun was registered to him, but he had reported the gun stolen three days before Williams was murdered with it."

"How do you account for his fingerprint being just on one small part of the cylinder?"

"My guess would be the cylinder was closed when the gun was wiped down and they didn't turn the cylinder to make sure they got all of it clean."

"That would explain it," I agreed. "Anything else?"

"Yeah. I found a smudged fingerprint on the frame of the gun just above the trigger under the cylinder. It seems whoever cleaned the gun didn't do a very good job of it there, either."

"Could you identify the print?"

"Yeah, but not enough to be of much help in court."

"Whose fingerprint was it?"

"It appears to be that of Stan Rickett."

I could hardly believe what he was saying. I knew Rickett to be an arrogant SOB. And I also knew him to be a very violent man, but I thought he was smart enough to remove his fingerprints from a gun.

"What finger was it? Could you tell?"

"It was a thumbprint. He must have left it there when he removed the shells from the cylinder before disposing of it."

"Were there any other prints?"

"No."

"God, how lucky can we get," I said as I smiled to myself.

"Don't get too excited. Like I said, I doubt that some of the prints will have enough points to hold up in court."

"Maybe not, but it will show Mac a clear connection between Royal and Rickett. It will also give him someone else to look at for a suspect. Reasonable doubt is enough to get my client off the hook."

"Well, it will give you reasonable doubt, that's for sure," John agreed. "What do you want me to do with the report?"

This was extremely important evidence, and I had no intentions of letting it fall into the wrong hands. With a cop involved, there's always the chance the evidence would mysteriously disappear. I couldn't let that happen.

"John, I want you to do me a favor. First of all, I want you to put the gun where it cannot fall into the hands of Royal or anyone else. Lock it up so no one can get at it.

"Secondly, I want to you make three copies of your findings. Send one by messenger to Captain MacDonald at his office as soon as possible, this morning if you can. Then mail the others, one to me at my post office box, and one to Mr. Tucker at the Tucker, Wade and Jones Law Offices. Mr. Tucker is Samantha's defense attorney."

"It will take a couple of days to get to you by mail," John said, the tone of his voice hinting that he wondered why I wanted to risk it being in the mail for so long.

"I know. I'm counting on that. The longer it's held up in the mail, the less chance Rickett has to get his hands on the information. Also, Mr. Tucker will get a chance to see the report when we talk to Captain MacDonald, and will get his own copy in a couple of days. That will keep it from disappearing from police files."

"Makes sense. I'll get it done right away."

"John, do me another favor. Do it yourself. I have no idea who I can trust."

"You've got it," he said, then the phone went dead.

I had known John for a long time. I had no doubt the reports would be in the mail within an hour, and the report to Mac would likely be in his hands before I had a chance to get there. I could get it from him to show Mr. Tucker before Mac interviewed Samantha.

I sat in the chair and began to think of what Mac might have to say about the report on the gun. He would not be happy that I went around him. In fact, he would be mad as hell that I had not turned the gun over to him in the first place. I was hoping he would understand why I did, and not be too upset with me.

MY THOUGHTS WERE INTERRUPTED by Samantha standing in the doorway looking at me. She was still in a nightgown with a shear robe over it. Except for the look on her face, she looked very sexy. I had no idea how long she had been standing there so I had no idea as to how much of my conversation she had heard.

"Good morning," I said with a smile.

"Was that good news or bad?"

"I think it was good with a little bad tossed in. My friend found fingerprints on the gun that will help us show Royal hid it behind your pool house. There were other fingerprints on the gun and they were those of Rickett and Mosser. Your fingerprints were not on the gun. That part is good. The bad part is that some of the fingerprints are not clear enough to hold up in court," I explained.

"Does that mean we can prove I didn't kill my husband?"

"It means we have other viable suspects. It also provides us with reasonable doubt."

"But it doesn't prove I didn't do it, does it?"

"Not really. In other words, it isn't over, yet."

I saw the disappointed look that came over Samantha's face. This whole thing had been hard on her, but we had made a serious dent in the police's thinking.

"Why don't you go get dressed and get some breakfast? It might turn out to be a very long day."

Samantha looked at me for a moment before she turned around and walked back toward the stairs.

THERE HAD TO BE A WAY to get one of our suspects to roll on the others. If that could be done, then there was a good chance of putting an end to this.

I knew Royal to be a tough cop who knew the ropes. He knew the tactics used to get people to talk and how to avoid the mistakes criminals often made, in spite of the fact that he left fingerprints on the bag with the gun. The fact he might lose his job as a cop might not be incentive enough to get him to roll on people like Rickett or Angilara. To roll on either of them would mean he was not likely to live very long. That was certainly incentive enough for him not to talk.

I still wasn't sure who he worked for, but it was most likely Rickett. Finding Rickett's thumbprint on the murder weapon, and Royal being the one who had hidden it, certainly did a lot to point me in that direction. I could only hope it would point Mac in the same direction.

The more I thought about it, the more I thought it might be best to work on Mosser. I had a hard time picturing him as the one who did the killing. He was the one who kept the money flowing in the organization. I doubted he would like the messy parts, such as murder. He didn't strike me as the type to want to get his hands dirty. As best I could figure, he was probably working for Rickett. I figured he would be the one most likely to roll.

The other one was Waterman. He had been in jail before so it would be nothing new to him. Yet, I didn't get the impression he was a hardened criminal. He was a fairly quiet man, but he would still be a hard nut to crack. I was pretty sure he worked for Angilara.

JUST THEN SAMATHA came to the door of the den again. She was wearing a pants suit outfit that showed off her curves very nicely, but was more conservative than the dress she had worn to my office the day I met her. In fact, the outfit made her look like a very successful professional businesswoman. There was one thing about Samantha; she knew how to dress for the occasion. The meeting with Mac was about as close to a business meeting as one could ever get, and the business of the day was to keep her out of jail.

"How is this?" she asked as she turned around slowly.

"That will do very nicely."

"I thought it would be better than a sun dress."

"Much better," I said as I got up and started toward the door.

Samantha and I went to the kitchen and sat down. I had a cup of coffee while she had breakfast. She didn't seem very hungry, but she ate just the same. Agnes had finished preparing the roast and had it in the oven. She sat down at the table with us.

"How long before we have to leave?" Samantha asked, her voice soft and whispery.

"We have a little while yet. I have to call that company in Los Angeles before we leave," I said as I got up to go to the den.

I CALLED THE COMPANY that had provided the inspector for Arnold. They told me the inspector's name and that he had not contacted them about the building yet, but confirmed he was in Denver. Before hanging up, I found out where the inspector was staying and placed a call to him.

"Hello?"

"Hello. Is this Mr. Stillman, Henry Stillman?"

"Yes it is. Who is this?"

"My name is Peter Blackstone. I work for Mrs. Arnold Williams. It is my understanding you are here to inspect the Ace Diamond Building in downtown Denver. Is that correct?"

"Yes it is, but why do you want to know?"

"Have you seen a newspaper or watched the news on television over the past couple of days?"

"No."

"In that case, it might be best if you know Mr. Arnold Williams was murdered last week."

"I don't believe you," Stillman said.

"You better if for no other reason than to understand your life may be in danger."

"I don't understand."

"Have you inspected the building, yet?"

"No. I got into town last evening. I'm getting ready to go over there this morning and start looking into it."

"I suggest you don't go. It would not be a good idea for you to be nosing around there right now, at least without a police escort."

"I still don't understand your interest in this. I'm to inspect the building and report back to my boss in LA what I find, that's all."

"I don't know if your boss knows what is going on here, or if he simply didn't tell you. But for your own safety, I suggest you meet me at the police station before, I repeat, before you go nosing around in the Ace Diamond Building."

I didn't hear anything for several minutes. He was apparently mulling over what I had told him. If he had any brains at all, he would take my suggestion and go to the police station.

"Which police station?" he asked.

"The downtown precinct," I said, then gave him directions.

"When you get there, ask for Captain MacDonald. He won't know you are coming. If you should get there before I do, tell him that I told you to go to him and that you are to wait until I get there. He is expecting me about ten this morning, but I'll try to get there as soon as I can."

"Okay."

"Have you talked to anyone at the Ace Diamond Building about the fact you are going to inspect the building?"

"Yes. I talked to a Ms Bradley. She's the . . ."

"I know who she is," I interrupted. "Listen to me. I want you to leave your hotel immediately and go directly to the police station now. I don't want you to wait. There's a chance the wrong people know you are in town. Go there now. I will join you there in about thirty to forty minutes."

"But,"

"Now, Mr. Stilman. If you value your life, you'll do as I say."

I hung up the phone without waiting for a response from him. I quickly left the den for the kitchen. Samantha looked up at me as I hurried toward her.

"What's the matter?"

"I think we need to get going. The inspector from LA is on his way to the police station. I want to have a talk with him before we talk to Mac."

"Peter, I saw the deputy sheriff nosing around Sam's house. If he should see your car, he might get suspicious and stop you," Agnes said with a worried look on her face.

"Is he out there now?"

"Yes."

"I guess we'll just have to take our chances."

"Why don't I drive you to the police station in my car? He wouldn't think twice about seeing it. The two of you can get down in the back seat."

"Good idea."

I watched the deputy from the kitchen window while Agnes went to get her keys. Since her car was in the attached garage, we didn't have to go outside to get in it.

Once we were in the car, we ducked down behind the seat as Agnes got in behind the wheel. She pressed the button that opened the garage door and backed up. She closed the garage door and headed down the driveway to the road.

"He's watching me. He's standing next to his car," she reported as she drove by. "I'll give him a wave so he doesn't think there is something wrong."

"Don't do anything you normally wouldn't do," I suggested.

"I always wave at him when I see him. He might get curious if I don't wave," she said as she waved at the officer.

She drove on down the road. When we had gone several miles, we sat up.

"Thank you, Agnes," I said.

"Oh, you're more than welcome. I haven't had so much fun in years."

I couldn't help but smile. I guess it was a pretty exciting game of hide and seek to her. It was far more than that to me.

CHAPTER EIGHTEEN

We arrived at the police station about thirty-five minutes after talking to Mr. Stillman. We parked in the visitor's parking lot and I hustled Samantha and Agnes into the building.

After I identified myself to the desk sergeant and told him why I was there, he called Mac. Mac came out and quickly ushered us into his office. When we entered, I saw a slim, fairly tall man with gray hair sitting in the corner.

"Peter, this is Mr. Stillman. He said you told him to come to my office and wait for you. Is that correct?"

"Yes, it is."

"Do you mind telling me what it's all about?"

"Certainly, but first I would like to introduce you to Samantha Williams, Arnold's wife, and Mrs. Agnes Holcombe her next door neighbor. Before you ask any questions, we'll wait for her attorney to arrive. She will say nothing until he gets here.

"In the meantime, I think Mrs. Holcombe has something to say to you. You might find interesting."

"Does it involve this case?"

"It most certainly does. Go ahead, Agnes, tell him what you told me about the day Arnold was killed."

Agnes told Mac about the man she had seen out by the pool house and the fact she had heard an ATV start up and go down the trail. Mac listened with a great deal of interest.

"Thank you for coming forward, Mrs. Holcombe. Would you mind waiting in the next room," Mac said as he stood up.

"Not at all," she replied with a polite smile.

"I would like Mrs. Williams and Mr. Stillman to stay with you until her attorney arrives, if it is all right with you, Peter. I would like to talk to you alone."

"Sure," I agreed.

Mac buzzed for an officer, then stood up and walked over next to the door. He had everyone escorted to another room.

AS SOON AS THEY WERE GONE, I sat down in a chair in front of Mac's desk. The look on Mac's face when he returned to his desk was not one I really wanted to see. I figured I was in a bit of trouble with him.

"Peter, what can you tell me about this forensic report I got this morning from the State Crime Lab?"

"Have you read it?"

"Yes."

"Then you know as much about it as I do. It's a report on the gun used to murder Arnold."

"I know that. What I want to know is how did you get your hands on it?"

"I dug it up from behind Samantha's pool house the morning after Royal hid it there."

"You're sure he hid it there?"

"Absolutely. He had it with him when he arrived at the house. He went around behind the pool house and came out without it."

"Where were you all that time?"

"I was watching him through Mrs. Holcombe's binoculars from her house."

"You'd like to see Royal lose his job, wouldn't you?"

"I don't need to make up stories to get to him. I could get him suspended just for the way he treated me when he picked me up. The problem is you have a dirty cop on your hands, and he's working for the mob. The only thing I don't know is which mobster he's in bed with for sure."

"Do you think the forensic evidence proves that?"

"Maybe not, but it goes a long ways toward convincing me that he's dirty. It's up to you what you do with it."

"What do you think I should do with it?"

"I think you should keep it quiet until you have something else to go with it. Then I would arrest him and send him to jail."

"It's not that simple."

"I know that, but if you want to look deep enough, you'll find what you need," I said.

"You know I could charge you with concealing evidence?"

"Sure you could, but you won't."

"Why is that?"

"Because you need to know everything I know if you're going to solve this case and get the higher-ups off your ass. The pictures I gave you did a lot to show you there is something going on at the Ace Diamond Building. And speaking of that, what did your people find out when they went through the financial records?"

"We found there was money being skimmed off and going to Rickett and Angilara through loan companies owned by them."

"Who was the accountant handling the transactions, as if I had to ask?"

"Jeffrey Mosser."

"That's who I thought, too. I've been thinking about him. I think he might be the key to getting to the rest."

"You think he'll roll over on the rest?"

"Maybe, but I wouldn't eliminate Waterman, either. It might prove interesting to play one against the other."

"You might have something there. Who do you think killed Williams?"

I wondered what he was really asking me. Never in all the years that I have known him had he ever asked me for my opinion as to who committed a crime. I felt he might be looking for something new, something he might have overlooked.

"You've seen and read the forensic report on the murder weapon, right?"

"Yeah."

"You've seen the pictures I took in front of the Ace Diamond Building, right?"

"Yeah."

"And you've had your people going over all the account books, right?

"Yeah."

"Then you know everyone involved as well as I do. That being the case, who do you think actually pulled the trigger and killed Arnold?"

"I think it could have been one of Rickett's enforcers."

"Why not Rickett himself?"

"I think he's smarter than that."

"But his fingerprints, namely his thumbprint were on the murder weapon. How do you explain that?"

"I don't."

"Well, to each his own," I said, then shrugged my shoulders.

I was about to say something about Angilara when there was a knock on the door. I turned to see who it was. It turned out to be the desk sergeant.

"There's a Mr. Tucker here to see Mrs. Williams. He says he's her lawyer.

"Go to the room next door and ask Mrs. Williams if she would join us. Be sure to tell her that her attorney is here."

"Yes, sir," he replied and closed the door.

I sat there looking at Mac. I had no idea what was going through his mind, but I was sure he was thinking about how complicated the case had become.

IT WAS ONLY A FEW MINUTES before Samantha entered the room followed by a good-looking older man in a very expensive suit. There was no doubt he was Jacob Tucker, attorney-at-law.

As soon as everyone had been properly introduced, we all sat down at a long table. Samantha and I sat on one side of the table, while Mr. Tucker sat at the end next to Samantha. Mac sat across from Samantha.

"Before you ask my client any questions," Mr. Tucker began. "I want it understood she had nothing to do with her husband's untimely death. She has been advised of her rights. I expect this to be a civil conversation. Mrs. Williams has come here of her own free will. She will cooperate with you as long as your questions are clear and related to her knowledge of the events surrounding her husband's death. Is that clear, Captain MacDonald?"

"Very clear. My first question is, are you aware that you are a suspect in your husband's murder?"

"Yes," she replied softly.

"Mrs. Williams, would you please tell me in your own words what you saw, what you heard and what you did on the morning your husband was murdered?"

Samantha glanced over at Mr. Tucker who indicated she should answer Mac's question. She began by telling Mac that she had finished her hour-long session with her personal trainer and was on her way to the shower when she heard Arnold come home. The story proceeded from there.

Samantha told Mac the same thing she had told me and said it with the same convincing tone and sincerity. It became hard for her to continue when she told Mac about what she saw in the den.

When she was done, she sat back and looked down at her lap. There were tears in her eyes and a couple of tears rolled down her cheek. I gave her my handkerchief.

No one said anything for several minutes. I wasn't sure if it was because they were trying to absorb what she had told them, or if it was to give Samantha a chance to gather her composure. Finally, Mac spoke.

"Did you see anyone around the house that didn't belong there?"

"No."

"You said Mr. Williams very rarely left the patio door from his den open."

"That's right."

"But you said it was open when you went to the den."

"Yes."

"Was that because you opened it?"

"No. I told you, I didn't go all the way into the den."

"That seems a little strange to me. You didn't even go into the den to check and see if your husband might still be alive?"

"No."

"Why not? If he had still been alive, you might have been able to save him."

Samantha was getting upset. She looked at me for help, but I had none to give her. If she needed any help, she had an attorney to help her. It seemed like a very logical question to me.

Samantha took a deep breath, and then said, "I don't know why I didn't go into the den to check on him. All I could see was Arnold slumped over his desk and the blood. There was blood all over the desk and on the wall behind him."

"You did have the presence of mind to call the police."

"Yes, I did," she admitted.

"Why not the presence of mind to check to see if he was still alive?"

"Captain MacDonald," Mr. Tucker said sharply in order to get his attention. "I believe you are aware of the different reactions people have to the same situation. At times of severe emotional stress, people often do things that would seem unusual or strange to those of us who have seen the same situation before. Don't you agree?"

Mac hesitated for a second before answering.

"Yes, but what I'm trying to figure out is why she did what she did."

"That's my point, Captain MacDonald. It is always easier to second-guess after the fact. In very unusual situations, I don't think anyone knows how they will react until faced with it."

I watched the expression on Mac's face as he looked at Tucker. If I had to guess, Mac was not happy with what Tucker had to say, but he understood what he was getting at. Mac turned and looked at me for a second. I wasn't sure what was going on in his mind. Then he turned and looked back at Samantha.

"Mrs. Williams, it is my understanding your husband had some concerns over the Ace Diamond Building and the allegation that it was unsafe. Is that true?" Mac asked.

"Yes," she replied.

"Do you know if your husband had done anything about the allegation?"

"Yes. He hired an independent building inspector to look over the building to see if the allegations were true."

"What were the results?"

"I don't know."

"Mac, Mr. Stillman is the inspector Arnold hired. He has not had a chance to inspect the building," I said.

"Oh," Mac said. "Peter seems to think Mr. Williams was about ready to pull his support of the building project because he found out there were several so called "mob bosses" who had invested heavily in the building. Is that correct?"

"Yes. When Arnold found out the mob was investing in the building and skimming money off it, he was getting ready to pull his support from the project," Samantha replied.

"How is it that you know all this?"

"Contrary to popular belief, Captain MacDonald, Arnold and I talked a great deal about what he was involved in. He wanted to share with me all aspects of his life. I know people think I married Arnold for his money, but I would have married him without it.

"Arnold and I shared a lot more than a bed. We shared our dreams as well as our frustrations. He shared the problems he was having with the project with me. He shared his concerns over the allegations of an unsafe building, as well as his concerns about some of those who were investing in the project," she said, speaking very clearly and staring Mac right in the eyes.

I had to smile to myself when I saw the look on Mac's face. He had just been told off, and it had been done with such class he couldn't argue with it.

"So he was thinking about pulling his support of the project?" Mac finally said, not knowing what else to say at the moment.

"Yes."

"If he was pulling his support, why did he bother to hire an independent building inspector?"

"Arnold didn't want the building to remain open if it was unsafe. He felt he couldn't trust the state inspectors. There was too much of a chance the mob might be paying them to submit false reports on the materials being used."

"Did he have any proof the inspectors were filing false reports on the safety of the building?"

"No, I don't believe so. Arnold wanted to make sure he had true and accurate reports that would be difficult to dispute. The only way for him to do that with any degree of certainty was to hire an independent firm to do a complete inspection of the building."

The look on Mac's face was hard to read. He might be thinking she had nothing to do with Arnold's death. One thing was clear, he was finding out she was a well-informed woman with a lot more than her good looks going for her.

"Mrs. Williams, do you know who might have had it in for your husband?"

"Not that I can prove, but I can think of several people who would not like it if Arnold had pulled his support from the project."

"And who might they be?"

"Well, there would be Mr. Angilara for one. He would stand to lose a great deal of money. Then there's Mr. Rickett."

"Do you know who these men are?"

"Yes. Peter, ah, Mr. Blackstone has told me who they are and what they are."

"Now that Arnold is dead, what happens to his support of the building?"

"I really don't know. I hope Arnold's support of the project can still be pulled out."

"Why is that? Could it be so you could get more money for yourself?"

"NO. I believe they killed, or had my husband killed, so what he had learned would not become public knowledge. I want the world to know what kind of men they are and see to it they get punished for what they did," Samantha said angrily.

"Captain MacDonald, Mrs. Williams has not been advised of her inheritance as of this time. As far as she knows, she will get nothing, not one red cent from Mr. Williams's estate," Tucker said.

"How's that?" Mac asked, looking a little confused.

"Mrs. Williams signed an agreement stating she would not receive any proceeds from Mr. Williams's estate if he died by any means other than by natural causes."

From the look on Mac's face, it was clear he had not checked into Samantha's inheritance. It was obvious he was thinking she would inherit big time and that was a good motive for killing or having her husband killed. That motive suddenly vanished into thin air like a puff of smoke with Mr. Tucker's statement. He looked as if he was kicking himself for failing to check it out for himself.

It was time for me to start sweating. Mac looked at me as if he was wondering if I already knew that, and why I hadn't told him. If Mac asked me if I knew anything about what Samantha was to inherit, I would not lie to him. I would have to tell him that she would get everything. Even if I told him that she didn't know, he would suspect she had found out somehow. I was hoping he wouldn't ask.

"Is there anything else, Captain MacDonald?" Tucker asked.

"Ah, no, not right now."

"Then can I assume she can go?"

"Yes," Mac replied.

"Are they done with her home?"

"No, not yet. It is still considered an active crime scene."

"Very well. If there are no other questions for my client, we will be leaving."

"That will be fine," Mac said, but I could see his mind was going a mile a minute. "Oh, be available if I should have any additional questions."

"If you call me, I will see to it she is available," Tucker replied as he pushed back his chair and stood up.

Samantha and I stood up. We followed Mr. Tucker to the door, but Mac stopped me.

"Peter, could you stay for a minute?"

"Sure, but give me a minute with Mr. Tucker first."

"Okay."

I FOLLOWED SAMANTHA and Mr. Tucker down the hall a little ways.

"Mr. Tucker, I want you to take Samantha back to your office. I don't want you to let her out of your sight."

"Do you really think that's necessary?"

"Yes. And take Agnes with you."

"How long will you be?" Samantha asked.

"Hopefully only a few minutes. I think Mac wants to talk to me with Mr. Stillman."

"Oh."

"Have Agnes leave her car keys with the desk sergeant."

"Okay," Samantha said with a smile.

I watched as Mr. Tucker and Samantha walked down the hall. I then returned to Mac's office.

"Have a seat," Mac said.

I sat back down at the table and waited for him to talk first.

"Do you think Samantha might be in danger?"

"Yes. If Rickett or Angilara think she now has control of Arnold's estate, she is in the same danger he was in. Look what happened to him."

"Earlier, just before Mr. Tucker showed up, I got the feeling you were about to say something. What was it?"

I had to think a minute before I could answer him. It took me a moment to remember what we had been talking about.

"Oh. I was about to ask you if I could take a go at Mosser. I think he might be the easiest one to get to roll on the others."

"What makes you think you can get him to talk?"

"I don't know if I can, but he might talk to me where he wouldn't talk to you. You see, I'm not a threat to him. I'm not a cop."

"But if I said yes, then when it comes time to go to court his defense attorney would claim I gave you permission to try to talk him, and in doing so you were acting as an agent for the police department."

"Then don't give me permission," I said with a grin.

"I'll do better than that, I'll tell you not to talk to him," Mac said with a slight grin on his face.

"Okay,"

"What about Mrs. Williams?"

"What about her?"

"Where are you hiding her? Is she staying with Mrs. Holcombe?"

"Yes. But since we had to come here with Mrs. Holcombe, I'm sure it wouldn't be hard for Rickett or Angilara to figure out Samantha has been staying at her place. The fact we came here is probably already known by Rickett and Angilara."

"You think so?"

"Why not? Royal works here. There's no doubt he has several eyes and ears keeping a watch on who goes in and out and who talks to you."

"I don't like that idea at all."

"Neither do I. It puts her in a great deal of danger."

"I could take her to a safe house?"

"There's no such thing as a safe house when one of the suspects is a cop."

"You have a point. What do you suggest?"

"I think it would be just as easy to protect her at Mrs. Holcombe's house if you can find two police officers who can be trusted to protect her. Do you have two officers you can trust?"

Mac sat there and looked at me for a couple of minutes. I know he didn't like what I had suggested about trusting his officers, but he knew I was right.

"I'll make the arrangements, personally. One of them will be a woman."

"Good. You can call me and tell me who they are. Then I'll get them out to Mrs. Holcomb's without anyone knowing."

"How do you suggest we do that?"

"Can you get them to Tucker's office in an hour?"

"I think so."

"Have them meet me at Mr. Tucker's office in an hour in civilian clothes. We'll sneak them into her house the same way we got out, in the back seat of Agnes's car."

"Okay. I'll see what I can do. Where will you be?"

"I'll be in Tucker's office. By the way, you might want to provide Mr. Stillman with a police escort when he inspects the Ace Diamond Building. What he comes up with might prove to be interesting," I said. "You might also explain to Mr. Stillman what's going on and why he needs protection."

"I'll take care of it."

"I'll be in touch."

"You better be."

I smiled and nodded that I understood what he was saying. I left his office and picked up the keys to Agnes's car from the desk sergeant.

CHAPTER NINETEEN

I drove over to Mr. Tucker's office, making sure I was not being followed. I found Agnes sitting with Samantha. She was crying on Agnes's shoulder.

"What's happened?"

"Sam was just told by Mr. Wade that she would inherit Arnold's entire estate."

"Then why is she crying?"

"She said she would rather have Arnold back."

I sat down in a chair to wait for the officers who were to guard Samantha. Time passed slowly as I watched Agnes try to comfort Samantha.

"Are we waiting for something?" Agnes asked.

"Yes. We're waiting for a couple of police officers. We're going to take them back to your house with us. We're going to sneak them into the house the same way you got us out."

It wasn't long before the two police officers showed up in civilian clothes. They were well armed. We went down to the building's parking garage and got in the car. I drove the car back to Agnes's house and into the garage before anyone got out.

ENTERING THE HOUSE was very pleasant. The kitchen was full of the smell of the roast Agnes had put in the oven before we left. I had thought the roast was pretty big this morning, but now with a couple more people to feed, it didn't seem all that big.

While Samantha and Agnes stayed in the kitchen to finish fixing dinner, I showed officers Bill Walker and Margaret Slone the layout of the house. We worked out a plan on how to protect Samantha. Since it wouldn't be difficult to figure out where Samantha was staying, it became more important than ever to have curtains and drapes closed in the evening. The last thing I wanted was for a sharpshooter to shoot her through a window.

Once the necessary plans to protect Samantha were made, we returned to the dining room to eat. Shortly after we finished, I decided I would drive back into Denver and see if I could find Mr. Mosser. I wanted to have a little heart to heart talk with him in the hope of finding out how deeply he was involved, and to see if I could get him to roll on the others.

I ARRIVED AT MOSSER'S office at about two in the afternoon. His secretary said he had called in sick and would not be in today, but he would be in tomorrow. She hinted he was probably hung over from going to a friend's home for a birthday party.

I thanked her, then headed for LoDo to his apartment. It didn't take long to find his place. It was in an old refurbished warehouse a couple of blocks from Coors Field.

Entering the building on the ground floor, I walked up the stairs to the second floor. I found the door to Mosser's loft, knocked on it, but I didn't get an answer. I tried knocking again, but got the same results.

The hall was empty so I took my handkerchief and spread it over my hand before reaching out and trying the door. The last thing I wanted to do was to leave fingerprints behind. To my surprise, it wasn't locked.

After stepping inside, I immediately had the urge to get out of there, but my curiosity got the best of me. The large room that served as the living room, dining room and kitchen areas was a mess. It looked like there had been a fight. Someone had been looking for something they apparently wanted very badly.

I wondered if Mosser had been out when his visitor came by. I started to slowly work my way around the large room looking for Mosser, but didn't find him.

There were three doors off the large room. The first opened into his home office. It had a computer desk with the latest computer I had ever seen, and it had been smashed to bits. There were several file cabinets and an office desk big enough to fill a small garage. It looked like everything that had been in the file cabinets and desk were scattered all over the place. Whatever they had been looking for, there was no way to know if they found it.

I backed out of the room being very careful not to disturb anything and went to the next door. It was the bathroom. When I first stepped into the bathroom I didn't notice anything out of the ordinary. As I turned to leave, I saw a red spot on the floor next to the large tub. It looked like it might be blood.

I checked the tub, but there was nothing there. I turned around and looked at the large shower with a frosted glass door. I couldn't see in, but there was something inside the shower stall. I reached under my coat and drew my gun. Gripping it in one hand, I reached out with the other and pulled the shower stall door open. Huddled on the floor of the shower was Jeffrey Mosser.

Whoever had been there had taken his time to work on Mosser. His face looked like it had been shoved through a meat grinder. The one hand I could see looked like every single finger had been broken. Whoever had worked him over had spared nothing to get him to talk.

I knelt down and reached out with my free hand to touch his neck. I wasn't sure if he was still alive or not. When I touched his neck to check for a pulse I could see a small trail of blood from behind his ear. I knew he was dead. With the beating that he had taken before he died, I wondered if whoever had done it had found what he was looking for.

Leaning over him to get a better look, I discovered a small hole at the base of his head behind his ear. He had been murdered. It looked like he had been shot with a small caliber gun, probably a .22 or .25 caliber. It had been fired at close range by the looks of the powder burns on the skin and hair.

I sat back on my heels and looked around as I thought about what I should do. There was a towel on the floor with a hole in it. If I was a betting man, I would have bet the towel had been used to muffle the shot.

My eyes went to what looked like a linen closet behind the bathroom door. At first I didn't know what it was about the closet door that bothered me, but then it came to me. Almost every cabinet, closet, desk, dresser drawers and the medicine cabinet had been opened. Yet, the linen closet was closed. The only thing on the floor was the towel with the hole in it, nothing else.

I went to the closet and opened it. I didn't really expect to find anything, but if I didn't look I would wonder what I might have missed. There was nothing I would not have expected to find in a bathroom linen closet.

When I looked behind the toilet paper and cleaning supplies, I found a white file folder. The color of the folder matched the color of the inside of the closet making it almost impossible to see. It was fitted up against the back of the closet. If it had not been for a small sliver of yellow legal paper sticking out of one corner, I never would have seen it.

I pulled the folder out of the closet and opened it. In it was a detailed accounting of the money that had been siphoned off the Ace Diamond Building project and who it went to. It was a sizeable amount of money. Most of it went to Rickett with a lesser amount to Angilara. There was nothing to let me know who had killed Williams or Hamilton, but it sure would provide proof of a motive.

The folder had been probably hidden there for Mosser to use as a bargaining chip if he was arrested for his part in helping to steal money from the project. He might have also thought it would help him get a better plea bargain if he was accused of murdering Williams or Hamilton. One thing was for sure, he didn't need a bargaining chip now.

The way I saw it, the best thing for me was to get the hell out of there before I called Mac. I didn't want to be there when the police arrived. I slipped the folder under my shirt and started for the front door. The last thing I wanted was to be seen coming in or out of Mosser's loft.

I opened the door carefully and peeked out into the hall. There was no one there. I slipped out, hurried down the stairs and out onto the street. I got in the car and headed away from LoDo.

I drove by the Ace Diamond Building on the way to my office. There were two police cars parked out in front. I smiled to myself as I thought about Mr. Stillman inspecting the building with a police escort. I wondered what he would find.

AS SOON AS I ARRIVED at my office, I picked up the phone and called Mac. He answered the phone almost immediately.

"What's up, Pete."

"I think it might be a good idea if you sent someone over to Mosser's loft in LoDo."

"Why?"

"He's dead."

"You kill him?"

"NO! It looks like somebody wanted something they were sure he had and he wouldn't give it to them. He had been worked over pretty good before he was shot with a small caliber gun behind the left ear."

"Sounds like the way Hamilton was shot."

"That makes three murders connected to the Ace Diamond Building."

"Are you sure he was involved in that?"

"It fits. He was at the meeting Hamilton never returned from. He was the accountant for the building. It sort of adds up."

"I'll get over there. Did you touch anything?" Mac asked.

"Nothing you'll find my fingerprints on."

"Okay. I'll get on it."

"One more thing. You might want to find out where Royal was at the time Mosser was killed. You might also try to find out where he was when Hamilton was killed."

"You might have something there. I'll look into it."

"Speaking of Hamilton, how's the inspection going?"

"They're over there now. I'll let you know."

"Thanks. Let me know if they find out Hamilton was killed some place else."

"Is that important?"

"Don't know, but it might be."

"Okay. I'll talk to you later."

I didn't say anything else. I simply hung up. I leaned back in my chair and looked at the file I had taken from Mosser's loft.

I SAT IN MY OFFICE and tried to put everything into perspective. There had been three people murdered and there was a solid connection between all three. They were all connected in some way to the Ace Diamond Building. Yet, their connections were all different.

Arnold was one of the major investors in the building. He also had a lot of input into the design and décor. According to Samantha, the building was his pet project.

Mosser was an accountant hired by Ace Diamond Company to keep track of expenses. There was substantial evidence that he had diverted money from the building project to the mob through businesses owned by the mob. He had maintained a set of false records to conceal the transactions from any audits, but kept an accurate set of records in case he needed them.

Hamilton was the rental agent for the building. He appeared to be on the up and up even if he did know who was involved in the building. He also had a fair idea of what was going on. The only reason I could see for his murder was that he knew too much, and it was discovered that he had passed on what he knew to Arnold. He was obviously murdered because of it.

It was fast becoming apparent that it was useless for me to sit in my office and try to figure out how all of it was going to play out. I was convinced Rickett and Angilara were behind the murders, but it was something else to prove it. Anything I could do could be done at Agnes's house where I would have Samantha to talk to while I was thinking.

I left my office and drove back to the foothills. I was again being very careful not to be followed.

IT WAS GETTING ON TOWARD five when I pulled into the driveway of Agnes's house. I drove the car into the barn. As I stepped into the house, I was greeted by Officer Slone. She had her gun pointed at me.

"It's just me," I said as I put my hands up.

"Can't be too careful," she said with a smile as she dropped her gun to her side.

"Just make sure that you are careful enough not to put a hole in me."

"Yes, sir," she replied with a slight chuckle.

I smiled and walked on past her. She followed me through the kitchen as far as the dining room.

"Mrs. Williams and Mrs. Holcombe are in the den," she said.

"Thanks."

I headed for the den. I found Agnes and Samantha sitting in chairs in front of the fireplace.

"Hi," Samantha said with a smile. "Where did you go?"

It seemed like a logical question. However, I wasn't sure how much I should tell her. I didn't want to scare her anymore than she already was without good reason.

"I went to see a man I thought might be able to help us."

"How did it go?"

"Not well, I'm afraid. He was unable to give me much help."

"I'm sorry to hear that," she said with a note of disappointment.

"Me, too. Where's Walker?"

"He's upstairs watching out one of the bedroom windows."

"What's he doing up there?"

"He said he could see anyone who might approach the house better from the second floor, and he could watch my house as well," Samantha said.

Her answer seemed logical enough on the surface, but it seemed to me there would be too much he couldn't see from up there. Having had the job of protecting someone before, I felt it would be better to be closer to those he was here to protect.

"Anything going on at your house?"

"I don't think so," Samantha replied.

"I think I'll go upstairs and see what Walker is doing."

Samantha simply nodded. I went to the stairs. As I was about to turn and go up, I saw Slone in the kitchen. She was sitting in a chair reading a paper. Her gun was on the table within easy reach.

I turned and went on up the stairs. When I got near the top of the stairs, I stopped. I thought I could hear someone talking, but I wasn't sure. I quickly sorted out in my mind where everyone was in the house and realized Walker should be upstairs alone.

I drew my gun and began moving up the stairs as quietly as possible. At the top of the stairs I stopped again to listen.

The voice I could hear was Walker's. Since I couldn't hear any replies or comments to what he said, I figured he was talking on the phone, not on his radio. I moved down the hall closer to the room he was in and listened.

"I don't know this Blackstone guy very well," I heard him say, and then there was a moment of silence before he spoke again.

"I'll make sure the patio door to the den is unlocked. Everyone should be asleep by then. You better make me look good on this. I have no intentions of rotting in jail," he said in almost a whisper.

It didn't take a rocket scientist to figure out what was going on. I had a mole in the house and it was of the two-legged variety. It was also clear there was going to be an attempt to get to Samantha, which meant they had no intentions of leaving anyone alive in the house. The last thing they wanted was to leave any witnesses.

Whether Walker knew it or not, he had just signed his own death warrant. There was no way they could leave him alive. They had to know the police would be looking at him as being involved in it. If things got too hot, he might talk to save his own skin. They couldn't let that happen.

There were three questions I wanted, no, needed answers to now. Who was coming to kill us? How many would there be? And when were they coming? All of these questions were important to how we would defend ourselves, but I doubted any of them would get answered soon.

There was no question we had a very big problem. Walker was not here to protect us. The question was is Slone involved in this, too? Apparently Captain MacDonald didn't know some of his people as well as he thought.

The way I saw it, we were on our own. It would most likely be impossible to call out without someone knowing. There was no one we could trust. I had to do something to protect Samantha and Agnes.

I could have taken Walker down right then, but I decided against it. At this point it would be his word against mine. If I took him out now I would have to take out Slone, too. I needed time to determine whose side she was on.

I quietly worked my way back down to the bottom of the stairs. As I got to the last step, I remembered the phone at the end of the railing. If we were going to be attacked, the first thing that would have to be done was to disable our contact to the outside world. I had to believe Walker would have thought of that, but I needed to know for sure.

I looked around to make sure no one could see me, then picked up the receiver and put it to my ear. The line was dead. The phone lines had already been cut. I reached for my cell phone, then remembered that I had left it on my desk. I was wishing that I hadn't left my cell phone in my office about now.

I RETURNED TO THE DEN. It would be in our best interest if Agnes and Samantha knew the phones were out. Since there was only Agnes, Samantha and myself in the den, I felt I could speak safely.

"Listen. The phones are out. We are on our own," I said in a whisper.

Agnes looked over at Samantha, and then looked back at me. She sat up straight, and then looked me in the eye.

"You think someone is going to try to get to Samantha here in my house?"

"Yes. I'm sure of it."

"When?" Samantha asked, the look on her face showed her fear.

"Probably sometime after dark."

"What do we do?"

"I'm working on that," I admitted.

I walked around behind the desk and sat down. I had to have a plan that would not give away the fact I knew what was coming.

"Agnes, did your husband have any guns other than the shotgun and rifle I've already seen?"

"Oh my, yes. There's a pistol in the top right hand drawer of the desk you're sitting at. There's also a gun in the bedside stand in my bedroom. Living alone, I need some protection."

"Good. We need to get to it before they find it."

We had at least three guns, four if I counted the backup I carried in an ankle holster. We also had a shotgun and a rifle if I could get to them. That gave us a pretty good chance. I was sure Agnes knew how to handle a gun, and I knew Samantha had done some target shooting with Arnold. The last thing I wanted was to get into a gunfight, but if I was left with no other choice we would be ready.

There was only one problem. I was the only one who had a gun at the moment. I had to get the guns into Agnes and Samantha's hands. Neither of the women were wearing jackets or sweaters or any kind of clothes that would make it easy to conceal a weapon.

Keeping one eye on the door, I slowly opened the top right-hand drawer of the desk. Under a couple of sheets of paper I found a .38 caliber snub nose revolver. It was small enough to be easily handled by a woman, but had enough punch to stop a man if he was hit solid.

Keeping the gun below the level of the desk, I checked it to make sure it was loaded. It had five rounds in it. A quick look in the desk revealed there were no extra cartridges for the gun.

I slipped the gun into the pocket of my pants where I could put my hand on it. I figured if I had to walk by Walker or Slone, it would be easy to cover it by putting my hand in my pocket.

I had no more than gotten the gun in my pocket when Walker came into the room. I hoped the women would not look too suspicious and cause Walker to wonder what was going on. I didn't want him to get nervous and start something before we were ready.

"Anything going on out there?" I asked in order to draw his attention away from the women as he looked around the room.

He quickly turned his head and looked at me before he answered, "No, nothing. It's quiet."

"Good, I'd like to keep it that way."

"Where's Slone?" Walker asked.

"In the kitchen, last I saw her," I replied.

"I'll go check on her. I think it would be a good idea if she was here in the den with the rest of you. It's starting to get dark outside."

I nodded that I understood, but didn't say anything. I had a feeling he wanted us all in the den so it would be easier for him to get and keep control of our movements. The last thing I wanted was for him to have control of the situation, but I also didn't know if Slone was involved.

"I think I would like to go upstairs. It's been a long day," Samantha said as she looked at me.

"I think that's a good idea," Agnes agreed.

"That sounds like a good idea. Walker and Slone can keep a watch down here. I'll take a position upstairs."

Walker turned and looked at me. I got the feeling he was trying to figure out how to keep us all together, but I didn't give him time to say anything without making him look either stupid or controlling. I didn't think he wanted to risk doing something that might seem to be the least bit suspicious.

"Yeah, that's probably a good idea," Walker said, but I got the feeling he didn't like the idea at all.

I slipped my hand over the gun in my pocket and followed Samantha and Agnes up the stairs. I could hear Walker telling Slone that she should take the kitchen end of the house and he would take the other end of the house, the other end being the den.

Once I reached the top of the stairs, I turned and looked back down. Walker was now standing at the bottom of the stairs looking up at me. The look on his face didn't conceal the fact he knew he was losing control of the situation. By letting us go upstairs, he had added to the difficulty of killing everyone quickly.

I gave Walker a slight nod to indicate everything was okay. He gave a causal little wave, then turned and headed toward the den.

I TURNED AROUND and found Agnes and Samantha standing on the landing near the top of the stairs. They were waiting for me. As I walked up to them, I pulled the gun from my pocket and handed it to Samantha.

"Don't use this unless you have to, but if you have to make sure you shoot to kill," I said as I looked into Samantha's eyes.

"Do you think it will come to that?"

"I don't know, I certainly hope not."

"What do you expect, Peter?" Agnes asked looking to me for answers.

"I'm not sure. The one thing we can expect is not to expect any help from Walker and Slone. I know Walker is involved. I don't know about Slone.

"Walker is to leave the den door unlocked. I doubt he will want to do any shooting with his service pistol. It would be too chancy. If he killed one of us, it would be darn hard for him to explain. It's my guess that three or four of Rickett's men will come in with the idea of killing everyone here."

"Even Walker?" Samantha asked.

"Yes. They're not going to leave any witnesses. I wouldn't be surprised if Rickett himself came with his men."

"Isn't that a little risky?" Agnes asked.

"Yeah. Rickett's got to know by now that the police are looking at him as a suspect. Royal would have told him how the case is shaping up. Rickett is a hands-on sort of guy. I seriously doubt he would trust his men to carry out the killing of everyone without supervising it to make sure it is done right."

"How do we get ready for this?" Agnes asked.

"I want you both in the same bedroom."

"I think my bedroom would be best. There's a deck off the back where we could hide if we needed to," Agnes said.

"That may not be the best place. As soon as they find out we are all in one room, they will have someone watching the outside for any escape attempt."

"If we're in any other room up here, we would be trapped," Agnes said with a worried look on her face.

"You've got a point. Use your bedroom, but stay in a corner; so if someone comes in from the deck you'll be behind him before he knows it and you can protect yourself."

"Where is the rifle? You had it the other day," Agnes asked.

"It's in our bedroom up against the wall next to the window," Samantha said.

"You might want it," Agnes suggested.

"Right. I'm going into the room Samantha and I had. I can see your door from there and will be able to cover it."

"You're not going to be with us?" Samantha asked.

"Not this time. Okay, let's get into position. Things could start at any time."

I watched as Samantha and Agnes went into Agnes's bedroom. I backed into the room Samantha and I had shared. There were a couple of lights still on downstairs, but they did nothing to light up the upstairs hallway. To me that was good. Agnes interrupted my thoughts.

"Peter," she called out in a whisper.

"Yeah?"

"My gun is missing."

Walker had obviously searched her room while we were all downstairs. He had found the gun and taken it. That reminded me of the rifle. I pulled back away from the door and went over next to the window where the rifle was still leaning against the wall. I slid open the bolt and found the rifle was empty. Walker had taken the cartridges.

I returned to the hall and knelt down. I took the small .38 caliber pistol from my ankle holster and held it out to Agnes. Agnes silently moved across the hall and took the gun.

"You'll have to do the best you can with this. It's loaded with Wad Cutters. Not big and powerful, but they have a lot of knockdown punch and can do a lot of damage. Be careful, it only has five shots," I whispered.

Agnes nodded and moved back to her bedroom. As I kept an eye on the hall, I took time to think. Being in the foothills where houses were some distance apart, a gunfight inside such a large house might go unnoticed.

There was also the problem of getting help. Even if we could notify the police when the shooting started, it would take them too long to get here to be of much help. Again, I was wishing that I had not left my cell phone on my desk in the office. It all boiled down to the fact that we were on our own.

Time passed slowly. Some of the lights downstairs had gone out. It was obvious Walker was shutting down everything he could that might give us even a slight advantage.

It was now very dark and very quiet in the house. I kept my eyes and ears open, hoping to see or hear something that would tell me the time had come. Agnes's house was big and spread out. Rickett and his men could be in the house before we would know it.

Keeping guard on the hall prevented me from being near a window where I could watch outside to see when they were coming. I took a deep breath, sat down on the floor and settled in next to the door. It was quiet. There was nothing going on as far as I could tell.

CHAPTER TWENTY

The silence of the night was broken by the slight sound of tennis shoes squeaking on the hardwood floor at the base of the stairs. I remembered Walker was wearing tennis shoes. I sat up and readied myself for anything, but nothing happened. I figured Walker was on his way to check on Slone.

"Everything okay here?" I heard Walker said.

"Yeah. All's quiet," Slone replied.

"What's that out there?"

I didn't hear an answer to Walker's question. What I did hear sent a chill down my spine. I heard the distinct sound of something hard fall on the kitchen floor. If I had to guess it was Slone's gun. I then heard the muffled sound of a body falling to the floor. What I didn't hear was Slone's reply. It answered the question of whose side Slone was on, not that it helped any.

The way I figured it, Walker had gotten her to turn her attention to something, and then disabled her. What he wanted her to look at was probably nothing, just a way to get her to turn her back to him.

Things were about to get interesting. It wouldn't be long before Walker's friends would be here, if they weren't already, and we would have to fight to stay alive.

I again heard the squeaking of tennis shoes on the hardwood floor as Walker went by the bottom of the stairs on his way back to the den. I wanted very much to take him out when he passed the bottom of the stairs. The stairway was too dark to make sure each and every shot counted.

There was a light switch at the top of the stairs. That gave me an idea. I moved out of the room to a place near the top of the stairs and waited.

I didn't have long to wait. It was only a few minutes before I heard the faint, almost inaudible sound of street shoes at the bottom of the stairs. Whoever was coming for us, they were already in the house. I prepared myself for what was to come.

The bottom two steps squeak from the weight of someone stepping on them. I reached up and flipped on the light switch. The stairs were immediately flooded with light. The fact that I was ready for the sudden light gave me the split second advantage I needed to see who was there. I opened fire and two big enforcers fell back to the floor at the bottom of the stairs. I then quickly turned the light off giving anyone who tried nothing to shoot at.

In the confusion that followed, I darted across the hall to Agnes's room. I took up a position at the door and waited. I could hear the moans of at least one person. That assured me at least one of them was injured, but I didn't know how bad.

I could hear voices talking downstairs, but I couldn't make out what was being said. I knew I had caught them off guard, but it was not likely to happen again. They would be ready next time.

"BLACKSTONE."

I'd heard that voice somewhere before, but I couldn't place it. I didn't answer him. This was a large house. It was still to my advantage if they didn't know where to find me.

"Blackstone, I know you're up there and I know what you have for firepower. That shoulder gun of yours is not going to be enough to get you out of this. You might as well give up."

I had no intentions of giving up. To do so would mean we would all be killed. The fact he thought he knew what we had for firepower, gave me additional hope. But I was still at a disadvantage. I didn't know how many of them there were.

I had listened very carefully to the voice in an effort to identify it. Then it came to me, it was Lieutenant Royal. If Royal was here and he was trying to kill me, then I was sure Rickett was close by.

"Okay, Blackstone. You're going to do this the hard way."

Without any further comment, the light in the stairway came on. I was sure there was no one standing at the bottom of the stairs. I laid down inside the bedroom at the bottom of the door. Whoever came up the stairs would not see me until it was too late. I waited and watched. It would not be long before things would come to a head. They had already lost the element of surprise. The longer they were here, the greater the chance of being discovered by a neighbor or someone passing by.

I looked back over my shoulder at Agnes and Samantha. They were difficult to see, but I could make them out. They were sitting in a corner behind a large dresser. The patio door to the deck over the den was only a few feet away from them. They would not be seen by anyone coming in that way, plus they were covering my back.

I turned my attention back to the stairway and waited. There was no doubt when trouble started this time, it was going to be all out. It was win or lose time for all of us.

I LAID ON THE FLOOR next to the door making myself as small a target as possible while still keeping an eye on the upstairs landing. I was sure it wouldn't be long before they tried to come up the stairs. Even though they had turned the lights back on in the stairwell and landing, we kept the bedroom dark.

The silence was broken by the sounds of someone on the stairs. Whoever it was, he was being very cautious. The last thing he would want was for me to see him first.

I aimed my gun at the place along the railing where I thought I would see the top of anyone's head as they tried to work their way to the top of the stairs. I held my gun steady. I was ready to pull the trigger.

It seemed to take forever before I saw just a hint of the top of someone's head at the base of the railing. It had stopped moving. I was sure he could see the top of the door, but he couldn't see me, yet.

He hesitated for what seemed like a lifetime. There was not enough of him showing so that I could be sure to hit him. Suddenly, he popped up and fire three quick rounds at the door. All of them hit well above my head, but startled the hell out of me just the same. I ducked back to protect myself from flying plaster and pieces of door molding.

He quickly ducked down and waited. I was sure he had expected some kind of a response and would have gotten one if I hadn't pulled back and ducked for cover. I had failed to hold my position. I had not taken advantage of him being where I might have been able to get him. I was sure that he would try it again, only I would be ready to return fire next time.

Once again I saw the top of his head move. There was no doubt in my mind that he was about to try it again. If Royal were running the show, he would not want to be here any longer than necessary. He would want to get it over with and clean up the mess so the forensic team wouldn't find anything to incriminate him or his boss.

All of a sudden the man jumped up again as if he was going to charge the bedroom door and began firing at the door. I fired two quick shots from my .38 caliber Smith and Wesson that caught him square in the chest. The big enforcer's face showed his surprise as his mouth fell open. He fell backwards and disappeared. I could hear him as he tumbled down the stairs.

I was busy watching to make sure no one else was going to come charging up the stairs when I heard a noise behind me. It was the sound of a gun firing and the breaking of glass as a bullet came crashing through the patio doors from the deck. The bullet hit just inches from me. I was in no position to return fire. I tried to roll out of the light in an effort to make it harder for him to see me and to get into a position where I could shoot back.

The guy on the deck was not going to give me a chance to return fire. He fired again as he stepped through the smashed patio door. By all rights, he should have hit me, but shooting while moving makes it harder to hit someone, and I was glad for that.

Just as I was about to return fire, a shot was fired from the corner of the room. The big man stopped in his tracks and slowly turned to look toward the corner. Then there was a second shot from the corner. The second shot doubled him over and sent him to the floor.

I jumped up and turned toward the door. I could hear someone running up the steps. I fired a couple of shots into the hallway, one of them putting out the hall light. It seemed to halt their advance for the moment.

I ran to the corner and got Agnes and Samantha to their feet. Grabbing Samantha by the arm, I pulled her out onto the deck. Agnes was close behind.

"Climb down and go to the barn. I'll hold them off," I whispered as I took the gun from Samantha because mine was empty.

Samantha looked at me, but Agnes was on her way down the fire escape ladder.

"Go," I insisted sharply.

Samantha reacted. She went to the ladder and climbed down. Agnes was waiting for her at the bottom. I saw her grab Samantha by the arm and pull on her. Together they ran toward the barn where my car had been hidden.

I turned around in time to see someone come into the bedroom. I fired a quick shot to slow them down, and then headed for the ladder. I didn't stick around long enough to see if I had hit anyone.

Just as I dropped to the ground, I heard someone inside the house yell. It was a warning to the others that we had gotten out of the house.

I no more than hit the ground when I heard someone come running around the corner. I quickly turned and fired. The shadowy figure doubled over and fell to the ground. I didn't wait to see if anyone else was dumb enough to come blindly running around the corner, I took off running toward the barn.

I RAN INTO THE BARN and began looking for Samantha and Agnes.

"Hold it right there," a deep voice said from behind me.

I straightened up and slowly turned around. It was none other than Stan Rickett. He was standing with his back to the wall just inside the barn door. He had one arm around Samantha and a gun in his hand that was pointed at her head.

"Get rid of the gun," he said. "I'd really hate to kill this pretty woman."

I knew it didn't matter if I got rid of the gun or not. He was going to kill us all anyway. I had to make a decision and make it quickly. I tossed the gun on the other side of the car. He made the mistake of taking his eyes off me for just a split second to see where it went.

When he did, I dove for cover in front of the car. I scrabbled around the car and picked up the gun. I then moved back toward the front of the car as quickly as I could.

"That wasn't very smart. Come out, now," he demanded sharply.

I slowly rose up from in front of the car, but this time I had my gun pointed right at Rickett's head.

"Now it's your turn to drop the gun," I said as I looked down the sights of my gun at his head.

"I still have little Miss Rich Bitch. I don't think you want her brains spread all over this barn."

He was right, but if I did as he wanted there was no chance for any of us. I didn't move.

"You kill her and I kill you," I said as I continued to hold my gun on him. I didn't figure he wanted to die any more than the rest of us.

"I guess this is a stand off," he said with a stupid grin.

He had let the end of the barrel of his gun drift away from the side of Samantha's head. It was no longer pointed directly at her. It was now or never.

"I guess you're right," I said as I pulled the trigger on my gun.

The barn was suddenly filled with a loud bang as my gun went off. A blank look came over Rickett's face as he began to fall backwards. I had hit him where I wanted, right between the eyes. He had died instantly, before his hand could even react.

As he fell, he took Samantha with him. I rushed to her and quickly pulled her to her feet and away from him, dropping my gun in the process. She threw her arms around me and held onto me so tightly I thought she would crush the breath out of me. I started to retrieve my gun when a voice caused me to freeze.

"Well, isn't this a pretty picture."

I swung around pushing Samantha behind me in an effort to protect her. Standing in the barn door was Royal. He had his gun pointed at me. There was an evil grin on his face as he glanced at Rickett lying on the ground with a hole in his head.

"I see you got him. Well, that's too bad. You know this isn't over?"

"Yeah," I said, not taking my eyes off him.

"You know what I have to do to protect myself?"

"It isn't that hard to figure out."

"Now I have to kill you. But once that's done, I'll be a hero. I can tell the shooting board I got here too late to save Mrs. Williams, but I got you and Rickett."

"What about Walker?"

"Oh, he's already dead. It seems one of your slugs got him. So you see, you'll end up getting blamed for the death of one police officer."

"What about the rest? How you going to explain that?" I asked in an effort to keep him talking while I tried to figure a way out.

"It won't be hard. I shouldn't have any trouble seeing as how most of those killed have a bullet from one of your guns in them," he said with a note of confidence.

I watched as Royal slowly lifted his gun up to take aim at me. Suddenly, there was the loud crack of a gun. Royal's body jerked as the bullet slammed into him from behind. His eyes got big, and then went blank. He fell on his face on the dirt floor of the barn.

For a second or two, I had no idea who had shot him. It wasn't until Slone slowly stepped into the light of the barn. She held her gun at her side, looked at me and smiled. Then the smile left her face and she collapsed on the floor at the door.

It wasn't until I ran to her aid that I noticed the blood on the side of her head. I checked her for a pulse. It was weak, but it was there.

I looked up and saw Samantha standing there with her hands over her mouth. She looked like she was in shock. The one person I didn't see was Agnes.

"Agnes?"

I heard a moan coming from a dark corner of the barn. I rushed over to find Agnes lying in a pile of straw in one of the stalls. She was only semiconscious. She had been struck on the head as she entered the barn.

I decided the best thing was to leave her there. I went back to Slone and took her phone off her belt. I called 9-1-1 for the police and an ambulance.

While I waited, I helped Samantha to the car and had her sit in the back seat. I helped Slone into the barn and laid her down on a pile of straw in an effort to make her as comfortable as possible.

IT WASN'T LONG before the police and ambulance arrived. Shortly after that, Captain MacDonald arrived. It was a little confusing for him, but once the injured had been taken care of and the dead taken away, we went into the den to talk.

"This place looks like it was a battle zone. There was a body upstairs in one of the rooms, one dead and one wounded at the bottom of the stairs, one pretty close to dying outside the house, and two dead bodies and two injured in the barn, two of them cops. What the hell happened here?"

"I can explain," I said as I sat down, took a deep breath and leaned back in the chair.

"I sure as hell hope so," he said as he sat down to listen.

I spent the next hour explaining to Mac what had happened, while the forensic team was going over the house and barn. I also told him about what Samantha had said about the involvement of Rickett, Angilara and the others in the Ace Diamond Building. I suggested that he might want to take a good look at Angilara because at least one of the men involved in the shooting was one of Angilara's enforcers. I recognized him when I blew him away on the stairwell landing.

Once I was finished telling Mac everything I could, he had everything he needed to put the rest of it together. He had the letter, the list of investors, and the records I had taken from Mosser's loft in LoDo. I told Mac that I would come to his office in the morning and answer any questions he had once he had had time to absorb all the evidence.

After Mac explained what he had been doing from his end, based on the information I had provided him earlier, he told me that I could go.

I DECIDED TO GO to the hospital to see how Samantha and Agnes were doing before going home. When I got there, there were officers posted at their doors. Fortunately, Mac had cleared it for me to see them. I visited Samantha first.

"Hi," she said as I stuck my head around the door to see if she was awake.

"Hi. How are you doing?"

"Okay, I guess. Thanks for saving my life."

"You're welcome."

"Why is a policeman outside my door?"

"It's not over yet. Once they have Angilara and his bunch in custody, it will be over. They don't think it will be very long. They've got enough on him to put him away for a very long time. It seems a wire tap on Angilara's office picked up a call between him and Rickett about getting rid of you. The District Attorney thinks it's enough to put him away, along with the information they found in the records kept by Mosser."

"That's great. Am I off the hook?"

"You are free and clear to do whatever you want."

"Why didn't you tell me that I would inherit everything of Arnold's?

"I found a copy of Arnold's new will a short time ago saying he was leaving everything to you. I'm sorry I couldn't tell you about it when I found it. As long as you didn't know, the police didn't have a good motive."

"That's okay, but what will I do with all that money?"

"Whatever you want. I'm sure you'll find a good use for it, maybe something Arnold would have liked."

"Yes. That sounds like a good idea."

"By the way, you might think about getting a new personal trainer. You're current one is going to be arrested.

"How come?"

"It seems he steals things that don't belong to him. He was probably working on a plan to steal something from you."

"Thanks for the warning. I'll find a new one."

"Good. Well, I think I should go and let you get some rest."

"Will I see you again?"

"Sure," I replied as I leaned over and gave her a light kiss on the cheek.

"I owe you more than I can ever repay. What can I do for you?"

"Oh, don't worry about it. Just pay the bill when you get it. Like I told you before, I don't come cheap," I said with a grin.

"I will, and gladly," she said with a smile.

I turned and walked out the door. I went on down the hall and looked in on Agnes. She was sleeping peacefully, so I decided not to bother her.

I made it a point to stop by the Intensive Care Unit to see how Slone was getting along. She was still listed as "critical, but stable". We could only hope for the best for her. It was time for me to go home.

I GOT IN MY CAR and headed out of the hospital parking lot and on toward downtown. As I passed in front of the Ace Diamond Building, I wondered what would become of it. I smiled to myself. I was sure that no matter what the inspector found, the building would be made safe and Samantha would see Arnold's dream came true.

I drove on to my apartment and parked the rental car in front of my garage. I could return it sometime tomorrow. I took a deep breath and started walking to my apartment. The adrenaline was starting to wear off and I was beginning to feel very tired.

As I stepped into my apartment, I dropped my keys on the table. After shutting off the light, I went to my bedroom. I turned on the bedroom light and was surprised to see Jennifer in my bed. She had been sleeping, but the light had awakened her.

"Hi," I said with a smile.

"Hi," she replied without sitting up.

"What are you doing here?"

"I came by to see you. When you weren't here, I decided to wait for you. It got late and I got tired, so I decided I would sleep here. Actually, I was hoping you would come back tonight. Are you hungry?"

"No. What I need more than anything right now is sleep," I said as I slumped down on the bed and began to undress.

"You don't need me?" she asked with a shy little grin that made her look so sexy.

"I'm sorry, honey," I said apologetically, as I stood up and took off the rest of my clothes. "It's been a long week and a tough night."

"It's okay," she said as she held up the covers for me. "Maybe, you will need me in the morning."

She was naked under the covers, but then she always slept in the nude. I had to smile. She was more than likely right. I would want her in the morning, maybe for all day.

I crawled in under the covers and rolled up against her. She took me in her arms and held me to her. I kissed her a couple of times before I drifted off to sleep.

Made in the USA
Monee, IL
20 January 2024

51517470R10144